Deatomizer

Robbie Portillo

Special thanks to CG for reading all my rough drafts and giving me the best input.

ISBN 978-1-971651-01-9
Deatomizer
Copyright © 2023 Robbie Portillo
All Rights Reserved.

Deatomizerbook.com

1

November 1st, 2026   0000 Indochina Time

On a typical Sunday morning in Ho Chi Minh City, Vietnam, the streets are alive with activity. People move throughout the city, engaging in their nightly routines. The vibrant nightlife blends seamlessly with the sounds of laughter from people passing by, while music pours out from nearby bars and clubs. Singles, couples, partygoers, and individuals from a variety of backgrounds all come together to enjoy the excitement and entertainment that the city offers. The mood is lively and energetic as crowds search for memorable experiences and nighttime fun in the heart of the city.

Throughout the city, the mood shifts suddenly as people reach for their phones, only to realize they cannot access the internet or make calls. Confusion quickly spreads among the crowd as individuals glance around, searching for someone who might have an explanation, but no one seems to have any answers. The mood grows increasingly uneasy as uncertainty takes hold.

As the tension mounts, attention turns skyward as eyes follow the path of roaring military aircraft flying east toward the Saigon River. In the buildings above, silhouettes press against windows, interested by the commotion outside. The city turns its focus to a massive, dark void descending over the water; its presence is both ominous and captivating. Instinctively, people attempt to document the extraordinary scene with their phones, but the darkness proves impossible to capture; no device can clearly make out the mysterious shape looming above.

As the mysterious object comes to a stop over the river, the water remains perfectly still; no waves disturb the surface, as if the river itself senses the unnatural presence overhead. The military aircraft circle the object tightly with their spotlights cutting through the darkness and illuminating its form. With the lights upon it, the true scale of the object finally becomes clear. The aircraft, once dominant and impressive, now appear minuscule; mere ants to the immense size of the hovering object.

Inside the Capitol Building in Hanoi, Kun Wen sits in his office, rubbing his tired eyes as his top advisor briefs him on the situation. Kun, a thirty-five-year-old Chinese man, is the leader of a mercenary group that recently seized control of Vietnam, Laos, Cambodia, and Thailand through a ruthless military occupation. Following his calculated rise to power, he has installed himself as the leader of all four countries, renaming the territory Kun's Unified Nation State. Now, this pressing crisis demands his full attention.

Across from Kun stands Zhen, his top advisor. Zhen is a forty-six-year-old man, notably overweight and bald, who appears visibly anxious as the crisis unfolds. He constantly dabs sweat from his forehead with a handkerchief. In his hand, he holds a tablet displaying an image of the mysterious object for Kun to see. "I'm getting reports that Ho Chi Minh City is under attack by an unknown adversary. The local government has shut off all connections to the outside world, and the military has already confronted whatever that thing is."

Kun leans forward, narrowing his gaze as he studies the image thoroughly. A deep wrinkle forms between his brows as he tries to make sense of the object in the picture. After several moments of silent inspection, he leans back in his chair, clearly unable to comprehend the full extent of what he is seeing. "Do we have a live feed? I want to see what this thing is doing in real time."

Zhen flips the screen back to him. His fingers quickly swipe through the interface to find what Kun wants. "Let me see if I can find one. Ah, I believe this will be it." He turns the screen back toward Kun. "This is a live feed from a military helicopter near the object. Only top government officials have access to this feed."

Kun's eyes widen as he takes in the massive size of the object. "That thing is huge. Are you sure this feed is secure? I don't want anyone outside the government seeing this."

Zhen gives a quick nod, then dabs his forehead once again. "Yes. The encryption is highly secure. Only a select few have access to this."

Kun opens his desk drawer and takes out a TV remote. With the press of the power button, the large TV mounted to the wall powers on. "Put the feed on the TV. I need you to get me in contact with our people in Hanoi. I need to know exactly what we're dealing with."

As Zhen moves to carry out the order, the office grows tense, with all eyes focusing on the unfolding crisis. The live feed becomes the focal point for Kun and his advisors as they work to understand and respond to the threat.

Back at the river in Ho Chi Minh City, a single warship has taken position. Its missile launchers lock onto the object, ready to strike at a moment's notice. Despite the readiness, the crew remains disciplined, holding off their attack while awaiting direct orders from Kun. The commotion from the military woke the nearby residents. Drawn in by curiosity and concern, thousands of onlookers gather along the banks of the river, struggling to comprehend the scene unfolding before them.

As a precautionary measure, the government immediately grounds and diverts all flights in the surrounding area. All anyone can do is wait and watch for any movement from the object. All attempts to communicate with it have failed; its frequency remains unknown. Without the illumination of spotlights from the circling aircraft, the object would be nearly invisible, existing only as a void in the sky.

Twenty minutes after the object's arrival, it remains motionless above the river. Without warning, a clear beam of light shoots out from its underside. Panic sweeps through the streets as people rush for cover, expecting the object to be powering to strike the city. However, their anxiety quickly turns into confusion when the beam refrains from causing any destruction. Instead, the light expands and forms a massive screen that faces toward the city. The unexpected phenomenon captivates everyone's attention.

On the screen, a series of images play, depicting strange creatures that resemble animals but are unlike anything known to man. The footage cycles through various species, each more bizarre than the last. Throughout these images, one particular species stands out among the rest. These beings somewhat resemble humans in shape, standing upright with slender frames and glossy hair that adorns their small, delicate faces. Their grayish skin provides a stark contrast to the piercing glow of their yellow eyes, making them impossible to ignore. Across their mouths, the creatures wear an unknown device. Occasionally, they remove this apparatus, briefly revealing their normal-looking mouths to the audience. The purpose of these mouthpieces remain unclear to the onlookers. As the footage continues to play, both civilians and military personnel struggle to understand the significance of what they are witnessing.

Kun's office crowds with curious secretaries and advisors, all watching the event unfold before them. The gravity of the moment quiets everyone in the room, with only Kun daring to break the silence. "It seems like we have guests from another world, and judging by what they're showing us, this is a declaration of peace."

"You can't be sure about that," says Zhen, unconvinced by the apparent message of peace. "This could be a ploy to lower our guard. What if they're here to conquer us?"

Kun shakes his head as he walks up to the TV, gazing deeply at the unknown object. "If that were the case, they would have just conquered us from the beginning. They wouldn't waste their time showing us this message." He turns to face everyone in the room. "No, I think they're up to something else. Have a look at our history. Only humans conquer foreign lands and claim them by force. Maybe they aren't like us. But we won't know for sure until we meet them."

The moment Kun finishes speaking, the room erupts with everyone talking over one another, trying to tell him that is a bad idea.

Kun raises his voice, sending a deafening echo throughout the room, instantly silencing the commotion. He scans the group with a stern gaze; his authority is absolute. "Be quiet, all of you. What I say is final. Do I make myself clear? This is your only warning." With the room now silent, Kun turns his hard gaze onto Zhen. "Let the general in charge know I want to establish contact with these beings. Under no circumstances does any soldier open fire."

Zhen swallows hard and gives a stiff nod. His face is noticeably pale, and his breath is short, but despite his visible anxiety, his words stand strong in the presence of Kun's commanding authority. "I'll get right on it."

The object's broadcast lasts for a full ten minutes before the beam shuts off. A purple light takes its place, appearing on the surrounding ground in a grid pattern to map the terrain. The light focuses on a flat piece of land at the Tan Son Nhat International Airport, in the center of Ho Chi Minh City. After a brief pause, the object moves silently through the night sky, steadily making its way toward the airport. The military is on high alert and has nearly tripled the number of aircraft circling it. Across the region, tension mounts as people prepare themselves for whatever might happen next.

Fifteen minutes later, it comes to rest above the airport's runway, and a concentrated beam of light pierces through the darkness, reaching down onto the runway below. In response, twenty military vehicles rush across the tarmac and witness several figures slowly descending from within the beam.

The military vehicles surround the perimeter of the light as four human-like creatures stand back-to-back, each one facing outward in a different direction. The surrounding soldiers point their weapons at these mysterious beings as terror overtakes them at the sight of these aliens, but no one fires a single shot. Kun's wrath outweigh the fear of these unknown visitors.

The aliens appear exactly as they do in the footage. Slender, glossy hair, and their gray skin almost looks metallic under the beam of light. The strange mask-like devices still cover their mouths, while their yellow eyes easily pierce through the night. Those eyes seem to study the soldiers' every movement, leaving a lasting impression on all who watch them.

The leading general slowly opens the hatch of a Humvee and cautiously peers out. Over a speaker, he speaks to them in English, trying hard not to mince his words. "If you make any sudden movements, we will not hesitate to shoot you."

An alien reacts instantly, quickly turning directly to address the general. Without hesitation, it talks back in fluent English. The voice comes from the device covering its mouth, sounding eerily human. "I understand many of you are afraid of us. You don't know why we are here. We are a peace-loving species that has come to your planet to bring you all hope and love."

The alien's words do nothing to ease the tension in the air. The soldiers freeze in place as fear intensifies with every passing moment. Each soldier waits in silence, uncertain of what will happen next as they wait for the order to open fire.

Among the four aliens, it quickly becomes apparent that, while they are nearly indistinguishable in appearance, one stands out from the rest. This individual's hair is noticeably brighter, setting him apart and suggesting a position of greater authority. He holds himself together with remarkable composure, despite the weapons pointed at him. He does not flinch or hesitate when he speaks. "We have come here to contact your leader and bring prosperity to this world."

Although Kun fills with delight at the extraordinary scene unfolding before him, he keeps his emotions hidden. He maintains a stern and composed demeanor, understanding that others might misinterpret any excitement he shows as weakness. Despite his efforts, Kun cannot suppress his curiosity. "I have to wonder though, out of all the places in the world, why did they come here to my territory?"

"I don't know," says Zhen, dabbing his forehead again. "But it looks like your meeting with them will happen. You can ask them yourself soon enough."

"Get back in touch with the general in charge there. Tell him I want to talk with these things personally," says Kun, focusing his deadly gaze on Zhen.

Zhen feels his intense gaze on him. He knows if he messes up, Kun will be out for his head. With slightly unsteady hands, he reaches for his phone and dials the general in charge at the airport. "Kun wants to speak with the aliens. Put them on the phone."

The general, whose head sticks out from the top of the Humvee, stares directly at the aliens. "You can't be serious. We don't know what they'll do to us yet."

Before the general can protest any further, Kun's patience finally snapped. With a swift and forceful motion, he snatches the phone from Zhen's hand, scratching Zhen's ear in the process. Anger builds in Kun, ready to explode at any moment. "You're not in charge; I am. Now get your ass down there so I can talk to them. And don't screw this up. You know what happens to those who don't do as they're told, or do I need to personally train you to follow my orders like the dog you are?"

The general squeezes his eyes shut and takes a deep breath to gather his nerve as the weight of Kun's demand presses onto him. After a few moments of steadying himself, he slowly opens his eyes and lifts the microphone to his mouth. One wrong word could cost him his life. "Our leader wants to have a word with you. I'll be coming down so he can talk with you." He ducks back inside the Humvee and puts the phone back to his ear. "I'm about to go outside."

The general steps out of the Humvee and approaches the aliens with caution. Four pairs of yellow eyes track his every movement, sending shivers down his spine. Only now as he stands before them does he realize how small they are. They are fairly short; barely standing four feet tall. They stare up at him with their beaming yellow eyes, almost like children lost in a mall.

The general hesitantly extends his phone toward the aliens, expecting one of them to take it, but they just stare at it. It dawns on him that they might not know what it is. "This is a communication device. The person you want to talk to is on the other side."

The alien who spoke earlier reaches up to take the phone from the general's hand. "Sorry, we didn't know what this was. I thought you were telling us it was your leader." He holds the phone up, examining it with curiosity. As he studies the phone, he makes a comment under his breath that the general can barely hear. "I read a report of a girl we studied who had one of these. She would constantly play with it and made friends with the other humans even though she didn't know their language." After a brief shake of his head, the alien drops the subject entirely, focusing his attention back on the matter at hand.

Kun watches the TV intently as the alien takes the phone. He starts talking first, so he is in control of the conversation. "This is Kun. Who do I have the pleasure of speaking with?"

The disembodied voice does not faze the little alien. He is calm and speaks without hesitation. "I go by Ignin. I'm in charge of this mission. It's an honor to speak with you."

"Likewise," says Kun. "What brings you here?"

"Our mission is to help beings reach their potential and bring prosperity to their civilization. We would like to meet you in person to discuss a few things," says Ignin.

"How do I know you won't kill me and take over this world?" asks Kun.

"That is a reasonable concern. I assure you we do not want that," says Ignin. "We have learned many languages of this planet. If we didn't want to help, we would not be here wasting your time."

Kun switches to speaking Chinese. He wants to confirm if what Ignin says is true. "You say you know more languages?"

Ignin responds to Kun in flawless Chinese, as if he spoke it his whole life. "Yes, we have learned seven of this planet's languages. Actually, that's not right. The devices around our mouths seamlessly translates our language into one of seven of your languages."

Kun switches back to speaking English. "That's impressive. How can we meet up?"

"Show us the location you want us to go, and we will travel there instantly," says Ignin.

"Give me a second," says Kun. He searches through his phone to locate the precise coordinates of his current position. Once he finds them, he sends the details over. "I just sent it to you. Give the phone back to the man in front of you, and he will show you where to go. I look forward to seeing you soon." Without waiting for a reply from Ignin, he ends the call and tosses the phone back to Zhen. As Zhen tries to catch the phone, he fumbles with it briefly before securing it with his hands.

Ignin examines the phone again before handing it back to the general. "He said he sent something to that device of yours that will show us the way to him."

The general takes back the phone and looks through his messages. "He sent me his location." He points the phone at Ignin, displaying their current location and the location of Kun in Hanoi. "Do you know how to read this?"

Ignin does not respond to the general's question. Instead, he removes his communication device and holds it up to the phone. A few seconds pass, and he places it back over his mouth. "The data has transferred over. We will be there soon."

Before the general can react, the beam lifts the aliens back into the object. In an instant, they are gone, leaving everyone scratching their heads.

Kun stands in the center of his office, preparing for the alien's arrival. He turns to Zhen and issues a series of urgent commands. "They'll be here soon. I want all connections to the outside world severed in all of my territories. We don't need any prying eyes. Ground all flights. No one will enter or leave until I say so. All military personnel and government workers abroad are to shelter in place until further notice. And round up any foreigners; lock them away for the time being. We'll deal with them later."

Zhen immediately obeys Kun's command. Without questioning or considering what Kun told him, he spins on his heel and exits the room.

Kun hears a commotion coming from outside. "It seems my guests have arrived." He hurries toward the exit with his guards following close behind. As they step outside, the object is now in plain view, showing off its sleek white surface. It hovers above the capitol building, no longer trying to conceal itself.

As the aliens descend, Kun steps toward the beam of light. His guards are on high alert, resting their hands on their firearms, ready to draw at any moment.

When their feet touch the ground, Ignin steps forward as his yellow eyes sparkle in the night. "Greetings, leader of this planet. We mean you and your people no harm." He places his hand on his chest. "I am the one you talked with moments ago."

"It's a pleasure to meet you in person, Ignin," says Kun as he gestures his hand toward the building. "Please come inside. We can discuss your reason for being here." As they move toward the entrance, he turns slightly and whispers to one of his generals. "Send a message to the people of Hanoi. Tell them this is a new military aircraft undergoing testing, and that there's nothing to worry about. It's only here because of technical issues." Kun learned long ago that controlling the flow of information meant controlling the people.

The general nods and hurries off to relay the message.

As Kun and his entourage head toward the building, the beam fades away. The object hovers motionless over the city as crowds snap photos and record videos. Excitement and curiosity quickly turns to confusion as those in the crowd try to share their findings online. The lack of information leaves many wondering what is truly happening above their city.

A few minutes later, phones in the surrounding area receive a message from Kun's government. "Do not be alarmed. This is a new military aircraft we are testing. Because of some internal issues, it will hover over the city for the time being. Internet and phone communications have been temporarily severed to prevent this information from leaking to our enemies. Connections will be back soon."

Kun leads the group through the grand halls of the capitol building and into a spacious meeting room with a long table surrounded by chairs. He gestures for everyone to sit, then takes a seat beside Ignin. A grin spreads across his face, eager to hear what the alien wants to offer. "First of all, I'd like to welcome you to our planet. It must have been a long journey here. I'm curious. Why did you land here, of all places?"

Ignin reaches for a glass of water in front of him. He removes his device and takes a drink as his yellow eyes briefly glance around the room. After setting the glass back down, he meets Kun's gaze as he slips the device back on. "When we arrived, we saw a large cluster of lights. We believed it was the main settlement on this planet. However, it would seem we were quite far off, but that does not matter anymore. We are part of a large colony from what you call the Andromeda Galaxy. You're the first species we came across in this galaxy. Our mission is to assist younger species like yourselves develop their planet in ways they could not otherwise. Here, let me show you." He removes his mask, and a translucent blue hologram appears in front of him, projecting a video for all present to see.

A narrator speaks as the hologram shows a ship identical to the one above the city traveling to a distant planet and meeting with its inhabitants. "There are many planets just like yours out there in the vast expanding universe that need a little help to progress. We know life can be very confusing at times, but it does not have to be. We meet other life forms and begin working on ways to improve their planet. With our help, we can help you thrive like never before. After advancing a species to their potential, we leave for the next planet to continue our work in the hopes that one day we can bring hope and love to the entire galaxy."

When the hologram ends, Ignin places the device back over his mouth and speaks without hesitation. "We want to bring happiness to your planet. Nothing brings us more satisfaction than that. If you need any help with anything, just let us know and we will provide the necessary tools to help you take care of it."

Kun remains silent for a long moment, processing what he just watched. An alien civilization, whose technology and understanding far surpass anything known to humanity, has arrived on Earth. By a stroke of fortune, Kun is the first leader to meet with them. He understands the gravity of the situation and the potential opportunities it presents. Before moving forward, he wants to be certain there is no misunderstanding about what Ignin is offering. "Anything you say?"

"Tell us how we can help you achieve your goals," says Ignin. "We want the leader of this planet and his people to thrive like never before."

Kun was not expecting the aliens to see him as Earth's ruler. However, he quickly realized the potential advantage in allowing them to continue believing this. Rather than correct Ignin's misunderstanding, Kun fully embraces the role. If the aliens regard him as the ruler of this world, then soon enough, he will be. The power and influence the aliens offer will be the leverage Kun needs to make the world submit to his authority, fulfilling his long-held desire for global dominance.

Through the night, Kun and Ignin talk about the future of his great empire. Kun recounts the history of the world in immaculate detail, ensuring Ignin understands the complexities and struggles his nation faces. Ignin attentively listens, absorbing the information and gaining insight into the ongoing conflicts. He came to realize that the other world powers are launching attacks against Kun's nation from every direction. Kun expresses his vision for the planet, describing his desire to unite humanity under his leadership and provide what he believes is best for its people. Kun's ambitions are clear. He wants to guide the world toward a brighter future while relying on Ignin and his advanced civilization.

As the first light of dawn filters through the city, the lengthy discussion between Kun and Ignin draws to a close. Ignin assures Kun that he will consult with his fellow peers regarding the ambitious vision that Kun outlined for the planet's future. He departs and makes his way back to his ship, and by evening he returns with three others, each individual carries an object. Kun's guards waste no time in escorting the visitors to Kun's office for the next stage of their meeting.

Kun stands tall on the other side of his desk as the aliens walk in. He refuses to show even a hint of weakness in front of them. "What are we thinking, Ignin?" His voice is calm, and he eagerly waits for a response.

The aliens line up in front of Kun's desk. Ignin steps forward, ready to present what he has to offer. "We have come to help you and your civilization to prosper like never before. We have brought you these items for you to achieve your goals. As I show them off, I would like you to meet my colleagues."

Kun stands silently as the three aliens arrange their items on his desk, with each one fixing their bright yellow eyes on him without saying a word.

Ignin turns his attention to the first alien standing beside him. "This is Gar, our navigator. He is responsible for ensuring our ship reaches any destination we set off to, no matter how distant or complex the journey may be." After the introduction, he gestures toward the first item on the desk. "The first item I would like to tell you about is this helmet." He lifts the device and holds it out for Kun to inspect. "It is designed to protect the wearer from harm. Try it on."

Without hesitation, Kun places it on his head. Instantly, a shimmering force field surrounds him. He reaches out to touch it, but it adapts to his movements, shifting and adjusting in real-time to accommodate his actions. "This is mind-blowing."

Zhen freaks out in disbelief. His eyes widen at the sight of Kun putting his trust in the aliens. "You shouldn't do that. You don't know what will happen." He reaches for the helmet, but Kun sharply swats his hand away.

Ignin turns his attention to the next alien standing in the middle. "This is Zilis. He is responsible for maintaining our ship's systems and ensuring that everything remains fully operational." He picks up the second item on the desk. "This weapon is modeled after the small handguns we have seen your people carrying." He hands Kun the gun. "When fired, this weapon sends an electric pulse throughout the target's body, stopping all internal organs from functioning, killing them instantly."

Kun studies the alien handgun from every angle, admiring every aspect of it. The urge to test its capabilities on someone in the room flashes through his mind, but he quickly suppresses it, recognizing that such an action would be reckless and send the wrong message to both his team and the aliens. Instead, Kun maintains his composure and continues to observe the weapon.

Ignin continues. "We can begin mass-producing these two items immediately on our ship if that's fine with you."

Kun takes his eyes off the gun and shifts his gaze to Ignin, then he slowly sets the gun back on the desk. "Yes, that's fine with me. Make as many as you can. But before we continue, I want to ask you something."

"Go right ahead," says Ignin.

"Didn't you say you're here to bring peace and prosperity? Why are you giving us these weapons?" asks Kun, wanting to test Ignin and see what his response will be.

"To achieve your goals, of course," says Ignin. "To bring peace to your civilization, you need to exterminate those who oppose you. Or did I misinterpret your words last night?"

Kun nods, coming to realize that the aliens' perspective is different from that of humans. "No, that's right. I'm just surprised by what I'm getting." He covers his mouth, concealing a sly, almost devilish smile as the magnitude of the opportunity before him sinks him. Once he regains his composure, he turns his attention toward the last item. Curiosity and caution fills him as he tries to guess its purpose.

Ignin turns to the last alien in the group. "This is Chatur. He is responsible for weapons manufacturing. And then we have this item. The pride and joy of our species." He picks up the spherical item with both hands and lifts it high for everyone to see. "This is only a replica because the real one is much bigger. This item is very delicate. A lot happens when it's activated. In short, this weapon disrupts the bonds holding atoms together, effectively disintegrating any material it touches at the molecular level."

Kun catches his breath as the weight of the item sinks in. He is speechless, grasping to find words to match his shock.

Ignin continues the explanation. "We already made adjustments to this weapon for this planet's usage. Using your measurement system, this weapon has a diameter of one hundred kilometers."

Kun takes the replica and holds it up to the light, turning it slowly in his hands. The object's color is light blue with a dark blue orb in the center. "A hundred kilometers, you say. How many of these do I get?"

"As many as you need to achieve your goal," says Ignin.

A huge smile washes over Kun's face, eager to get things started. "Give my team two days to come up with the number we need, and I'll get back to you."

Two Days Later November 3rd, 2026 1900 Indochina Time

Kun steps outside and waves at the ship, signaling to Ignin that he is ready for him to come back down and greet him. Two aliens descend from the ship and greet Kun. Without delay, they return to Kun's office, where Zhen is spreading a map of the world across his desk for Ignin to see. Once Zhen finishes arranging the map, he steps back, giving Kun control of the discussion.

Kun stands beside Ignin, gesturing confidently at the map spread out before them. "After thorough consideration, we have identified eighty targets we want to destroy. However, upon further analysis, we narrowed the list down to just twenty-two locations. We believe any more than that would be overkill and against our best interests. Each black X represents a target we want to hit. Knowing that, when can we launch the attack?"

Ignin leans in, narrowing his eyes as he carefully examines the map intently. He studies each marked target with focus, silently considering the logistical challenges involved in preparing twenty-two items. "With the production of the helmets and guns underway, we are looking at about seventy hours."

"That's plenty of time for us to tie up all loose ends," says Kun.

"If that's all, I'll be heading back to my ship to give the orders to begin the manufacturing," says Ignin. "I'll also be leaving one of my assistants with you. Her name is Taf. She is the intermediary on our ship and will make it easier for you to contact me."

"It's a pleasure to meet you," says Taf, walking up to Kun. "Feel free to ask me anything. I'll help you in any way I can." She quickly settles in. Upon her arrival, Kun's assistants respond to her every request without hesitation or question. Whatever Taf needs, Kun's team ensures she receives it promptly and efficiently.

Two hours later, Kun calls for a meeting with his advisors to discuss what he expects to be carried out. "I want all military personnel and embassy workers from around the world to come back immediately. We will provide the necessary transportation to pick anyone up. If anyone refuses these orders or contacts anyone from the outside, they are to be killed on sight. Do I make myself clear?"

His advisors nod in unison, then spring into action without hesitation.

A nasty smile spreads across Kun's face. He glances at his advisors as his eyes gleam with anticipation and confidence. "Days from now, the world will come to fear my strength."

November 3rd, 2026 1000 Eastern Standard Time

At the same time, President of the United States, Charles Whiteford, sits in a Pentagon conference room, meeting with all the four-star generals. They are going over the global crisis after Kun shutdown all communications with his territories. The room falls silent as an advisor walks to the front of the room to give a presentation.

"As you all know, it has been three days since we last spoke to any representative from Kun's Unified Nation State. The only thing we were going on was rumors until we made a breakthrough yesterday." The presentation behind him advances to the next slide. "We were looking over satellite photos when we found a large object hovering over Hanoi, Vietnam. These photos have been released to the public, and people are coming up with their own theories of what's happening in Vietnam. We've been in talks with the United Nations, and they are also conducting their own investigation. So far, none of the embassies from KUNS have reached out to their respective countries. We have yet to receive a distress signal from any of our embassies within Kun's territories. We expect the worst. Regarding this object, either Kun's military has come up with a new type of aircraft that can hover in place for what looks like an extended period, or we are witnessing the first encounter of the third kind, which I believe to be the case." He turns to the screen and clicks a remote to switch to the next slide. "We have estimated the near-spherical object to be roughly two thousand feet in diameter."

The entire room fills with gasps as the revelation settles in. No one can believe that an object that big can hover in place. Faces around the table reflect a mix of disbelief, concern, and awe. Murmurs break out as everyone tries to grasp the full implications of what is going on.

President Whiteford leans forward. His voice, steady but firm, brings a sense of order to the tense room, which calms everyone down. "All right, I'm skeptical this is alien-made. But I'll go with my intelligence's best judgement." He turns his attention to the general sitting beside him. "What's your recommendation, General Turner?"

Seated beside the president is an older man with a high and tight haircut; an imposing figure. He is the chairman of the Joint Chiefs of Staff, the highest-ranking military officer in the United States Armed Forces. He meticulously reviews his notes, ensuring he fully understands the situation. After carefully analyzing all the information given to him, General Angus Turner comes to a solution with a stern expression on his face. "This situation is unprecedented. Until we know exactly what we're dealing with, I'd advise you to keep this contained. We should only confirm information to the public what they absolutely need to know. Let the theories go on as is."

Across the table, a middle-aged general scoffs at the suggestion of restraint. Robert Jackson, a thin and muscular man, interrupts General Turner to voice his concerns. "What we need to do is strengthen our defenses in case of an attack. We have no idea what's going on in Kun's head. That thing could be a weapon. We need to be ready for an attack."

General Turner turns to him and shakes his head. "Mobilizing our forces would be seen as an act of aggression and could cause an unnecessary escalation. Kun is a merciless man who took over Southern Asia at the cost of millions of lives. If we were to just go in there, he'll justify that as an act of war and do whatever he can to attack us. There's still a lot we don't know about this situation. I would rather get more intel than make any unnecessary risks."

"That's even more of a reason to strengthen our defenses," says General Jackson. "We don't know what's happening, so we should be ready for the worst. It has worked perfectly in the past and will work again. If we keep sitting here, twiddling our thumbs, we could be at a tremendous disadvantage if something were to happen. All I want is to be prepared for the worst-case scenario."

"I'm not saying we do nothing," says General Turner. "We need to proceed carefully. There are ways to prepare ourselves without strengthening up our defenses. As of now, we will adjust accordingly to whatever Kun does." He then looks back at the president. "We need to find the best course of action. I have already thought of a few ways we can prepare ourselves that don't require military escalation. I just need your thoughts."

Before the president can respond, the conference room doors burst open and a Pentagon analyst rushes inside. Her urgency immediately captures the attention of everyone present. "We just got word Kun has ordered all military personnel and diplomatic workers from all across the world to head back to his territory."

The sudden news blindsides General Turner. He straightens his posture, and his eyes lock firmly on the analyst. "When were you given this information?"

"A few moments ago," says the analyst, nearly out of breath. "It wasn't a formal notice. Kun's government reestablished connections with only their military and embassies, and told them to leave immediately. The news is already covering it. No country was given a heads up."

General Turner narrows his eyes, trying to make sense of Kun's sudden recall of his personnel. "Has anyone asked any of Kun's personnel what the hell is going on and why they are all being called back?"

The analyst shakes her head. "The reports are coming in slowly, but all the information is the same no matter who we ask. They don't have the slightest idea why they are being called back after all this time."

General Turner furrows his brow as he tries to process the latest information. He speaks his thoughts aloud as he attempts to make sense of this. "Kun has cut his territory off from the world for three days, and now they're recalling their people. It doesn't add up." He looks at the president with uncertainty in his eyes. "We need to let the public know about our findings. I believe something is about to happen."

Two hours later, President Whiteford is at the White House, about to address the nation. The room quiets down as he approaches the microphone, and cameras lock onto his every movement. Without hesitation, he speaks. "We are keeping a close eye on the situation in Southern Asia. Unfortunately, we have yet to get in contact with anyone. Our calls have gone unanswered. A few hours ago, we received news that Kun has ordered all of his military personnel and diplomatic workers to return. We have asked many of their personnel what's going on, but all they told us is they have been ordered to remain silent; anyone who breaks that order will be killed on sight. Also, none of his warships or aircraft respond when we try to communicate with them. Only the bare minimum is being said when they need to cross a country's border. We have reports of diplomatic workers in Europe being killed for not following his orders. The diplomatic workers at the embassy in London were massacred when they tried to rebel. The UK government has gotten involved; they have taken over the embassy, and the people responsible for the massacre have been taken into custody; however, they refuse to talk. The UK has already searched the embassy for any clues about what is going on, but they found nothing useful. This is pure chaos and inhumane. The embassy in Washington, DC has already been vacated about an hour ago. Under international law, we could not force them to stay or answer any of our questions. All we can do is make sure they are escorted to an aircraft safely. At this time, this is all the information we have. We will keep everyone up to date with what is happening on our official social media pages."

Amidst the flurry of questions, one reporter calls out to the president, "Does this have anything to do with the aliens we have been getting reports about?"

"It's hard to say. We haven't confirmed any aliens at this time. It's only speculation," says President Whiteford.

The president points at a reporter for the next question. "Last year, Kun and his mercenary group rose to power by forcefully overthrowing four leaders simultaneously. What is the US and UN doing to make sure that Kun doesn't spread his group's influence elsewhere?"

"All the countries in the UN have put massive sanctions on Kun's foreign assets," says President Whiteford. "We thought he would play by the rules after having a talk with him earlier this year, but it seems we were wrong."

Another reporter yells out, attempting to catch President Whiteford's attention amid the commotion. "Why not send a group to find out what is happening?"

"I'm not going to risk the lives of my men," says President Whiteford. "Kun is ruthless and will treat that as a declaration of war. That is something we do not want happening." He looks to his right as someone waves to him. "And that will be all the questions I will take for now." He walks off stage as reporters swarm him with more questions.

As President Whiteford leaves the room, the press secretary hurries to the podium to take questions. The doors swing shut behind him, muffling the sound of reporters urgently calling out for more information.

As the president moves through the halls of the White House, tense conversations fill the air. Upon reaching the Oval Office, he finds his team of advisors waiting for him. He closes the door behind him, ensuring privacy for the critical discussion ahead. "We need answers. I'm at a complete loss. None of this makes sense. The American people deserve better than this."

"What's our next move, sir?" asks a senior advisor.

The president thinks for a moment. He knows if he does not handle this with care, it could be difficult to win the support of the American people when he decides what to do. "I need someone to talk to Congress on my behalf because we're in desperate need of emergency legislation. I need Congress to pass a bill that empowers the government to act effectively in case Kun does something rash. We do not want to be blindsided by whatever he's doing."

"I'll get right on it," says the advisor. "I should be able to get about five House members on our side by tomorrow morning. That should be enough to draft an emergency bill and push it to the floor."

"That's a good start," says President Whiteford. "I'll leave the funding up to you. I need to be getting to New York now. The meeting with the UN over this is starting in three hours."

Over the course of two days, President Whiteford receives regular updates on the situation. Despite the steady stream of reports, there have been no significant changes. Once every military unit, embassy worker, and overseas official returned to Kun's territory, those regions went into full lockdown. The only intelligence the US gathers comes from fragments of satellite images and intercepted chatter, none of it useful.

His advisor goes to Congress to persuade several key House members to support the allocation of emergency funding. He met with lawmakers, outlining the urgency of the situation. Despite his efforts, the request is shot down before it can gain traction. Many members of Congress dismiss the crisis, treating it as a distant issue rather than an immediate threat.

Across the nation, news anchors argue over what might be happening behind Kun's silence. Their speculation only feeds the fire as people on social media burn with paranoia as each new theory becomes wilder than the last.

In the Oval Office, President Whiteford stands at the windows with his hands behind his back as his reflection stares back at him. He wants to do everything in his power to uncover the truth, but his resources are limited. Despite his resolve, the situation leaves him with only a few options. For now, all he can do is wait to see what happens.

2

November 5th, 2026   2100 Japan Standard Time

In a quiet studio in the heart of Tokyo, the members of Amazing Spring, a talented musical group, gather for a rehearsal to prepare for an upcoming performance on Saturday. At the front of the studio stands Kazuo Ryouichi, the group's lead choreographer. He has been the guiding force since the group's beginning, shaping Amazing Spring's identity over the past five years, with his unmatched talent and vision. At thirty-eight, Kazuo is widely recognized as Japan's best choreographer, known for his outgoing and energetic personality and music style. His journey in the arts began at age ten, showing early dedication and promise. His commitment led him to graduate at the top of his class from Tokyo University with a degree in fine arts. By the age of twenty-two, his reputation had grown significantly, with companies across the country eager to work with him and benefit from his creative brilliance.

His sharp, rhythmic claps resonate through the room as he directs the group through each movement of their routine. "Come on, ladies, we're only two days away from your big show. Let's give the best performance you ever have." The members respond in perfect synchronization; every step reflects their years of dedication and practice. Kazuo watches their performance closely and, satisfied with their progress, stops the music. "All right, we can stop here for tonight. Good work ladies. The last train leaves in an hour, so make sure you all get home safely."

The nine idols turn toward Kazuo, expressing their gratitude for his direction and support with a graceful bow. In response, he offers a respectful nod before quietly exiting the studio without saying a word.

The idols quietly chat among themselves as they make their way toward the wide studio window that overlooks Tokyo's sprawling skyline. Along the wall beneath the window, their bags and water bottles sit neatly in a row.

Their leader, Haruka, leans casually against the wall, gazing out the window to the glowing city. "Before we go home, does anyone want to do karaoke?"

"If you think about it, we just finished karaoke. Plus, we danced as well. Do you really want to do more?" asks Kaede, chuckling as she picks up her water bottle.

"I'm only kidding," says Haruka, playfully nudging Kaede. "I was looking for a reason to get a parfait with someone."

Ayane moves in and shares in the laughs. "If that's what you want, you should have just said so. I'll tag along."

She picks up her bag and pulls out her phone. The screen lights up with a few missed calls and unread texts from her mom. She opens the messages, and her heart sinks as she reads the urgent message. *Your grandfather is in the hospital. He fell down while working. Call me now.* She suddenly puts down her phone and quickly gathers her belongings. "Something just came up. I'll have to pass on the parfait." Without pausing for further explanation or goodbyes, she hurries out of the room. Once in the hallway, she immediately pulls out her phone and calls her mother.

Her mom answers immediately, her voice filled with concern. "Ayane, I've been calling you for over an hour. Why didn't you pick up your phone?"

"Sorry, Mom, I was in the middle of practice," says Ayane. "I didn't see your message until now. How's Grandpa?"

"He's hanging on, but we don't know how long he has left. We need you to come to Nagoya," says her mom.

"I'm on a tight schedule. There's a show in two days. I don't have time to make it," says Ayane.

From his office's doorway, Kazuo overhears the urgent conversation and steps into the hall. "As long as you're back by Saturday, you'll be fine. Family's important. Go be with them."

Ayane turns to him as her eyes shine with heartfelt gratitude, then she bows deeply. "This means a lot. Thank you." She lifts her phone back to her ear, and her expression shifts as she refocuses on her mother's voice. "I'll be there tomorrow morning once the trains start running."

Ayane hangs up and prepares to head home. But before she leaves, another colleague grabs her attention. "Wait, Ayane. Is it okay if I tag along?"

"Of course, Sachi," says Ayane, smiling back at her. "I'll message you the details later."

Kazuo crosses his arms and leans on the doorframe as he watches them head toward the exit. "Remember, ladies, be back by Saturday."

They both turn around and synchronize. "Yeah, we will."

Ayane rushes through the narrow hallway of her apartment. Her mind and heart race as she grabs a suitcase from her closet and tosses it onto her bed. Her hands tremble as she throws in clean clothes for her trip to Nagoya. One by one, messages from her friends light up the screen, with each wishing her the best of luck. They overheard enough to understand something serious must have happened, and their words carry warmth and support.

November 5th, 2026   1200 Eastern Standard Time

General Angus Turner sits in his office at the Pentagon while on a video call with the commanding officer of Fort Liberty in North Carolina. "I told the president I'd handle all matters concerning Kun and the unknown ship. I don't think faulty equipment falls under that category."

As the other general speaks about his problem, a woman in her early thirties steps into the office with a pitcher of water and quietly pours him a glass. Without saying a word, she moves behind him with her hands resting slightly below her waist and quietly waits for the video call to end.

The general at Fort Liberty finishes his update. "Those are my thoughts on the matter. We need you to send some specialists to assess our base."

Angus leans back, considering what to do. "I can arrange that."

The woman behind him leans forward to whisper into his ear. "It's kind of odd this is happening to the biggest base we have. With what's going on with Kun, I think it would be in our best interest to go there and see what's going on. I can clear your schedule for today and tomorrow."

Angus nods slightly before speaking to the commanding officer. "After discussing it with my senior advisor, I think it's best for me to fly down there personally to see what's going on firsthand. If it's true that the entire base is experiencing a mass equipment failure, our national security could be at risk. What are the odds that a foreign entity is involved?"

"From the data we've gathered, that's likely the case," says the general. "Unfortunately, we need more people to help locate the source of our problems. Like I said, none of our equipment is working."

Angus turns his head back to the woman, who gives a subtle nod. He then returns his attention to the call. "I'll get the specialists you are asking for there by tonight. For now, I want you to close the base and turn off anything connected to the internet. No one enters or leaves either. If it's some kind of virus, I don't want it to spread. Do I make myself clear?"

The general straightens his posture, salutes Angus, and ends the video call.

Angus stands from his chair, and the woman hands him his coat. "Paula, I need you to set up a flight down to North Carolina. I'm going to talk with Robert."

"I'll get right on it," says Paula. "Also, that general sent me some files about what's going on. Let me print them so you can review them on the plane."

As Paula makes the arrangements, Angus makes his way down the hall toward Robert's office. The door is wide open, revealing him inside, deep in conversation on a call.

Angus taps on the door twice while glancing around the well-organized room. "I hope I'm not interrupting anything."

Robert raises his index finger up at Angus. "I have to go now. Angus is standing at my door. Love you too, honey." After ending the call, he looks at Angus. "What's up?"

"I just got off an interesting call with Fort Liberty. They said nothing's working," says Angus.

Robert shoots him a strange look as he slides his phone into his pocket. "Like what?"

"Anything electronic related," says Angus. "Communications, defense systems, and basic infrastructures are down. I'm sending a team of specialists to see what's going on. We're also going."

"Now hold on just a moment," says Robert, leaning back in his chair and crossing his arms. "If nothing's working, how were they able to call you?"

"They claim the only call that would go through was to me," says Angus, shrugging. "This situation piques my interest, and I want to see what's going on."

"That's weird," says Robert, leaning forward. "I guess I'll bite. Could this be a trap by ISIS or some other terrorist organization to cause the US more problems?"

"I took that into consideration, but I don't think that's the case," says Angus. "I don't think a terrorist organization has the capabilities of taking out one of our military bases."

"Let's hope not. We don't want any foreign adversary helping Kun," says Robert. "What time are we leaving?"

Before Angus can respond, Paula squeezes past him and positions herself between the two generals. "Right now, Robert. The plane leaves in thirty minutes. Pack your things and let's go." She slaps a folder against Angus' chest. "Here's the printed notes. Have a look at it when we get on the plane. I've also talked with the secretary about getting us those specialists."

Robert stands and gathers his belongings. He retrieves his coat and slips it on. "Then what are we waiting for? Let's head out."

Angus, Robert, and Paula leave the Pentagon and head straight for a black SUV that is waiting for them outside. The ride to Ronald Reagan Washington Airport is brief. Instead of stopping at the airport terminal, their vehicle drives straight onto the runway. There, a private military jet waits to depart. Without delay, they board and find their seats, ready for takeoff.

Once Angus settles into his seat, he opens the folder Paula handed him earlier. He carefully reads through the documents, scanning each page with care. "So this is all the information we know at this time?"

Paula unbuttons her coat, places it over her seat, and settles down beside Angus. "Those were all the files he sent me."

Angus leans across the aisle and passes the folder to Robert. After giving it a quick read, Robert hands it back to Angus. "So the base only started experiencing this five hours ago? Something still feels off about this. I can't seem to figure out what though."

Paula leans past Angus so she can make eye contact with Robert. "I thought so too. I've been keeping notes of anything I deem important. What stands out to me is this." She angles her phone screen toward Angus and Robert, showing what she has written.

Robert glances at the screen and lets out a mocking scoff. "You expect me to believe that? That's a pretty big assumption."

"Someone's trying to get Angus' attention diverted elsewhere, like they want him away from the Pentagon," says Paula.

"Let's not jump to conclusions before we know the full scope of the situation," says Robert. "Did you tell anyone else about this?"

"You two are the only ones I shared this with," says Paula. "When we were driving here, I messaged the Secretary of Defense to keep an eye out for anything or anyone suspicious."

As the two of them continue their conversation, Angus leans back in his seat, closes his eyes, and allows himself to get lost in his own thoughts. He focuses on assessing the situation and trying to plan out a mental outline of the next steps they should take. Shortly after, the plane takes off.

An hour later, they touch down in North Carolina. As they disembark the plane, a convoy of military vehicles is already waiting for them on the runway. Armed soldiers escort them to one of the military vehicles. They step inside, where the commanding general of Fort Liberty, General Zachary Dillon, greets them.

"Has there been any changes to the situation?" asks Angus.

"It's a full blackout," says General Dillon. "The blackout is within a one-mile radius of the base. We moved some equipment outside of the affected area, and it all started working again."

Paula sits quietly with her pen in hand as she carefully records her thoughts in a notebook. Something feels off, though she cannot quite put her finger on it. "Could something inside the base be emitting a signal that's disrupting everything?"

"We've searched for any signals from inside the base, but there's nothing. It's a dead zone," says General Dillon. "With all the equipment turned off, we should have found something by now."

Paula looks over her notes while tapping the end of her pen against the notebook before looking back at General Dillon. "Are only electronics affected?"

"Anything with an electronic component is affected," says General Dillon. "That includes vehicles and generators. Shoot, even the automatic doors have stopped working."

"None of this adds up," says Paula, placing the pen onto the paper. "I've never heard of anything like this happening before." She glances at Angus. "I think what I said earlier is true."

Angus takes a moment to consider what Paula told him. As much as he wants to dismiss her theory, something about this situation feels orchestrated. Realizing that speculation alone will not produce the answers they need, he lets out a slow breath and forces himself to concentrate on the task. "Have the specialists arrived?"

"A few have," says General Dillon. "We'll be arriving there soon as well."

Throughout the rest of the day, Angus, Paula, and Robert dedicate their time to conducting thorough investigations at the base. They meet with the specialists and watch them work tirelessly to find the issue. Despite everyone's efforts, they are no closer to an answer by nightfall. By the end of the day, the three make their way to the hotel they are staying at.

Angus stretches his neck and lets out a long yawn. "Get some rest, you two. We're heading back to DC early in the morning." With that, he takes his room key and disappears down the hall. Once inside his room, he takes a hot shower, scrubbing away the day's stress and grime. By ten o'clock, he collapses onto the firm mattress, nearly falling asleep until his phone rings on the nightstand. He groans as he grabs to see who it is. Recognizing the caller, he answers. "Angus speaking."

"Sorry for waking you, but everything in the affected area works now," says General Dillon.

Angus sits up, rubbing his eyes. "Really? That's odd. What changed?"

"I don't know," says General Dillon. "This is bizarre."

"I'm heading back now," says Angus, not wasting another second with his response. He ends the call and immediately throws off the covers. As he hurries to put his uniform back on, he dials Paula and Robert, telling them to get ready as well.

Throughout the night they monitor the situation closely. But despite everything working normally, nothing happens.

November 6th, 2026	0500 Japan Standard Time

Ayane wakes up at dawn and throws the covers off. She sits up, stretching and rubbing her eyes, then sends a message to Sachi, letting her know the time she will be at the train station. After having breakfast and taking a shower, she exits her apartment, and locks up before she leaves. The morning air is chilly for her liking, so she bundles up in a cozy jacket.

At the station, Sachi is already waiting, wrapped in a scarf. When she notices Ayane approaching, she raises her arm and waves. The two friends exchange a quick hello before they hurry onto the platform just as their train arrives on schedule. They waste no time boarding, and Sachi slides into her seat by the window. She breathes on the glass to draw a smiley face with her finger.

The train pulls out of the station and speeds through the Tokyo suburbs. The cityscape gradually gives way to stretches of open countryside. They chat quietly to pass the time, and two and a half hours later, the train pulls into Nagoya Station at 8:30. Outside the station, Ayane's father, Tatsuya, is waiting for them. A warm grin spreads across his face as he sees them approach.

The moment Ayane sees her father, she sets her bags on the pavement and goes in for a hug, wrapping herself in her father's tight embrace. "It's good to see you, Dad. It's been so long."

"I hope Tokyo has been kind to you," says Tatsuya. He lets go and his gaze shifts to the girl standing behind her. "Who's your friend?"

Ayane steps back toward Sachi, eager to introduce her. "This is Sachi. I told you about her over the phone. She's a friend who wanted to come with me."

Sachi politely waves at Tatsuya. "It's nice to meet you."

Tatsuya smiles back, but before he can say anything, Ayane interrupts him as her expression suddenly turns serious. "How's Grandpa doing?"

"I haven't seen him yet," says Tatsuya. "I just got off work at eight and rushed here to pick you both up." He recognizes the worried look in his daughter's eyes and gently pats her on the back to comfort her. "I wouldn't worry too much about him. I've known that man for many years. He's a fighter. A little fall like this won't take him out." He walks over to Ayane's bags and bends down to gather them. He gestures for Ayane and Sachi to follow him to where he parked his car.

The hospital is located two miles away from the station, making the drive a quick and easy one. After the brief journey, they soon arrive at their destination. They step through the sliding glass doors and enter the bright, bustling lobby, where Ayane's mother, Hana, is waiting for them.

"How's Grandpa doing?" asks Ayane.

"I'll take you to him so you can see for yourself," says Hana.

Hana leads them down the hall to the room where Ayane's grandfather is recovering. Ayane steps forward, hesitating briefly before she opens the door. Inside, her grandfather is sitting upright in bed, talking in a friendly conversation with the nurse. His mood seems relaxed and cheerful, showing no visible signs of distress.

As Ayane enters, his expression shifts from casual to pleasantly surprised as his eyes brighten when he sees her. "Ayane? I wasn't expecting to see you."

Ayane approaches him as a look of confusion washes over her face. She hesitates before speaking, her voice carrying a mixture of worry and relief. "How are you feeling, Grandpa? You don't look hurt. Mom said, you didn't have long left."

He tilts his head and furrows his brow as he responds to Ayane's concern. "I don't have long left before I leave the hospital." They both glance at Hana, who stands quietly in the doorway, returning their worried looks with a gentle smile. He rolls his eyes and looks back at Ayane. "You know your mother. She overreacts to the littlest things. I'm fine. My only problem is my ankle." He pulls the sheets back to reveal his swollen ankle. "I tripped while working. This stupid metal rod appeared out of nowhere. Nothing bad at all. A few days of rest is all I need, and I'll be as good as new." He reaches out his arm to Ayane, and she steps forward, embracing him in a warm hug.

"I was so worried," says Ayane. "I didn't get any sleep last night. I left Tokyo early this morning just to see you."

After they finish their embrace, Tatsuya steps forward with a wide grin. "I'm glad to see you are still hanging in there, Toshiro."

Toshiro glances back toward the doorway where Hana is standing. "Did Hana invite the whole town to see me? A simple phone call would have been enough."

"So, everything's good, Ayane?" asks Sachi, poking her head through the doorway.

"That seems to be the case," says Ayane. She turns back to Toshiro and gives the bed a loving pat. "Since you're fine, we need to be getting back to Tokyo."

Toshiro reaches out and gently takes Ayane's hand, shaking his head with a reassuring smile. "Nonsense, you're already here. You might as well stay for the day." He then turns his attention to Sachi, extending the same invitation. "That goes for you too."

Ayane shakes her head and waves her hands back and forth. "I would love to, but we need to get back to work. We need to practice with our group. We have an important show tomorrow."

"You both came all this way expecting to stay the night," says Toshiro. "Why not practice here together, and first thing in the morning, you can head out?"

After going back-and-forth with each other, Ayane caves with a sigh. "Fine, we'll stay the night."

Toshiro reaches over to the table beside him and picks up his phone. A smile spreads over his face as he calls his wife. "Terrific. Let me call Akemi and tell her we're having Ayane and her friend over tonight."

"I'll only stay for lunch," says Sachi, stepping fully into the room. "I was expecting to leave tonight, anyway. There are other things I have to take care of before our show."

Hana turns to her, clasping her hands around Sachi's hands. "Are you sure? It wouldn't be a problem if you stayed the night."

Sachi shakes her head firmly, sending her hair flying everywhere. "I'm sorry, but I have to leave by three."

"Don't force the little lady," says Toshiro. "She's just as important as Ayane. If she needs to be somewhere, we shouldn't stop her."

Ayane looks at the nurse. "When is he going to be released from the hospital?"

"All he has is a sprained ankle," says the nurse. "We can release him now if he wants."

"That settles it," says Toshiro. "Sign me out so I can spend time with my granddaughter. Who knows the next time I'll have this chance."

Once the nurse confirm that Toshiro is okay to be released, the group moves into action. Toshiro carefully moves into a wheelchair, and together, everyone helps to gather his belongings, ensuring nothing gets left behind. With everything packed, they make their way out of the hospital's front entrance.

Tatsuya pulls the vehicle around to the entrance. He steps out to help Toshiro into the vehicle. Once Toshiro is secure, the rest of the group climbs in, and Tatsuya drives away.

"I'm going home so I can sleep," says Tatsuya. "You can spend the day at your grandparents' house, Ayane. I'll see you later tonight for dinner."

When they arrive at the grandparents' house, Ayane and Sachi work together to help Toshiro out of the vehicle. As they approach the front entrance, the door swings open and Akemi steps outside, and her face lights up at the sight of her family. "It's been so long, Ayane. You've gotten bigger since the last time I saw you."

Ayane lets go of Toshiro and eagerly hurries into Akemi's arms. She smiles warmly as she embraces her grandmother. "It's good to see you too, Granny. Are my brothers here?"

"They both are still in their clubs at school. They'll be here later," says Akemi.

Ayane goes back to supporting Toshiro as they make their way toward the house. "This is Sachi, Granny. She came to make sure I arrived safely."

"It's nice to meet you, dear," says Akemi. "I hope my granddaughter has kept you out of trouble."

"She keeps me grounded. Without her, I wouldn't be able to perform at my best," says Sachi.

"That's good to hear. Let's get Toshiro inside. We can set him on the couch," says Akemi.

The afternoon passes by quickly for Ayane and Sachi. After enjoying a delicious home-cooked lunch made by Akemi, the two idols sit together at the dining table, listening to stories from Ayane's childhood. Laughter fills the room as Akemi recalls fond memories, and Sachi delights in learning more about Ayane's past. Afterward, Ayane and Sachi move to the backyard to practice their dance routine. The yard becomes lively with music as the two work together, encouraging each other and perfecting their moves. At three o'clock, Hana offers to drive Sachi to the train station, and Ayane joins them for the ride.

When Hana pulls up to the front of the station, she turns to Sachi with a gentle smile. "It was nice to meet you. You're welcome to come back anytime."

"I had a great time today. I'll definitely make time to come back soon," says Sachi. She steps out of the vehicle and closes the door behind her.

As Hana drives away, she glimpses Sachi waving goodbye through the rearview mirror. The gesture brings a warm smile to her face. "She's a good kid. I was worried you wouldn't make any friends in Tokyo."

Ayane gazes out the window as she watches the passing scenery. "It was scary at first, but once I settled in, it wasn't bad. I'll tell you all about it when we get home."

For the rest of the day, Ayane sits with her mother and grandparents. She shares stories about life in Tokyo, recounting moments from her job and the challenges she faces.

In the middle of the story, Akemi looks at a clock hanging on the wall. "Six already? I should start making dinner."

"I can help," says Ayane, standing with her.

"Come now. You're the guest," says Akemi. "Keep your grandpa company, and Hana will help me."

As Hana follows Akemi to the kitchen, she pauses for a moment to glance at Ayane. "Your brothers will be here in an hour. Dinner should be ready by then."

Ayane nods and continues talking with Toshiro.

About an hour later, Tatsuya arrives with Ayane's brothers, Kado and Shun, all eager for dinner. As the aroma of Akemi's cooking fills the house, ten more family members unexpectedly arrive, much to Ayane's delight. After dinner, the group gathers in the living room to catch up with Ayane until it is time for everyone to leave. Each relative hugs Ayane, offering her words of encouragement for her upcoming performance.

"Well, I need to head to work," says Tatsuya, standing from his chair. "Are you staying here at your grandparents' place tonight, Ayane?"

"Yes, I want to spend some more time with them," says Ayane.

"What time are you leaving tomorrow?" asks Tatsuya. "I get off of work at eight. I can drop you off at the train station."

"I was planning on leaving at six, but if you want to drop me off, I can leave at nine instead." says Ayane.

"Will that give you enough time to make it back to Tokyo?" asks Tatsuya.

Ayane taps her finger on her lips and tilts her head up to the ceiling as she considers her plans for the following day. "The train ride is about three hours. I'll be there by noon. The show doesn't start until seven anyway. I'll have plenty of time." She hugs Akemi, and a big smile washes over her face. "I can also eat Granny's breakfast tomorrow morning."

Before he leaves, Tatsuya pulls Ayane in for a hug and a kiss on the forehead. "I'll see you tomorrow morning then."

Ayane spends the evening deep in conversation with her mother and her grandparents well past eleven o'clock. Suddenly, a soft blue dome of light catches their attention from the living room window.

The light shimmers far in the distance, noticeably getting bigger with each passing moment. For about a minute, it continues to expand, captivating everyone in the room. Without warning, the light stops growing. The family sits in silence with their eyes fixed on the spectacle outside. Another minute passes, and a darker light abruptly overtakes the shimmering blue light and fades away, leaving no trace it was there. Ayane and her family struggle to make sense of what they witnessed. They brush off the strange phenomenon, assuming it must have been part of a local light festival. With the event behind them, the family calls it a night, and each person heads to their room.

As the house settles into silence and darkness, everyone is already in bed for the night. Ayane's phone rests on the counter beside the refrigerator. Suddenly, the screen lights up with an incoming call. However, she has it on vibrate, so the call goes unnoticed by anyone in the house. After a moment, the screen dims again, but a notification appears saying it has three missed calls.

November 6th, 2026   1015 Eastern Standard Time

At the same time, Angus and Paula stands in the well-lit hotel lobby, waiting for Robert to meet up with them.

Paula checks her watch, watching the second hand tick away. "What is taking him so long?" She glances at Angus with concern in her voice. "You don't think something happened to him, do you?"

Angus stands with his arms crossed, gazing down the hallway where Robert should come from. "It's odd he isn't here. He's always strict with his schedule. Have you called him?"

"Not yet," says Paula, pulling out her phone.

Before she can hit the call button, Angus glances over his shoulder, catching sight of a commotion across the lobby. A small group of people gather in front of a TV mounted on the wall. Sensing something urgent has happened, he taps Paula on the shoulder. "Something's going on."

Paula looks up from her phone just as Angus makes his way toward the TV. "What? Hey, wait up." She quickly tucks her phone away and hurries after him. "What's going on?"

On the TV, a reporter narrates from a helicopter hovering over a scene of devastation. The live footage reveals an enormous hole as water rushes inside to fill it. The camera pans across the edge of the void, capturing the scale of destruction, while the reporter struggles to find the words to describe what he is witnessing. Angus and Paula stand frozen, unable to speak as a headline flashes across the screen saying this used to be New York City.

Robert sits on the edge of his bed, focusing on the same broadcast. The harsh glow from the TV illuminates his face, casting shadows that deepen the terror and disbelief in his expression. Beside him, his phone lies forgotten. The fractured screen faintly displays his wallpaper with him, his wife, and two kids. As the reality of the situation sets in, Robert clenches his hands into tight fists and his fingernails dig into his skin. His chest tightens under the weight of fear and disbelief. "This can't be." Tears slip silently down his cheeks. Then he snaps; his voice explodes into the room with raw emotion. "What the hell is going on?"

3

November 6th, 2026   1000 Eastern Standard Time

All major news networks across the US suddenly cut to black, leaving viewers to wonder what is happening. At first, many assume the disruption is an isolated technical error affecting only one network. However, as they switch between news channels, they soon discover that the same problem occurs. This widespread outage confirms that something significant is happening, even though viewers are unaware of the disaster that has just taken place. Amid the uncertainty, only a single network returns to the air.

A twenty-two-year-old woman with dark red hair sits in front of a camera at the bustling news headquarters in Atlanta, Georgia. The scene behind her is one of barely controlled chaos as staff rush to restore the regularly scheduled program back on the air. Despite the commotion, she maintains her professionalism, addressing the viewers directly. "It seems we've lost connection with our network in New York City. I'm Brittney Taber and for now, I'll be reporting until we can get the connection back."

Brittney continues to cover the latest news stories. Suddenly, someone off-screen interrupts her and says something that catches her attention. "Are you serious? That can't be true." For a moment, she sits in stunned silence before coming to her senses. "We're getting unconfirmed reports that a bomb went off in New York City. We're trying to get in contact with anyone in New York to confirm this. As of now, it looks like the bomb took out communications with our studio in New York City and forced them off the grid. This may take some time to fix."

A sudden, piercing scream comes from somewhere behind her, causing Brittney to flinch. She turns to speak with someone off-screen, and her face drains of color as she slowly turns back to the camera. "We just received a video showing what happened in New York City. Please be aware that this footage is disturbing. If you have children in the room, or if you can't handle sensitive content, I'd recommend turning away at this time."

The footage, captured on a mobile phone at Port Jersey in New Jersey, opens with a clear view of the New York City skyline in the distance from across the Hudson River. In the foreground, the Statue of Liberty stands tall and resolute, with her iconic torch rising high against the clear blue sky. People go about their day, unaware of the catastrophe about to occur. Without warning, a shimmering clear blue dome expands over the city. The phenomenon quickly engulfs the towering skyscrapers and bridges, advancing steadily until it envelops the Statue of Liberty and comes to a sudden stop. Onlookers watch in awe, unsure of what is unfolding before their eyes.

A dark blue dome emerges, trailing behind the see-through dome. As this second dome covers the city, a piercing sound reverberates through the air, similar to the sound of ice falling in a storm. The dark dome stops precisely where the clear dome boundary stopped before. Then, almost as quickly as it began, both domes dissipate, revealing the aftermath.

Back in the newsroom, voices yell in terror as the sound of rushing water grows louder in the footage. New York City and the vast majority of its surrounding areas are completely gone without a trace. All that remains is a massive hole where the once great city stood. The footage comes to an abrupt end.

Brittney sits frozen at the news desk, struggling to make sense of what she sees unfolding on the screen before her. The disaster leaves her speechless, and a flood of emotions washes over her, but despite the chaos and confusion swirling around the newsroom, she forces herself to maintain composure. She remembers her responsibility as a reporter and the importance of keeping the public informed during such a crisis. "Can we get a helicopter out there to confirm this footage?"

"We're already getting one from New Jersey. It should be there soon," says someone off-screen as their voice trembles with fear.

Moments later, the helicopter reaches the site where New York City once stood. As it hovers above the scene, the camera pans across the vast hole as the reporter aboard struggles to comprehend the devastation below. "I don't know if you can see what I'm seeing, but the city is gone. It's gone. There's nothing left." The camera operator shifts focus to the relentless surge of ocean water rushing to fill the hole. The water pours in, sweeping boats and debris into the void where the city once thrived.

Brittney's attention remains on the live broadcast. Her hands tremble on the desk as she watches people caught in the water struggle to stay afloat. She tries to stay calm, but her face displays her fear. "I can't find the words to describe what's going on. The city is just...gone. How is that even possible?"

A fellow reporter rushes to Brittney's side, keeping her head turned away from the camera, trying to conceal her fear from the viewers. "Reports are coming in that another city is gone."

Britteny's expression drops as she tries to process the shocking news. She stares blankly at the woman as her eyes widen in disbelief. "What? Really? What other city?"

The other reporter leans in and whispers to her, so the viewers cannot hear her.

She turns back to face the camera. She tries to hold herself together, but the panic is impossible to hide. "Reports are coming in saying that Washington, DC is also gone." She glances around the newsroom, searching for someone who might have the answer or further information. "Do we have any live footage of DC? We do? Put that footage on." The broadcast quickly shifts to the live feed of Washington, DC. The scene resembles New York City; an enormous, empty crater where the city once stood. The broadcast cuts to another aerial shot of water pouring into a gaping hole where the nation's capital once stood. Brittney speaks over the footage; her voice cracks under the weight of the situation as she delivers an urgent update. "I have more breaking news. We are getting reports that other locations across the world have also disappeared."

Within an hour, confirmation of additional cities to have disappeared continue to arrive. The disappearance of major metropolitan areas triggers worldwide panic, with communities fearing their city might be next. All anyone can do is wait for what might happen next.

November 7th, 2026   0100 Japan Standard Time

A sudden, loud noise startles Ayane awake. She swings her legs over the edge of the bed. Her movements are sluggish and unsteady as she struggles to shake off the lingering effects of sleep. She stumbles across the room toward the door. As she turns the handle and opens it, her father stands there, startling her fully awake.

Before she can say a word, Tatsuya steps forward and wraps his arms around her in a tight hug. "Ayane, I was worried you had already left. You wouldn't answer your phone."

"What's going on?" asks Ayane.

Tatsuya pulls back to look her in the eyes, then wipes the sweat from his forehead. "You need to see what just happened in Tokyo."

"What about Tokyo?" asks Ayane, rubbing her eyes.

Tatsuya takes her hand, guiding her out of the bedroom and into the living room. The TV glows with the latest news as the images cast a sobering light across the room. Hana sits on the couch as her eyes fixates on the screen, with her hands pressed tightly over her mouth.

The news broadcast shows a live aerial shot of the massive hole where part of Tokyo used to be. The sight is overwhelming, and Ayane collapses to the floor as the world around her blurs; sounds and voices fade into a muffled haze.

"Ayane...Ayane..." says Hana.

Ayane's breath becomes heavy as her mind races to make sense of what is going on, with each rapid heartbeat echoing her mounting anxiety.

Hana grabs Ayane's wrist and shakes her urgently. "Ayane, wake up."

Ayane takes a deep breath, forcing herself to regain composure as reality sets in. She stares at her parents with her mouth slightly parted in shock, but the words she wants to say refuse to come out.

The commotion wakes Ayane's grandparents, and they come into the living room. Toshiro struggles to stand, so he leans against the wall for support as he surveys the tense scene. "What's going on so early in the morning?"

"Have a look for yourself," says Tatsuya, pointing at the TV.

Toshiro turns his gaze to the TV as the rest of the family speaks quietly among themselves. Ayane, however, finds herself unable to focus on their conversations. Her attention snaps to a faint vibrating sound that echoes somewhere in the distance. She closes her eyes for a moment, concentrating to identify the noise. When she realizes what it is, she springs to her feet and dashes toward the kitchen. On the counter, her phone buzzes persistently. The family's attention shifts to her as she picks up the phone and answers it. On the other end, a familiar voice greets her.

"Ayane, it's about time you picked up. I've been calling you for over two hours," says Kazuo.

Hearing Kazuo's voice triggers a surge of emotions within Ayane, and tears well up in her eyes as she clutches the phone tightly to her ear. "Where are the others?"

"We don't know. We're waiting to hear from them," says Kazuo. "Listen, Ayane, I'm expecting the worst."

Ayane tries to say something, but nothing comes out.

"I'll keep in touch when we hear from anyone," says Kazuo. "If you need to talk, call me. I'll have my phone with me."

Ayane calms herself and takes a steadying breath as she attempts to regain control over her emotions. With great effort, she utters a single word. "Okay."

The call ends abruptly, and Ayane stands motionless as she stares at her reflection on the phone's darkened screen. A heavy silence fills the room. Then, without speaking, Tatsuya gently places a hand on the back of her head and pulls her close toward him. Overwhelmed by emotion, Ayane buries her face in his shirt, letting out a deafening scream.

The night is long for Ayane. Hours stretch by endlessly as she sits curled on the couch, wide awake but numb, unable to fall back to sleep. She clutches a pillow to her chest, hoping to hear from the others at any moment.

November 6th, 2026   1400 Eastern Standard Time

Four hours have passed since the crisis began, and Brittney remains on the air, tirelessly covering the unfolding events. Despite her exhaustion, she continues to deliver updates, uncertain if her efforts are providing comfort to those watching. "From all the reports we've received, we can now confirm that twenty-two major cities, along with their surrounding areas, have been wiped off the map. Of the twenty-two, three cities have vanished here in the US. The three cities are: New York City, Washington DC, and Los Angeles. For simplicity's sake, we here at the studio have chosen to name this event the Disappearance."

At this time, the National Guard has mobilized in both California and New York. Each state's forces are offering assistance wherever possible. Their efforts focus on rescuing individuals from the water. But despite their tireless work, many people have already drowned, and the rescue teams have only recovered dead bodies so far.

In the wake of the Disappearance, Washington, DC suffered an unprecedented blow to its leadership. Nearly all members of Congress, the nine justices of the Supreme Court, everyone at the

Pentagon, the White House including the president, vice president, all cabinet members, and any other politician who happened to be in the city are gone. Amidst the chaos and confusion, the nation desperately searches for answers. With everyone in the line of succession missing, people scramble to determine who, if anyone, is around to assume the presidency.

By two in the afternoon, Angus, Robert, and Paula arrive at the massive hole where Washington, DC once stood. As they approach the edge of the devastation, a news camera catches sight of them. The footage quickly makes it to networks around the globe, providing undeniable proof that these three survived the Disappearance.

Brittney promptly identifies the military generals; she picks up a piece of paper containing details about them. "Let's see here. General Angus Turner was appointed the chairman of the Joint Chiefs of Staff last year in October, along with his vice chairman, General Robert Jackson. We are doing everything in our power to get an interview with them." She looks exhausted but continues, ensuring the public remains informed. "We just received new footage out of California." The video reveals people glowing with a blue hue as the National Guard takes them away. "We are getting reports of what can only be described as 'blue people.' Our experts believe these people were caught in the initial blue dome but managed to leave the affected area before the darkened dome enveloped everything." Brittney pauses as someone off-screen tells her urgent news. She nods grimly and turns back to the camera. "We just got another video. This one is from outside of Santa Clarita, the town north of Los Angeles."

The footage captures the moment traffic came to a standstill on the southbound lanes of Interstate five as the wall of the darkened dome swallowed Los Angeles. The same ominous sound previously recorded in the New York City footage echoes throughout the video. Meanwhile, on the northbound side of the highway, vehicles glowing blue have come to a stop. Drivers and passengers exit their cars, transfixed as they witness the city being swallowed up by the advancing dome. What began as awe quickly turns to horror. As the dome reaches the boundary of the other dome, it looks as though the phenomenon reached its conclusion. Mere seconds later, everything that glows blue fades away, disappearing completely and without a trace. Onlookers collapse in shock as people vanish before their eyes. The terror on these people's faces as they fade away leaves many people sick to their stomachs. After a certain distance, the blue objects are unscathed.

November 7th and 8th, 2026

Within the following two days, nations around the world scrambled to recover. Eighteen countries fell victim, forcing their governments to move their capitals and reorganize their leadership structures. While some countries can adapt to the crisis, others plunge into turmoil. Power vacuums arise in certain regions, and a handful of nations collapse entirely.

Russia plunges into chaos. With Moscow gone, rival factions try to take control, leading to a civil war that destabilizes the entire country.

Israel faces a similar fate after the disappearance of Jerusalem. This sparks violent clashes among religious groups, each desperately trying to gain power and influence over the country.

India lost two cities; Mumbai, and its capital, New Delhi. The situation is further complicated by invasions from neighboring countries, intensifying the nation's crisis.

Two countries cease to exist altogether. Singapore and South Korea were erased entirely from the map. With the capital of South Korea, Seoul, gone, North Korea quickly took advantage of the situation. Within hours, the North Korean forces seized the opportunity, launching an invasion into South Korea. The remaining South Korean military surrendered five hours later, and the peninsula reunites under one name: Korea.

The other countries that suffer devastating blows are the capitals of Japan, Malaysia, The Philippines, Indonesia, China, Australia lost Melbourne and Sydney, France, Italy's capital along with

Vatican City, England, Brazil, Mexico, the three cities in the US, and Toronto, Canada. The estimated death toll is around half a billion.

By November eighth, the US capital moved back to Philadelphia, Pennsylvania. Many lawmakers, who had previously served in Congress, assembled there, determined to help the country recover and rebuild its legislative framework. During the disappearance, eight representatives were out of town. These individuals immediately took over and accepted help from any former member of Congress. However, several of those lawmakers sought to advance their party's agenda and tried to take advantage of the situation. Since they were not voted in to represent their state's people, a law has to be written up by the surviving Congress members to stop anyone from making any bills that would benefit one party. No new laws will be enacted until the states vote in their own representatives. For the time being, the House and Senate are merged into one body. The biggest problem they face is finding a new president and vice president.

Japan suffers the most devastating loss in the wake of the Disappearance. Tokyo, home to twenty-six million residents, accounts for the largest human casualties of the catastrophe. The country's economy revolves heavily around its capital. Within the first hours after the event, the Japanese yen rapidly losses its value as there is no longer anything to support it. Over the next twenty-four hours, businesses across the nation shut down for good. Then, after a full day passes, the Japanese stock market crashes, leading them into a depression. Local governments did their best to intervene and halt the market crash, but their efforts were ultimately unsuccessful. Fortunately, relief came when the US reestablishes its Congress. Among the first bills passed is a relief bill, designed to aid nations affected by the Disappearance. With economies in disarray and currencies failing globally, the US dollar quickly becomes the most sought-after currency, offering a measure of stability in the uncertain world.

November 7th, 2026   0600 Japan Standard Time

The first light of dawn creeps across the sky. Ayane sits motionless as her eyes anxiously drifting between the TV and her phone in her hand. News anchors solemnly report on the countless cities that have vanished. As the morning drags into midday, Ayane confronts the devastating reality that her idol group, the companions who meant so much to her, are gone. Overcome with grief, she curls herself into a tight ball on the couch, clutching a pillow against her chest. She uncontrollably weeps until the world finally becomes a blur and she slips into a restless sleep.

Ayane dreams she is singing alone on a vast, empty theater stage. A single spotlight shines down, illuminating her as she stands at the center, dressed in a fluffy light-purple dress. There is no music playing; only her voice fills the space as she sings her part of the song. When her singing ends, she transitions into her dancing, and moves gracefully around the stage; each step and turn echoes off the wooden floor. When her routine comes to a close, Ayane stands quietly, gazing out into the sea of empty seats.

A faint voice drifts softly from somewhere in the distance, barely audible yet unmistakably familiar. "Become what we tried to be. Never forget, Ayane." The words echo throughout the theater, lingering in the air before gradually fading away.

A bright white light appears behind Ayane, and she wakes with the vivid memory of her dream lingering in her mind. Still curled up on the couch, she comes to realize that she is clutching her phone tightly to her chest. As she brings the phone into view, she notices that the time is already six in the evening. Her hands tremble as she unlocks her phone and scrolls through her contacts. When she finds Kazuo's name, she hesitates only briefly before tapping the call button. Kazuo quickly answers her call, but before he can respond, Ayane interrupts him. "I'm going to continue to be an idol so I can be the light the world needs. I need your help, please."

Kazuo stays silent for a moment to gather his thoughts before responding. "You know that's going to be hard, right? An unknown force devastated the world. Are you sure you don't want to take some time off for yourself?"

"I owe it to everyone to continue this journey," says Ayane. "Even though they are gone, I'm still here. I want the world to know that."

"If that's what you really want, then who am I to stand in your way?" asks Kazuo. "I'll help you, but only on one condition. You need to become the best idol the world has ever known. Do that, and I'll help you."

Ayane sits up on the couch with resolve shining in her eyes. "I will. You can count on it."

November 8th, 2026   1400 Japan Standard Time

Kazuo arrives in Nagoya the following day, driving a moving truck filled with his belongings. As soon as he pulls into the driveway of his new home, he takes out his phone and calls Ayane. "I just arrived. I'll text you the address so we can talk in person."

When Ayane pulls up, she parks on the street and steps out, taking a moment to admire the house. "Pretty big house for one person." She then walks to the gate and calls out. "Kazuo, are you in there?"

"Hey, Ayane, come inside," says Kazuo.

Ayane walks through the front gate and enters the house. The living room is welcoming, and she notices Kazuo carefully arranging decorations to brighten the space up. He has a few colorful vases on the shelves and framed photos on the wall.

Kazuo notices Ayane standing at the entrance and quickly approaches her, offering a friendly pat on the back. "I'm happy to see you are doing well." He then stretches his arms above his head and lets out a long yawn. "Sorry, I haven't been able to get any sleep."

"I'm the same way," says Ayane, forcing a smile. "So much has happened. I don't know what else to do."

"There's someone here I want you to meet," says Kazuo.

From the kitchen, a woman's voice calls out. "Is she here? Give me a second." A beautiful woman steps into the living room and stand beside Kazuo. "So, this is the girl you are going to be mentoring."

"Ayane, I'd like to introduce you to my wife, Miyu," says Kazuo, wrapping his arm around the woman's waist.

Ayane freezes in place with her mouth slightly open in surprise. "You never mentioned that you were married to one of the most popular singers of our time."

"Oh, so you know who she is?" asks Kazuo.

"Who wouldn't know Miyu Yoshioka?" asks Ayane. "She was only voted the best singer of this generation. I've seen her face in all the popular music magazines."

"We've kept this marriage a secret until today," says Kazuo. "We didn't want either of our successes ruining the other's career. However, after everything that's happened, we decided it was time everyone should know."

"It was so scary," says Miyu, wiping away her tears. "We were coming up with new songs when we noticed a bright light out our window. At first, we thought it was the neighbors with new lights, but when we opened the blinds, the entire city was inside a blue dome. We didn't know what to make of it. As fast as it appeared, it was gone just as quickly."

"I was talking with my mom, and we noticed it as well. We didn't give it a second thought," says Ayane.

"When morning came, we saw the damage that was left behind," says Kazuo, letting go of Miyu. "From our house, we could clearly see the hole. When you called me last night, we made up our minds to leave Tokyo and move here."

"How were you able to buy this place?" asks Ayane, tilting her head to the side. "Our money became worthless when the economy crashed."

"This is a friend's place. I asked them if we could move in for the time being," says Kazuo. "Before all of this, both of us had a small fortune, but it's gone now. It's whatever though. We're looking toward our future. What's done is done."

"Then why?" asks Ayane. "Why move here? You didn't have to do that."

"We lost everything but our belongings in Tokyo," says Kazuo, as a sad expression spreads across his face.

Ayane comes to realize that Kazuo and Miyu have spent their entire lives in Tokyo. They grew up, went to school, built friendships, and eventually met one another. Tokyo was more than just a place to live; it was the backdrop to all of their memories and the foundation of their relationships. Now with everything and everyone they once cherished swept away, Ayane understands why they could not stay. The loss they experienced was personal. Suddenly, reality hits her. She comes to realize that she is in the same situation. While she did not grow up in Tokyo, she made lots of friends and memories that are now gone.

"Ayane, I want you to be my pupil," says Kazuo. "I will teach you everything I know. I want your idol career to flourish under my guidance."

"If I won't be a bother to you or Miyu, then I accept," says Ayane, wiping away tears.

"Give us a few hours to settle in and we can start going over a few things I expect from you," says Kazuo.

Three hours later, after settling into their new home, Kazuo and Miyu sit close on their couch, holding hands and facing a camera. They go live on social media to share an update about their circumstances and the recent changes in their lives.

"Good evening, everyone," says Kazuo. "We are happy you're all here. We have a few announcements to make. First off, yes, Miyu and I are married. We've been married for three years."

The comments on the stream explode with reactions as viewers react to the news. Some flood the chat with joyful emojis to celebrate the news, while others respond with tears and broken hearts. A few of them sent sharp words and angry emojis, lashing out in frustration and disbelief. The chat is a chaotic mix of hope, sorrow, and rage.

"Second, we moved to Nagoya," says Kazuo. "We could see the hole from our home in Tokyo and it put us in an awful state of mind, which brings us to our last announcement." He waves Ayane over, and she sits on the couch beside Miyu. "I have decided to take on a pupil. You may remember her from the idol group Amazing Spring that I was teaching. To all of you who don't know who she is, this is Ayane Sugita."

The comments flood again with people saying they thought she was gone as well. Messages of encouragement mingle with heartfelt expressions of grief, and the screen fills with the crying and heart emojis.

"Both Miyu and I plan on teaching her everything we know," says Kazuo. "We will make her the best performer Japan has ever known." They gracefully bow their heads toward the camera. "We hope you can look forward to what we bring you."

As soon as the stream ends, the story quickly catches the attention of Japanese news outlets. Their phones ring almost immediately, with reporters and producers eager to feature Kazuo, Miyu, and Ayane on TV that very evening Without delay, the three agree, ready to share their message and plans with the world.

November 9th, 2026   0700 Eastern Standard Time

General Angus Turner and General Robert Jackson face each other in the back of an armored vehicle. Members of the Secret Service escort them toward downtown Philadelphia as they silently listen to a DJ on the radio.

"Good morning, Philadelphia. It's Monday, the ninth, at seven. The weather for today is clear, with a high of fifty-eight; the temperature right now is forty-six. Time for your top headlines to start off your day. Our top story: overnight, Kun announced caused the Disappearance. The United Nations held another emergency meeting, and things got heated. Kun made his demands clear. He wants all governments to kneel to him, and have given the world leaders a week to decide. Kun also confirmed that aliens, in fact, did contact him earlier this month. The US has yet to issue an official response. NATO representatives have met and are in talks to invoke Article Five against Kun within the next few days. Next, Congress expects to pass a bill later today to help countries affected by the Disappearance. Many people disagree with them, saying Congress has an obligation to prioritize the American people first before anyone else. Next, yesterday, after spending hours considering who the next president and vice president should be, Congress came to an agreement behind closed doors on who will take over as the commander-in-chief. The announcement will happen at ten, followed by their swearing-in at twelve. And finally, public concern about the blue people continues to grow. Some want to get rid of them, saying they could cause another disappearance. Congress has not addressed these concerns directly, but has moved anything glowing blue to secure locations away from the populace and is monitoring them twenty-four seven. And those are your top headlines for today. This has been your news at seven." The DJ ends the news segment, and music plays in the background.

Robert crosses his arms, and his sharp gaze locks onto Angus. A look of disappointment settles over him as he takes in the unfolding chaos. "So that's what they're calling this tragedy: the Disappearance?" He then shifts his attention toward Noel, the secret service agent sitting beside Angus.

"It would seem that's what people have coined it," says Noel.

Robert lets out a long, weary sigh. He is already exhausted, and all he wants is for the day to be over. "Turn off the radio. I'm tired of hearing music after these world-shaking events. People have died."

"Robert, you don't need to look so annoyed. We'll finish this ceremony soon enough," says Angus.

"I'm not annoyed. I'm just concerned, that's all," says Robert. "We are about a hundred miles from what used to be New York City and Washington, DC, and top officials are gathering in a single place for a ceremony to announce the next people in charge. It would be better if this was in a hidden location or over a webcam instead."

"We need to show the world we are as strong as ever," says Angus. "We need to be seen so no one will think we are weak. The best way to show power is to be in the open."

Robert stays quiet for a moment. He runs his hands down the sides of his face as he gathers his thoughts. "I understand that better than anyone. However, our enemy has a weapon the world has never seen before from aliens we just got confirmation of existing. We don't even know the true range of that weapon. All the disaster sites may have shown us the same-sized hole, but they could easily have a weapon that gets much bigger than that and wipe us all out in an instant."

Everyone stays quiet for the remaining ride, thinking about what he said. Minutes later, the vehicle comes to a stop in front of Philadelphia City Hall, where a massive crowd of reporters and onlookers wait for the generals to step out.

The driver steps out and quickly opens the door for the generals. As they step onto the pavement, the reporters bombard them with endless questions about the future of the US and Kun's demands.

The generals keep their focus and walk with confidence toward the building. Once inside, security staff close the doors behind them. They make their way to the meeting room where the eight surviving members of Congress and other military officers are waiting. The upcoming discussion will center on the latest intelligence reports, the Disappearance, and the critical announcements at ten o'clock.

After two hours of intense discussion and analysis, the meeting wraps up. A congressman stands from his seat and walks to the front of the room. "To wrap things up, there are two more things we want to talk about. To anyone who doesn't know me, I am Scott Hage, the representative of this fine city, Philadelphia, and one of the eight members who was out of town when Washington, DC disappeared. I also have the honor of being the Speaker of Congress. A title used only in this special circumstance." The room dims as the lights shut off. A projector turns on, casting blurry photos of the weapon that caused the Disappearance. "We don't have any clear images or videos of the weapon used. However, last night Kun was nice enough to show us what he used. So we have sketches of it." He turns to the next slide, which is a drawn picture of it. "It's a round object, around the size of a normal-sized car; roughly fifteen feet in diameter. This weapon has two parts to it that we labeled the outer and inner parts for simplicity's sakes. The outer part is light blue, while the inner part is dark blue. The inner portion is the size of a tire, roughly three feet. These two parts expand, forming the dome we see in all the footage."

Robert intervenes in the presentation, cutting off Scott. "Are we seriously supposed to believe the information Kun provided? An object no bigger than a car wiping out entire cities, leaving nothing behind? Even nuclear bombs leave some kind of radiation behind."

"Yes, that's exactly what you're supposed to believe," says Scott, meeting Robert's gaze. "The experts analyzing this information assured me it's most likely correct. If they had any doubts, you wouldn't be seeing any of this." He turns back to the presentation and continues where he left off. "The affected area covers a hundred kilometers or sixty-two miles. After carefully looking at what this weapon has done, our team has decided on a name."

Everyone straightens up and is on the edge of their seats, waiting for the reveal.

"They have chosen the name Deatomizer," says Scott, clicking to the next slide. "They chose this name because of its properties. The 'De' stands for destruction, while 'atomizer' describes its function. What people are calling the Disappearance is that weapon forcibly separating every atom it comes into contact with. That's why this weapon gives the illusion that nothing remains; it's all deconstructed from the atomic level. The experts also made a video for you to see so you can understand it better." He puts on the video and narrates what is happening. "So, there are two stages to this weapon. The first stage sends the outer blue light out, covering an area. In this stage, it looks like the weapon puts the atoms in comes into contact with into an active state. The second stage sends out an inner dark blue light that engulfs the outer one. We believe that the dark blue light separates the atoms, as seen in the video from California of the people disappearing. We don't fully understand why people outside the dome disappeared. Our best conclusion is that the darker light actually doesn't stop at the edge of the other blue light. We just can't see it continuing. Anyone farther than a thousand feet from the dome that glows blue didn't disappear. It was probably designed like that to make sure if anyone can leave the light blue area, it gives them a sense of safety and they stop outside only to still be affected and finished off. Our next part in the video is finding out why it extends up into the sky nearly thirty-three miles, but only descends into the ground sixteen hundred feet. Unfortunately, they got nothing. They couldn't think of a definitive answer. They said it could be a feature added to the weapon, so that it doesn't destroy the planet it's used on. Thirty-three miles underground would be catastrophic for us. End of times." The video ends with the planet engulfing in lava from the massive hole. The lights turn back on. "So, any questions?"

Angus is the only person raising his hand. "What's that hissing sound we can hear in all the videos?"

"While not in the information, that's most likely the sound of atoms being forced apart, but they aren't too sure. Any more questions?" asks Scott, scanning the quiet room. "Well, if that is all, then the presentation is finished."

As the room fills with conversations, Angus leans over to Noel, who is sitting beside him. "Do you know if James Peterson will attend the ceremony?"

"My intel says he will. He thinks he's going to be talking at the ceremony," says Noel.

"Well, we'll see how that plays out for him," says Angus. He stands from the table and turns his attention toward Scott. "This was a very productive meeting. Thank you, Congressman Hage, for the presentation. Robert and I are leaving now so we can get ready for today's events." He makes it to the door but stops to turn back toward Scott. "Only one last thing: are you the same Hage that is going to be delivering the announcements today?"

"Yes, I'll be giving a shorter version of what I presented here," says Scott.

"Sounds good, Scott. We'll see you then," says Angus.

Angus and Robert exit the building and into the lingering crowd. At the sight of them, the reporters shout questions, hoping for a response. However, both generals remain silent, choosing not to acknowledge the calls as they make their way back to their armored vehicle. Once inside, they swiftly leave and go to a hotel where Paula is waiting for them.

As the car slows to a stop in front of Paula, she steps forward and opens the door for them to step out. "I hope your briefing went well."

Angus steps out first, pausing for a moment to take a deep breath of the fresh morning air. "It was very insightful. That Scott guy really knows how to put on a show."

Robert steps out from behind Angus, with an annoyed expression. "I would've preferred a straightforward briefing to a showman's circus. It takes away from the severity of the situation."

"You should have spoken up to let him know," says Angus.

"I let him know," says Robert. "When you left the room, I told him not to put on a show when he gives his speech in front of the world."

"If you follow me this way, gentlemen, I'll show you to the conference room," says Paula, gesturing toward the hotel entrance. "You'll have an early lunch before the big event. Today's going to be a long day. I hope you're prepared."

The hotel is in the heart of downtown Philadelphia, close to where the announcements will take place. Inside, the lobby is full of people from various branches of the military, each engaged in their own conversations. As they walk through, everyone they pass greets them. Angus normally is not one to pass up the pleasantries of conversation, but today he has more important matters to deal with. All he can do is walk by and wave. At the far end of the lobby, they arrive at a set of doors guarded by two secret service agents.

Paula retrieves her ID from her purse and holds it up for the agents to see. "I have brought General Turner and General Jackson so they can get ready for today's events."

The agent barely looks at her ID before he opens the door. "We've been expecting the three of you. Please make yourselves comfortable. Lunch will be out shortly."

The doors open up onto a large conference room, bustling with activity. The space is full of even more people, ranging from military personnel to politicians.

"The room is pretty lively," says Angus.

Paula puts her ID in her purse and quickly moves to rejoin Angus. "What else would you expect? All these people are here to find out who the next president is."

As Robert scans the room, he trails behind them with a sour expression. "Back to what I was saying earlier. Why do we need all these important people gathering in one place? Have we learned nothing?"

Angus shrugs off Robert's concerns and keeps moving through the room. "There's nothing we can do about it. Let's just find a place to sit and have lunch." As he surveys the crowd, his eyes settle on a familiar face. With Paula and Robert following behind, he leads them toward a table near the center of the room. "Well, well, well. If it isn't Mitch. How long has it been?"

A man in his early fifties turns around at the sound of his name and gasps at the sight of Angus. "Oh, Angus. It's been too long. And Robert's here too? Please have a seat." He tries to stand, but Angus puts out his hand for him to stay seated.

Robert pulls out the chair beside Mitch and settles into it. "So they flew you out here as well?"

"Drove, actually," says Mitch. "It's been a good minute since we last spoke. The Army moved me out to Pittsburgh last year." He gives Robert a firm pat on his shoulder. "I heard about your family. I'm sorry."

"Don't be," says Robert, jerking his shoulder forward, forcing Mitch's hand away. "It's my burden to deal with."

Angus and Paula sit across from them. As they settle in, Mitch shifts his attention to Paula, offering her a warm smile. "So, who is this lovely lady?"

"This is Paula. You've met her before," says Angus.

"Paula? It's been ages. I remember when you were this tall," says Mitch, putting his hand out to show her height from years ago. "So what, you follow these two around now?"

"Good to see you too, Mitch," says Paula. "As you can see, I'm the senior advisor for these two."

"What have you been up to?" asks Angus.

"Besides the military, took up a new hobby," says Mitch. "Have either of you heard of disc golf?"

"Isn't that where you use a Frisbee and try to throw it into a chained goal?" asks Robert.

"Some people I work with invited me to play one day, and I haven't stopped since. It really helps me relax, especially with what happened recently," says Mitch. "What about you two? From what I've seen, you both have been busy with Pentagon stuff."

"This month has been crazy," says Angus, letting out a sigh. "First with the alien sightings and now with the whole Disappearance. Our plates have been full."

"I've been with Angus the whole time. Following him everywhere," says Robert.

Mitch leans forward, resting his elbows on the table and interlocking his fingers. "Let's get down to the nitty-gritty of things. Do you know who the next president is going to be? I have a bet with a few others here that it's going to be that James Peterson guy."

"That's classified information," says Robert. "And even if we know, why would we tell you?"

"To help me win money, of course," says Mitch. He turns his gaze to Paula. "Come on now. You should know."

"Your guess is as good as mine," says Paula, closing her eyes and shrugging. "Put me down for James as well."

"You guys are tight-lipped," says Mitch, giving a sigh and shaking his head. "I guess I'll wait to see what happens."

Moments later, lunch arrives. Angus and Robert eat without delay. The conversation continues as they enjoy their meal. Once Angus finishes his last bite, he wipes his mouth was a napkin and stands to his feet. "It's been a pleasure talking with you, Mitch. Let's keep in touch."

Mitch drops his fork abruptly and jumps to his feet with a mouthful of food. "Give me your number."

The group pulls out their phones and exchanges contact information, making sure that they will reach one another in the future.

"I'll be seeing you later," says Angus.

Mitch waves goodbye as Paula guides Angus and Robert out of the room. She leads them down the hallway to their rooms to freshen up, and within twenty minutes, they head to East Fairmount Park, where the announcements and ceremony are taking place.

A massive crowd fills the park for this historical moment. News outlets from across the world are here, ready for what is going to be said. Backstage, Scott waits to be ushered out. Sitting in the front row are many important people with the most notable being the two generals and James Peterson. They are sitting beside one another.

James Peterson, a tall and slender man in his early forties, leans toward the generals with a confident smirk. His sharp eyes and unwavering posture show he is a man who always gets his way. He never accepts no for an answer. "As the candidate who ran against the president in the last election, it's only fair that I take his place. When I'm called onto that stage and become president, the first thing I'm going to do is accept Kun's offer. I'll be very hard on him for what he did. My administration will quickly make a peace deal. Mark my words."

Angus and Robert hold back; choosing not to antagonize James. Instead, they respond carefully, maintaining a diplomatic tone throughout the exchange. They discuss the shifting political landscape and how the past few days have reshaped everything.

As the clock strikes ten o'clock, Scott steps onto the stage, and the crowd quiets down. He approaches the podium and begins his presentation, starting with the details about the Deatomizer. When he finishes, he begins the next announcement of who the next president and vice president will be. The world holds its breath as Scott speaks.

Most expect that James Peterson will take over, since he was the candidate during the last election. Some believe the new leader will come from the same party as the previous president. A few hold out for a neutral figure who has no affiliation with any party and will be a placeholder until a new election happens.

Scott takes one last look at his notes before looking out at the crowd. "Congress had to select a new president and vice president. That was not a simple task by any means. After much debating, we have concluded who we are picking. Without further ado, the next president and vice president of the United States are General Angus Turner and General Robert Jackson."

4

November 9th, 2026   1025 Eastern Standard Time

"The next president and vice president of the United States are General Angus Turner and General Robert Jackson," says Scott as he points at the two generals.

Before Angus and Robert can stand, James bursts from his chair. His face flushes a deep, furious red. "This is bullshit. I was the next candidate in line for the presidency. I deserve to be the next president, not these two."

Angus rises from his seat with a calm composure, locking eyes with James' fiery glare and holding steady without the slightest hint of hesitation. "You need to sit back down and know where you are. You've made it clear what you want for the US, and that does not fly."

James' frustration boils over as he steps forward, squaring his shoulders and pushing his chest against Angus. "Who do you think you are? I'm not going to be lectured by someone who doesn't deserve to be president."

The Secret Service moves toward the altercation, ready to intervene, but Angus quickly raises his hand, signaling them to hold back and not get involved just yet. He pushes back against James with equal force, refusing to yield or let James intimidate him. Both men stand their ground, locked in a tense standoff that intensifies with each passing moment. "Well, I think I'm the next president of the United States of America while you're just a little whiny baby who can't get his way."

James reaches his breaking point and suddenly throws a punch at Angus.

Robert forces his way in between them, grabbing James' wrist before the punch lands. He scowls at James, daring him to throw a punch, but this time at him. "Have you forgotten where you are? Trying to attack Angus gives you a bad look. That temper is why you weren't chosen to be the next president. You're too hot-headed to be given the presidency and the power it holds. You said it yourself; you'd side with our enemies to get what you want. This is bigger than you can imagine. Twenty-million Americans have died, and here you are, making a fool of yourself." He looks directly at the Secret Service agents gathered nearby. With a sharp tilt of his head, he signals for them to intervene and remove James from the park. Responding immediately, two agents grab James by the arms and forcefully remove him from the venue.

James struggles against the agents as they take him away. His eyes remain fixed on Angus and Robert, filled with anger and defiance. Refusing to slip away quietly, he spits out one last remark. His voice echoes through the venue before he disappears from sight behind the curtains. "Mark my words, I'll get my way even if it is the last thing I do."

At the back of the venue, Brittney stands with a microphone in hand, reporting on the unfolding event. "Things are getting very heated." She glances at the cameraman, motioning him toward the scene. "Frank, get a close-up shot of James before he's gone."

Frank captures James' last glare before he disappears behind the curtains. After the tension finally settles, he focuses the camera back on Angus and Robert making their way onto the stage. Scott steps aside, allowing Angus space to take the mic.

Angus pauses, letting his gaze sweep over the crowd before lifting the microphone to his mouth. "I'd like to thank Congressman Hage for helping with today's event. While I only met him today, he has been very helpful in getting all this information out to the public. I'd also like to thank all the members of Congress for placing their trust in myself and Robert to lead this nation in its time of need. We have talked about the actions the US should and will take against Kun for his crimes against humanity. We also talked with NATO, and they agreed with our plan going forward. Kun Wen is a newly established leader with no past leadership positions to speak of. He rose to power because of the military occupation he started nearly a year ago. He's a madman who has killed all who have stood in his way. Kun has not responded when we've tried to contact him. A representative only told us to announce publicly our loyalty to their country. We do not abide by their demands and will not be siding with them after the atrocities they have committed. Our intel has shown us he loves power and will obtain it in any way he can. Today, that will change. The United States will not kneel to him or his regime. With that being said, I am announcing today that we are declaring war against him and his group for what they have done. They will learn that they cannot bully us into submitting to their demands. Their actions have consequences, and they are going to learn what happens when they mess with the world. War is the only path we have to keep our great nation free from tyranny."

The crowd erupts in enthusiastic cheers as Angus and Robert make their way backstage. Reporters eagerly shout out questions for immediate reactions and further details, but they go unanswered. Angus and Robert remain focused, choosing not to say any more than is necessary.

Brittney steps back in front of the camera, ensuring that the viewers are kept well informed of the upcoming events. "With that, we're going to take a break. We'll continue bringing updates as the events unfold. I'll be back here at noon for the inauguration. Back to you at the studio."

The broadcast ends, prompting Frank to lower his camera to his side. He glances at Brittney, aware that they have a brief window of downtime before the next major event. "We have an hour and a half until the inauguration starts. Want to have an early lunch?"

"Yeah, let's go. We might not get a chance later," says Brittney.

Frank gathers the camera equipment and hands it off to the accompanying crew that came along with them. He and Brittney head to a nearby diner, not wanting to stray too far from the park just in case their food takes longer than expected.

Once at the diner, a server shows them to a table. Frank gets comfortable, leaning back in his chair as he tries to relax after the tense morning. "So how's life as a reporter treating you? I know that for a newbie, it can be quite hard adjusting to this lifestyle. As you know, I used to be a reporter until I shifted my focus to operating the camera. So don't be shy to ask me questions."

Brittney does not answer right away. Instead, she stares out the window, lost in her thoughts. The weight of the recent events clearly hangs over her. After a long pause, she finally turns to Frank. "It's nice and all, but I don't like how I got thrust into this position. So many of my colleagues had to die."

"I know how you feel," says Frank. "I've worked with many of them these past thirty years. I'm still trying to wrap my head around this. It's going to be a long time before I can come to terms with what happened. I know I share this feeling with the vast majority of Americans, or at least, that's what I want to believe. All we can do is report whatever happens. We owe the American people that much."

"I just don't know how to feel," says Brittney. "Do you think going to war is the right thing to do? Shouldn't we be focusing on helping those affected by this?"

"I can't make that call," says Frank. "On one hand, I see war being necessary; they took the lives of millions. That can't go unpunished. But if we go to war, we're only going to lose more lives. Then, if we don't go to war, we could be back in this situation with even more cities gone. It's a tricky situation for sure. I feel sorry for Angus having to make that call."

"Maybe the best thing to do is to comply with Kun's demands," says Brittney.

"And live under his iron thumb?" asks Frank. "I think I'll pass on that."

"We have a lot of bright people all across the world," says Brittney. "I bet we could work out some sort of deal that would benefit the US in the long run."

"Listen Brittney. You're young. You don't know the horrors of the world like I do," says Frank. "I've been to the Middle East and saw firsthand what the horror of war does to people. Just because one side gives in doesn't mean the oppressors are going to stop. They will strip away all of your rights. You will be nothing to them. We're reporters. We're the first to die in that situation. If they don't like a group of people for whatever reason, what will stop Kun from launching these weapons again? Someone needs to stand up to him and tell them enough is enough. We cannot fall to him. We have to fight back in whatever way possible."

"Even if that means we could be spared another day of suffering?" asks Brittney.

"Life will only be suffering under his rule," says Frank.

After talking for a while longer, their meal arrives. They eat slowly, allowing themselves to get lost in the conversation. When they finish, they hurry back to the park, arriving with twenty minutes to spare before the inauguration begins.

At noon, the inauguration ceremony for Angus and Robert starts. Both men stand before the crowd, and, following tradition, they place their hands on a Bible and take the oath of office. With the completion of the swearing-in, they officially become the leaders of the United States.

Angus walks up to the mic with a folder in his hands. He holds it up high for the people to see. The crowd quiets as they wait in anticipation for his words. Angus stands tall as he prepares to address the nation for the first time as its leader. "In this folder lies the declaration of war Congress has given me to sign. It was a tough decision to come to this conclusion in this short amount of time, but we believe this is the right choice. Under normal circumstances, Congress would have been the only one debating this declaration. However, since there are no rules established for allowing unelected members of Congress to declare war, we brought all government parties together and talk about this declaration." He opens the folder and takes out the paper. "Over the past few days, we didn't know who was to blame for this atrocity, so we were talking about what action we would take when we found out. Now that we know who's responsible, we will take action." He reaches into his suit's pocket and pulls out a pen, holding it high for everyone to see. "With this pen, I will sign my name to officialize this declaration of war." A podium is brought over, and Angus lays the paper down. The crowd watches intensely, holding their breath until he finishes signing it. He puts the pen back in his pocket and raises the paper up high for everyone to see. "I will put an end to all this needless suffering and bring justice back to the world."

For the rest of the day, Angus and Robert meet with the leaders of the UN and NATO in hopes that other countries share their fighting spirit. Despite their earnest attempts, they are swiftly let down. One by one, representatives from other countries turned their backs toward the US. They do not share the same goals as the US, leaving them to fight alone in this war.

November 10th, 2026   1330 Eastern Standard Time

"What do you mean you won't help?" asks Robert. His voice echoes through the room as he speaks urgently into the phone, reaching out to a foreign leader to secure help.

"We believe it's in our best interest to side with Kun. I'm sorry." The call ends abruptly, leaving Robert furious.

"How dare they not side with us," says Robert, hurling the phone to the floor. "This makes eighty countries already. If they lost a city, they would be crying and begging for our help."

"I've never seen you this mad before," says Angus, sitting at his desk, only a few feet from Robert.

"I've never been put in a situation where cities just up and vanished, but here we are," says Robert with a bit of sarcasm. He leans back in his chair, forcefully exhaling. "It's already been a full day since we took this position, and I feel like we haven't made any progress. So what if we declare war? It doesn't mean shit if no one will back us. You know what? It's been a long day. I'm going to have lunch now."

As he reaches the door, Angus watches him closely with concern in his eyes. "I know you're stressed, Robert. Just don't go picking up smoking again."

"I quit that over two decades ago," says Robert, resting his forehead against the door. "I'm not planning on starting again. My wife would kill me if she found out." With those words, he opens the door, and steps out of the room with his head held high.

Across from where Robert was sitting, Angus' two top advisors, Paula and Xavier, focused intently on their paperwork.

"We have no other choice but to contact the media and let them know about this grim information. The people need to know," says Xavier.

"All right, Paula, call whoever you want and tell them the grim news," says Angus.

"I'll get right on it, sir," says Paula, pulling out her phone to make the call.

Angus leans back in his chair, staring out the window as the warm sunlight hits his face. "We are in desperate need of a miracle."

Meanwhile, Robert takes a brief walk to the dining room, his mind still occupied with thoughts about the endless rejections. Upon reaching the entrance, a staff member greets him. "Ah, Mr. Jackson. I was beginning to wonder when you and Mr. Turner were going to have lunch." The staffer glances behind Robert. "I don't see Mr. Turner, though."

"He's occupied with work. It's only me," says Robert.

"That's quite all right," says the staffer. "Please make yourself at home, and lunch will be brought out shortly."

Robert nods and takes a seat in the center of the room, choosing a comfortable spot to relax. The sunlight filters through the windows, giving the room a warm feeling. A TV hangs on the wall showing the news, with Brittney as the reporter. "This just in, another country has sided with Kun."

Robert rolls his eyes and zones out the TV. He closes his eyes and gets lost in thought. *What's going to happen to the US if no one sides with us? Can we even afford this war? What kinds of weapons has Kun been given?* He opens his eyes and shakes off that idea. *No need to play what-if games. I need to come up with definite answers to this problem.*

The staffer approaches Robert with his lunch on a tray. She sits it down gently in front of him and offers him a warm smile. "I hope you enjoy the meal, hun."

"It looks great," says Robert.

The main dish includes meat-and-potato casserole, served alongside steamed broccoli and a portion of coleslaw. For dessert, he enjoys a slice of pumpkin pie. While he usually opts for water with his meals, today he chose a Coke. Robert is a man of great etiquette. He prefers to put his napkin on his lap, keeps his elbows off the table, and leans over the table when eating so as not to allow anything to fall on his nice clothes. Halfway through the meal, he takes a drink of his Coke, and tunes back into the TV.

Suddenly, Brittney's eyes widen in surprise. "We just got some more breaking news."

"Here we go again," says Robert, rolling his eyes.

"Japan has just confirmed they'll side with the US," says Brittney.

Robert chokes on his Coke hearing the shocking news. He sets down the soda, jumps from his seat, and rushes back to the office, stopping at the doorway. "Is what I just heard true? Is Japan really siding with us?"

"I just got off the phone with their representative," says Xavier. "They said we have been a massive help to their country, and they want to help us in any way they can."

Robert lets out a loud cheer, pumping his fists into the air. His excitement echoes throughout the building. "Hell yeah. We finally got someone to fight on our side."

"Don't get too excited yet, Robert," says Angus. "This is only one country. We need more if we plan on standing a chance against Kun."

"You're right, but I see Japan siding with us as a major push forward. We need this to be covered by all media outlets," says Robert.

Paula quickly types out a message on her phone; Her fingers move rapidly across the screen as she composes an update about the recent development. With the message sent, she looks up at Angus. "I just sent out a message on our social media accounts about this. I agree with Robert. We cannot let this momentum slow down."

"Do what you can to keep talks up. I do not want this to die down either," says Angus.

Throughout the day, Paula and Xavier work tirelessly to ensure that the news of Japan's alliance reaches every corner of the internet and all major media outlets. Their efforts paid off quickly. The confirmation of Japan's support acts as the catalyst, prompting other nations to reconsider their stance on the conflict. Canada is the next country to step forward, announcing its decision to join the US and Japan. The momentum continues as several European countries reverse their positions. One by one, these nations declare their support, gradually tipping the balance of global alliances. Notably, Russia remains silent, unable to respond to the invitation because of its ongoing civil war. Meanwhile, several other countries chose not to join, citing reasons such as internal conflict, fear of repercussions, or a general lack of concern regarding Kun's actions. By nine at night, the allied countries officially declare war against Kun, marking a significant escalation in the conflict and solidifying the international response.

November 11th, 2026   0600 Japan Standard Time

Ayane approaches an abandoned, rundown house standing in the middle of nowhere. The paint on the exterior is fading and chipping away. All of its windows are shattered, revealing the pitch-black interior. The setting sun casts its eerie orange light over the scene.

Ayane steps up to the door and knocks three times, with her knuckles echoing against the warn wood. Faint voices murmur on the other side, their words too muffled to understand. Undeterred, she knocks harder three more times.

Voices come from inside. "She wants to be let in."

"She can't be let in."

The door slowly creeps open, revealing the brightly lit interior. She steps inside without hesitation. Everything within the house is white: the walls, the floors, the ceiling, and the furniture. Once inside, the door slams shut behind her and locks abruptly. Unintelligible whispers fill the air, surrounding her and heightening her sense of unease. Drawn in by the sound of the TV, Ayane cautiously makes her way toward the living room. The room is dark except for the glow coming from the TV. On the screen, Amazing Spring is performing, but she notices she is missing from the lineup. Between her and the TV, the silhouette of a figure is partially visible, peeking from behind the couch. Ayane feels a chill run through her body as she approaches; her heartbeat quickens with every step. As she circles the couch and finally sees the figure's face, a wave of horror washes over her, leaving her stomach in knots.

Sitting on the couch is Sachi. Her posture is rigid and unnatural as every muscle in her body contorts beyond comfort. Blood streaks down her face, leaving jagged lines across her torn skin, and her clothing is in complete disarray, saturated with dark-red stains. The extent of her injuries and the chaotic state of her appearance make her seem barely human. Without warning, Sachi suddenly snaps her head to face Ayane. "You were supposed to die with us, Ayane. Why are you still alive?" She jumps onto the couch, yelling at Ayane.

Overwhelmed by terror and the horrific sight before her, Ayane lets out a piercing scream. The intensity of the moment buckles her legs, sending her collapsing to the floor. Her body shakes uncontrollably, and tears streak down her face as she tries to process what she is seeing.

Sachi jumps down to her and grabs her by the neck, lifting her from the floor. "Answer me, Ayane. Don't you dare forget."

From the shadows, additional figures emerge. The remaining members of Amazing Spring step into the room. Their faces are expressionless, and their eyes are vacant, devoid of any warmth or recognition. As they approach, they chant and shout at Ayane. Ayane desperately covers her ears to block out the noise.

Suddenly, a voice cuts through the chaos. "Wake up, Ayane." A blinding white light overtakes Ayane. As she opens her eyes and regains her bearings, the voice persists with concern. "Ayane, can you hear me? Are the nightmares happening again?"

Ayane lies motionless on the bed, her mind clouded and her breathing is shallow. She scans her surroundings and gradually realizes she is in a hotel room. Miyu stands over her with a worried expression. "You started screaming, so I came here to make sure you're all right."

Tears well in Ayane's eyes as the terror of the nightmare continues to haunt her. She hesitates for a moment before reaching out to Miyu in search of comfort. Ayane wraps her arms around Miyu, seeking solace in her friend's reassuring presence. Miyu responds with gentle care, holding Ayane close and softly rubbing her back to soothe her nerves.

After a few quiet moments, Ayane slowly pulls away. She wipes the tears from her eyes, still visibly shaken and unable to calm herself enough to try sleeping again. "Do you want to get something to eat?"

"Sure," says Miyu, smiling at Ayane. "I saw a restaurant next door when we arrived last night. Let's see if it's open this early."

After gathering their belongings, Ayane and Miyu leave the hotel, ready to begin their day in Kyoto, the new capital of Japan. They are here for an interview that will promote Ayane and generate excitement for an upcoming concert scheduled for the fourteenth. The city outside is quiet, offering a peaceful moment as they make their way to the nearby restaurant.

As they enter the establishment, Ayane and Miyu immediately notice a TV broadcasting news about Japan's recent agreement to join the US in war. The report hangs in the background as the host greets them and escorts them to their seats.

Miyu wants to get Ayane's mind off of what happened, so she talks about the first thing that comes to mind. "When I was a little girl, I had many opportunities laid out in front of me, but none of them led me to be the singer I am today."

Ayane tilts her head to the side and stares at Miyu with a confused look. "Am I the right person you should talk to about this?"

"You are the only person I should talk to about this," says Miyu. "So anyway, I was always told what to do and how to act. The only musical training I got was playing the piano."

"So, you were a spoiled rich girl?" asks Ayane.

"You could say that," says Miyu, chuckling. "It wasn't until I got to high school that my true colors came out. On a whim, I joined the music club, and the rest is history. I became Japan's most famous singer. I've met a lot of different people along the way. Some good and some not so good, but I never let that discourage me from moving forward." She reaches across the table and places her hands gently over Ayane's hands. "I know these nightmares can be rough. I'd be lying if I said I never had to deal with that. If you ever need help, I'm here to talk to you."

"Thank you, Miyu," says Ayane, taking a napkin and dabbing the tears forming in her eyes.

"Let me tell you a story of another singer I know. Do you know who Yuko Kusumoto is?" asks Miyu.

Ayane crumples the napkin and nods. "She's just as famous as you."

For a heartbeat, silence fills the space between them. The warmth of the café fades into the background, leaving only the faint hum of distant chatter. Miyu lowers her eyes and traces the rim of her cup with her fingers as she gathers her composure. When she finally lifts her gaze, her expression has softened as she narrates her story. "Nearly six years ago, I was recording my second studio album. Kazuo was producing the music. But at that time, we barely knew each other, so we weren't together yet."

In the recording studio, Miyu stands in front of a microphone, focusing on her performance. On the other side of the glass, Kazuo observes her, monitoring the session's progress. His voice comes through the studio speakers as Miyu wraps up the last take. "That's good, Miyu. That should be enough to finish the vocals for your album."

Miyu turns toward the glass and bows toward Kazuo. "Thank you for your help."

"Come to this side," says Kazuo. "Someone's here that I would like you to meet."

Miyu's voice softens as her gaze drifts past Ayane. She lets out a quiet breath, gathering her thoughts before continuing her story. "At the time, I couldn't think of why Kazuo would want me to meet anyone. My first album had lackluster sales, but regardless, I still went with a smile on my face."

"I would like you to meet Yuko Kusumoto," says Kazuo. "I've had the lucky opportunity to work with her, and I thought it would be a fitting time for you both to meet and hopefully make a connection with each other."

"It's a pleasure to meet you," says Yuko. "What Kazuo didn't tell you is that I wanted to meet you ever since he told me you both are working together. I'm a huge fan of yours."

Miyu regains her focus and looks back at Ayane. "It came as a complete shock that a singer I thought was more famous than me would want to meet me. From then on, the two of us became close friends. We lean on each other when times get hard."

"Have you been able to get in touch with her?" asks Ayane.

Miyu shakes her head, and her voice trembles with emotion. "I haven't been able to get in touch with any of my friends. I think it's too late at this point." The realization weighs on her as she lowers her head. A quiet sniffle escapes her as she fights back tears.

Ayane realizes Miyu is struggling with her own pain. She reaches across the table, mimicking the comforting gesture Miyu made earlier. "If you need to talk with someone about what you've been through, you can tell me."

Miyu lifts her gaze. Her eyes shimmer with unshed tears. Emotions threaten to overwhelm her, yet she draws in a steady breath and manages a gentle smile at Ayane. "Thank you. I'll do just that."

An hour passes as Miyu finds comfort in Ayane. Miyu receives a message from Kazuo asking where she is. She responds promptly, informing him she and Ayane are having breakfast down the road and invites Kazuo to join them. For the rest of the morning, they prepare for an upcoming interview scheduled for twelve o'clock.

They arrive at the studio, and the interview opens with Kazuo proudly showing off Ayane and responding to various questions. As the interview draws to a close, Kazuo shares an important update regarding the upcoming concert. "As I have said before, the concert will be held on the fourteenth. We have gotten the go ahead with performing in Okinawa. Along with Ayane and my wife, as of right now, there will be thirty-five acts performing. Yesterday, I got many people on board with this concert. I'm expecting more people and groups to join. Right now, I'm talking with the local government about holding a festival around the island. On Saturday, Miyu, Ayane, and I will be brought to Okinawa by a cruise ship, and they'll perform songs onboard. On Sunday, they will be up on a stage in Okinawa. This event will also be televised for everyone to see."

The interview ends, and excitement quickly spreads across social media. People post messages of support and enthusiasm for the upcoming event.

November 11th, 2026   2055 Eastern Standard Time

"All current members of the military have been activated," says Robert, reporting to Angus about their allies. "It's only been a day, and everyone's ready. We just got word from our allies that they also have their militaries on standby. Have we heard anything from Kun?"

"Nothing. He is still keeping us at arm's length," says Angus.

"We should attack him before he can attack us again," says Robert.

"We still don't know the weapons they have. The one we know about can wipe an entire city off the map," says Angus.

"Even more of a reason to attack," says Robert. "We don't know what these aliens are providing them, and frankly, I don't want to wait to find out."

Angus crosses his arms. He keeps a stern tone, not wavering in his decision. "It's better we get more prepared and find the best way to combat them."

"Stubborn as always," says Robert, rolling his eyes. "What if we're wasting time and this is our only chance to hit them? I want to—"

Xavier bursts into the room, cutting off Robert. "You both need to get to the situation room right now. Russia just launched nukes at Kun's territories."

Angus immediately stands, and he grabs his coat as he makes his way to the door. "We'll pick up this conversation later." Without hesitation, they hurry down the hallway to the situation room. Upon entering the room, a group of high-ranking military officials and advisors gathered to address the crisis at hand. Angus wastes no time and steps forward. "What's the situation?"

Paula pulls up a live satellite feed over Russia. "At approximately 8:54, Russia launched eighteen nuclear warheads. Their target is undoubtedly the capital of Vietnam. From what we can tell, each nuclear weapon was launched from different locations across Russia. Our intel thought these locations were abandoned since the fall of the Soviet Union."

On the TV, a detailed map displays the current locations of the nukes as they advance toward Vietnam.

"I thought Russia was in chaos," says Angus, analyzing the TV closely. "How were they able to launch this many nukes without us knowing?"

"We don't know," says Paula. "I can only speculate that it's because of a plan they put in place a long time ago just in case Moscow were to fall. I'm talking well before the collapse of the Soviet Union."

"This is going to result in mutual destruction of both of them," says Robert as his jaw drops and eyes fill with terror. "May God have mercy on our souls."

Within minutes of the nuclear launch, Kun mobilizes his military forces. Missiles launch to intercept the incoming warheads. Simultaneously, fighter jets scramble into Chinese airspace, working to confirm the precise locations of each nuke. After twenty minutes, all eighteen warheads are accounted for. The nukes will cross into Vietnam within minutes, sending the nation into a state of chaos. In response, Kun's government urgently instructs its citizens to shelter in place. Meanwhile, four of the nukes get intercepted over Russia while six more get intercepted above China.

Xavier puts the trajectories of the remaining nukes on the screen. "We just calculated where the remaining eight are heading. They're all going to Hanoi."

"What are the chances they hit their target?" asks Angus.

"Less than one percent," says Xavier.

As the crisis intensifies, news outlets worldwide broadcast the unfolding events in real time. The entire world is gripped with uncertainty, with millions watching anxiously. World leaders brace themselves for the worst outcome. Another twenty minutes pass, and the countdown to disaster nears its end. The nukes are now just two minutes away from reaching Hanoi. Kun's military is frantically launching missiles to intercept them. Many of the missiles miss their target. With only a minute remaining until impact, three nukes remain. Everyone is on the edge of their seat expecting a nuke to hit. Two are shot down, with only one remaining. A final missile launches, but it misses the nuke by mere inches. The last nuke descends over Hanoi and explodes.

The situation room has gone quiet as everyone watches the satellite feed of a mushroom cloud forming over Hanoi. News outlets are sharing the news of what just unfolded. Kun's military ceased all offensive operations. There are no further missile launches and no deployment of any unknown weaponry. War appears to be averted.

"I want a full report of the damage. Kun's reign is over," says Angus.

"Once the mushroom cloud dissipates, we'll be able to see the damage left behind," says Paula.

"How is Kun's military responding to this?" asks Angus.

"They haven't responded. They're not retaliating," says Paula.

"Good to hear," says Angus. "Keep me updated if any new information comes in."

Then, without warning, the mushroom cloud gets instantly blown away, revealing a force field shielding Hanoi from certain doom as the huge object floats menacingly over the city.

"Is that the alien aircraft?" asks Angus.

"Yes, sir," says Paula. "I can't believe prevented a nuke from destroying the city."

Robert stands at a loss. Then, he slams his hand down on the table with a force that echoes through the room. "So that's another trick they have. I never would have thought I would see the day when nukes have no effect."

Moments later, Kun's military retaliates against Russia. Over the next five hours, they bomb every major city, causing the death of millions. The devastating horrors are broadcast worldwide, leaving no doubt of Kun's terrifying power. By dawn, Russia ceases to exist, allowing Kun to take over the territory. After witnessing the power Kun now holds, every European country gives in to his demands, leaving the United States, Canada, and Japan alone in the war against Kun.

5

November 14th, 2026   0600 Japan Standard Time

Ayane makes her way through the dimly lit halls of the cruise ship, heading toward her room. Most of the lights are off except for the ones on the floor, lighting her way. The ship is almost silent; the only sound comes from the waves splashing against the hull. After what feels like a long walk, she reaches her room. She fumbles with the keys, struggling to find the lock in the darkness. After a few attempts, she finally unlocks the door and steps inside.

The room is pitch black. Ayane presses her hand along the wall, searching for the light switch. When she flips the switch, the lights stay off. She flips it many times, but nothing happens. After a few more attempts, she gives up and reaches into her bag to take out her phone, only to realize it is not there. As she continues to look through her bag, a powerful gust of wind sweeps through the room. She turns to see that the balcony door is wide open, letting the pale moonlight illuminate the space. In front of her stands a dark silhouette. For a moment, it remains motionless. Then, without warning, it lunges at her.

Ayane's knees buckle, and she drops to the cold floor in fear. Though her mind screams for her to move, her body stays frozen, unwilling to accept what her eyes are seeing. "Not this again. This has been happening every night. Just leave me alone."

The silhouette looms over her with a heavy presence. It tilts its head, carefully studying her every movement. It slowly crouches to be at her eye level. "Why haven't you killed yourself, Ayane?"

Ayane squeezes her eyes shut and clamps her hands over her ears, shutting out everything. "You're not real. You can't hurt me."

The silhouette grabs Ayane's hair, yanking her to her feet. It slams her back against the door and lifts her off the floor by her hair. "Look at us when we speak to you." Ayane struggles and kicks wildly, but nothing happens. An icy hand clamps around her jaw, tilting her head until she is staring straight at it. Its face shifts, morphing through the faces of her idol friends. "Did you forget us, Ayane? This is all your fault."

Ayane's screams echo through the darkness, piercing through the silence of the room. Suddenly, a blinding white light envelops her, washing away the shadowy figure. When she comes to her senses, Miyu is by her side, trying to wake her up.

"Here, Ayane, drink this," says Miyu, handing her a bottled water.

Ayane takes a gulp of the water. When she lowers the bottle, her eyes meet Miyu, and a quiet sadness lingers between them.

"Was it the same nightmare?" asks Miyu.

Ayane stares at her trembling hands as tears streak down her face. "I can't take this anymore. Every night it keeps getting worse. I beg, but they won't stop coming. It should have been me who died, not them."

Miyu wraps her arms around Ayane and pulls her close in a comforting embrace. "Don't say that. Don't throw your life away because you survived. Live your life for all of those you've lost." Miyu pulls back slightly and rests a hand gently on Ayane's shoulder. "Now, come on. We need to get ready. We have a big day ahead of us."

On the island of Okinawa   0900 Japan Standard Time

A twelve-year-old Japanese girl rests quietly in her hospital bed, with a white beanie covering her head. Sitting beside her is her father, a Caucasian-American soldier dressed in a US Army uniform, holding her hand.

There is a knock on the door, and a doctor steps in with a clipboard. "I have the test results. Are you ready to go over them?"

"We are," says the man.

The doctor pulls up a chair and sits beside the bed. She flips through the papers attached to the clipboard. "Looking at the results, Justin, I'm happy to say Lilly has finished her chemo treatment."

Justin leans over and wraps his arms around Lilly, smiling through his tears. "You hear that, baby girl? You made it through. Your mom would be so proud of you." After the hug, he sits back in his chair, shifting his gaze toward the doctor. "Thank you for being with us every step of the way, Doctor Ogawa. I don't think I would have been able to make it without you."

"Now that she's in remission, we'll keep monitoring her to make sure her recovery stays on track," says Dr. Ogawa.

"Will she be able to go out today for the festival?" asks Justin. "She's been looking forward to it since the beginning of the week."

"We need to keep an eye on her today," says Dr. Ogawa. "She only finished chemo a few hours ago, and her body needs time to regain its strength. We don't want something bad happening to her." She turns toward Lilly and winks. "However, if she doesn't have any complications by the end of the day, we can let her go out tomorrow as long as she has an adult accompanying her everywhere she goes." She looks at Justin, hoping he catches the hint.

"I'll be looking forward to tomorrow then," says Justin as a warm smile spreads across his face. "I know you're a big girl; you got this." He extends his fist, and Lilly responds with a cheerful bump. Justin stands, then heads toward the door alongside Dr. Ogawa. "I need to get back to the field to finish some work. I'll be back around one or two." He stops at the doorway and turns around to look at Lilly. "Your grandparents will be here at noon with lunch and to check on you. I'll see you later tonight. Bye, honey." He steps out of the room with Dr. Ogawa following behind.

"Dad, wait," says Lilly.

Justin turns around to peek into the room once more. "What is it?"

Lilly looks at her father as determination shines in her eyes. She extends her arm and holds out her pinky finger. "Make a pinky promise with me. I want you to promise me you will take me to the festival tomorrow. She'll be there on stage. I don't want to miss it."

Justin smiles and also puts his pinky out. "It's a promise, Lilly. When I get back, we can talk all about what you want to do tomorrow. Now get some rest." He closes the door behind him and walks down the hall.

"I know these past two years have been very hard for you," says Dr. Ogawa. "You look tired. Have you not been resting?"

"I'll get some rest when this is over," says Justin, rubbing his eyes. "Right now, my time and energy is best spent on Lilly. It's been hard for her. She should be playing with her friends and doing what kids do best. I just hope that starting next week she can start being a kid again. Not having a mother and fighting cancer is too much for a child. That's why I'll always be here for her." He makes it to the elevator and presses the only button available. "I'm just happy she has a great view of Okinawa and the ocean from her window. I think that scenery helped her through these past two years."

The elevator door slides open, and Justin steps inside. Dr. Ogawa stands in the hallway, waving goodbye with a smile. "Take care, Justin. We'll see you later."

The hospital is located in Nanjo, on the southeastern part of the island. Outside its entrance, a car waits patiently for Justin. Inside the vehicle, a young man dressed in a Japanese military uniform reclines in the driver's seat. "How did everything go?"

Justin steps into the passenger side and closes the door with a firm thud. "Everything went great, Yuuto. Today was her last day of chemo. If everything goes well, I'll be able to take her to the festival tomorrow."

Yuuto straightens his seat and, brimming with excitement, give the steering wheel a slap. "That's great news. After work today, I'm going to take you out for drinks. I bet William will come with us." Without wasting another moment, he starts the car and quickly pulls out, eager to get their day underway.

"Sounds good to me," says Justin. "We can go at five. I made a promise to Lilly that I would be back after work. Also, didn't your wife get mad the last time you went out for drinks?"

"That was last time. This time is different. We're celebrating your daughter's recovery. She'll understand," says Yuuto.

"Sounds to me you just want an excuse to drink," says Justin.

"What? Me? No," says Yuuto sarcastically. "My wife lets me drink whenever. I swear she lets me."

"Sure, let's go with that. What is the report for today?" asks Justin as he takes out his phone.

"Besides the ominous warships to the west of the island Kun sent to show off his power, all we have for today is an inspection of the new construction in Itoman to make sure it's up to code," says Yuuto.

"Ah, yes, the new military warehouse," says Justin. "Didn't the construction start back in January? I can't believe this year is almost over."

On the cruise ship   0955 Japan Standard Time

"Are you ready to go, Ayane?" asks Miyu.

"In a moment. I'm finishing my makeup," says Ayane, in front of a mirror, putting the final touches on her lipstick.

They are in the dressing room backstage, preparing to walk onto the main stage of the cruise ship's theater for the first of two performances. This event marks the opening of the festival, and both Miyu and Ayane are wearing matching dresses. Miyu's dress is vibrant red, while Ayane's is a striking blue. Each dress sparkles under the lights, the shimmering fabric catching every glimmer. The dresses fit tightly around their figures, making it difficult for them to move.

The stage is at the front of the ship, opening to a grand, three-story theater that can accommodate up to eight hundred guests. The ship itself spans nearly a thousand feet from bow to stern and carries close to four thousand passengers, though today, the ship is holding nearly three thousand passengers and crew. At six in the morning, the ship arrived at Naha port but remained anchored in open water alongside eight other cruise ships. They are scheduled to dock at 5:30 this afternoon following the conclusion of the second performance.

Onstage, a man in a sailor's uniform walks out and speaks in English. "Good morning everyone, I hope you're as excited about this performance as I am. Many of you already know who I am, but for those watching at home, I'm the captain of this fine ship, Captain Louis." Beside him, a translator speaks in Japanese.

Backstage, Miyu steps in front of Kazuo. She twirls gracefully, allowing him a full view of her attire. "How do I look, Kazuo?"

Kazuo slips an arm around Miyu's waist, drawing her closer. With his free hand, he softly lifts her chin, gazing into her eyes. "As beautiful as the day I met you."

Behind them, Ayane's face turns red from secondhand embarrassment at the sight of them flirting.

Miyu notices Ayane's flushed expression and breaks into laughter. Afterward, she holds out her hand toward her. "Come on, we're about to be called out."

Ayane takes Miyu's hand and gets whisked to the side of the stage, beyond the view of the audience.

Captain Louis glances over his shoulder and notices the singers waiting for him to introduce them. "And today's guests of honor, we have the legendary Miyu Yoshioka, along with Ayane Sugita." He turns toward them and claps.

Miyu walks onto the stage first, waving confidently at the roaring crowd.

Ayane follows close behind while also waving. As she walks on stage, the bright stage lights blind her and, for a fleeting moment, she forgets all that has happened. A calm and relaxing feeling overtakes her, and she feels at peace, even if it is only for a moment. She believes everyone in the room also shares the same feeling as her.

From the other side of the stage, the translator walks up to greet them in Japanese. "It's a pleasure to meet the two of you. I will translate what you both say into English."

Captain Louis offers Miyu and Ayane a friendly nod as he walks off the stage.

Miyu closes her eyes, savoring the moment as the crowd continues cheering. "I'd like to say we came here for a better reason, but today is about remembrance; remembering all who we lost. This is for them. This weekend's concert and festivities are about bringing peace back to the world. Let's show them love can conquer all." Miyu takes a step back, allowing the spotlight to fall on Ayane.

"I've struggled these past few days with the loss of my friends," says Ayane. "With the help of Miyu and Kazuo, I plan to continue my music career. It's because of them that I found the strength to keep moving forward. I hope I can touch the hearts of all who are watching. So here's hoping this festival is a massive success." She throws her fist into the air as the crowd chants their names.

Miyu steps back beside Ayane, flashing her a warm smile. "Are you ready?"

Ayane nods, and the show begins.

Over the next hour, Miyu and Ayane's voices harmonize beautifully, reaching every corner of the theater. Each song flows seamlessly into the next, carefully crafted to fit the mood of the recent events. Their notes carry the weight of their emotions, and the audience feels it as if the singers are speaking directly to them. Their voices tremble, struggling to hold back their raw emotions as they get lost in their music, but they remain fully present in the shared energy between them and the crowd. When the final note fades, the theater erupts with cheers and applause that seem to go on forever. Miyu and Ayane stand side by side under the stage lights as they sweat and breathe hard. They look at each other and smile. They gave the best performance they had ever given.

Miyu takes Ayane's hand and raises it high into the air. "Thank you all. This has been such an incredible show. Make sure to be back here at five to see us perform again. You don't want to miss it." The theater lights turn on, and they slowly walk offstage while waving at the audience.

Backstage, Kazuo waits with two water bottles in hand. "That was a great performance."

In the background, Captain Louis is back on stage to deliver his last remarks. "Be sure to be back here before five for the last performance. Like Miyu said, you do not want to miss it."

Miyu playfully bumps Ayane's shoulder and gives her a wink. "You hear that, Ayane? We still have one more performance today. I hope you can keep up with me."

"You can count on me. I'm still revving to go," says Ayane. She smiles softly as she twists open her water bottle and takes a refreshing sip.

Kazuo glances down at his watch, then claps his hands together. "Until then, you both have a meet-and-greet with your fans soon."

"We'll start at twelve," says Miyu, stretching her arm above her head. "We need to freshen up and eat lunch. So until then, our fans can wait." She takes Ayane's hand and sits her in front of a mirror. "Let me fix your makeup before you go. We can't have anyone seeing you this sweaty."

Once they are ready, the three of them step into a service elevator that takes them a few stories up. The doors slide open, revealing the ship's interior on the deck where the lifeboats are. Performers use this elevator to help them get to the theater room quickly while staying hidden from the guests. Once they step out, they pause to choose from one of the many restaurants the ship has to offer. After settling on a spot, Kazuo takes the lead, guiding them through the maze of corridors toward the restaurant.

Inside the restaurant, the hostess steps forward with a warm smile to greet them as they enter. "How many are in your party?"

"Just the three of us," says Kazuo.

Before the hostess can lead them to their seats, a voice calls out from behind them. "Make that a table for four." They turn around to see a woman waving at them. "Long time no see, Miyu. Let's chat and catch up."

Miyu's face lights up with joy. "Yuko, is that you?" Without giving Yuko a chance to respond, she wraps her arms around her, pulling her into a tight hug.

Yuko taps Miyu's shoulder. "That's enough. You can let go of me now."

"You never returned my calls. I thought you were dead," says Miyu, squeezing even tighter.

"I'm about to be If you keep hugging me," says Yuko, out of breath.

Miyu finally lets go and takes a step back. "Why didn't you return any of my calls?"

Yuko takes a deep breath and discreetly wipes the saliva from her lips. "A lot has happened this past week. Let's go inside so we can talk at the table."

"Oh my God, it's Yuko Kusumoto," says Ayane, star-struck.

The hostess leads them through the softly lit restaurant. She stops at a table by the window, which offers a view of the ocean. The sunlight dances on the water's surface, and the horizon stretches endlessly. The group settles into their seats, taking a moment to appreciate both the scenery and the comfortable atmosphere before turning their attention to the menus.

As they look over the menu and place their orders, Miyu keeps her eyes fixed on Yuko. "I didn't know you were on this ship. Why didn't you meet with us sooner?"

"I wasn't," says Yuko. "I boarded not too long ago. My plane arrived in Okinawa at ten. So I asked if I could get on this ship to see an old friend and was told I could. To answer your question of why I haven't returned your calls. Well, my place was lost in the disaster. I was lucky to be away picking up some midnight snacks from the store. I left my phone in my apartment and poof, just like that, it was gone." She slips her hand into her pocket and pulls out a phone. "I got a new phone with a new number. I also lost your contact information."

Miyu reaches into her purse and pulls out her phone. She unlocks the screen and holds it out to Yuko. The two friends lean in, carefully typing in their contact details and confirming each other's numbers.

Ayane tries to hold back her excitement, but her bright eyes give her away. "Miyu recently told me the story of how you both met."

"Oh, did she now?" asks Yuko. "Seeing how you look excited to see me, I'm assuming you know all about my career."

"Yes, I do," says Ayane. "I know you were a child prodigy, and when you started your music career, you skyrocketed through the charts. Kazuo, at one point, was your mixer and introduced you to Miyu."

Yuko's face turns red, and she quickly covers Ayane's mouth with her hands. "Okay, okay, stop. I wasn't expecting you to know about how the three of us met. Anyway, I met Miyu a few times after that. We worked on a few projects together, but nothing ever came out. The higher-ups at the record company said our voices don't match. They don't know what they're talking about."

"We tried singing together multiple times," says Miyu, chiming in. "We even had Kazuo making our music, but it never worked out. Our music styles are just too different."

"Have you seen what's off in the distance?" asks Yuko, shifting her attention to the ocean. "It terrified me when I first saw it from the plane. The word around is they are preparing for an attack."

Their eyes drift to look out the window, where in the distance, silhouettes of Kun's warships loom on the horizon.

"I thought those were US warships," says Kazuo.

"Nope, have a look at this," says Yuko, shaking her head. She points her phone screen toward Kazuo, showing the news talking about the warships. "The reporters are saying an attack could happen at any time. But I wouldn't worry about it too much. The military base has all its people on standby, ready for anything."

In that moment, a low rumble reverberates through the ship as jets streak across the sky, heading toward the looming warships visible on the horizon. The restaurant goes quiet in anticipation of an attack. For several tense seconds, time seems to stand still. Then, just as suddenly as they appeared, the jets bank sharply to the right, turning away from the warships and heading back toward land. A collective sigh of relief ripples through the restaurant, breaking the silence as everyone relaxes and resumes chatting.

"See, nothing to worry about," says Yuko, smiling.

At the hospital   1150 Japan Standard Time

Lilly lies in bed, her heart fluttering with excitement for tomorrow. For the past two years, she has been in and out of the hospital. She was diagnosed with cancer at ten, but through all the hardships, she learned to find joy in the small things, like the breathtaking view of the ocean stretching endlessly beyond her window. On warm summer days, she opens the window to let the salty breeze drift inside and listens to the outside world. Even though she is on the top floor, she can still hear the ocean splashing on the shore. At night, she can hear it better when the city is asleep.

Lilly has been a devoted fan of Amazing Spring since it formed five years ago. Their music became her lifeline that helped her through her treatments. She was heartbroken when she found out all but Ayane died. Ever since Ayane said she was going to continue to be an idol, Lilly has been watching her closely, following every update. She hopes that tomorrow she can meet Ayane at the festival and tell her how much she means to her.

"How are you feeling, Lilly?" asks Dr. Ogawa, checking in on her.

"I feel fine. Nothing to worry about," says Lilly, flexing her arm muscles.

Dr. Ogawa chuckles softly as she checks Lilly's vitals. "Good to hear. Has the festival started streaming yet?"

"It started at ten, with Ayane singing," says Lilly, with sparkling eyes. "Right now, the news people are interviewing people. The big event starts at twelve."

Dr. Ogawa looks at her watch. "Oh, so in ten minutes."

"Yep," says Lilly with a big smile.

"Okay, everything looks good," says Dr. Ogawa, finishing her check-up. "If you need me, I'll be down the hall."

Lilly waves cheerfully as Dr. Ogawa turns to leave, and the doctor returns the gesture with a kind smile before closing the door behind her.

The festival officially kicks off at twelve o'clock, with many singers and bands performing across Okinawa. Shortly after, Lilly's grandparents arrive with lunch. For the next hour, they stay with her to keep her company and watch the festival. Even though Lilly has been in and out of the hospital, she does not mind it. She keeps in touch with her family and friends. Someone always visits her, so she never feels alone. She remains a happy-go-lucky girl.

Two hours ago   0955 Japan Standard Time

Justin and Yuuto arrive at the job site, where Yuuto parks the car alongside a group of military Humvees.

"The hardhats are in the back. Let me get them," says Yuuto. As he reaches into the back seat, something falls from his uniform onto Justin's lap. He brings the hardhats to the front, looking at the item now in Justin's hand. "Oh, whoops. How did that get there?"

Justin lets out a sigh and, without making eye contact, returns the item to Yuuto. "You might have gotten me the first time, but the hundredth time is different."

"You're no fun," says Yuuto, swiping the item from Justin. "Fine, I'll get someone else then. I heard we're getting a recruit today." He puts the item back in his pocket.

Justin ignores him, stepping out of the vehicle and securing his hardhat firmly on his head. He takes out his phone to review the construction details again as a group of soldiers approaches him.

An American man in his seventies waves his hand. "Hey Justin, how did everything at the hospital go?"

Justin looks up and smiles. "Everything went great, Will. If we're lucky, Lilly will be able to go out tomorrow."

"That's great news," says William, grinning and slapping Justin on the back. "We need to celebrate. After work, let's go get some drinks. Alcohol's on me tonight." The soldiers around him cheer, only for him to cut them off. "I'm not paying for any of you."

"Already a step ahead of you, William," says Yuuto, stepping out of the vehicle. "We talked about going out for drinks on the way here."

As they make their way toward the warehouse, the soldiers congratulate Justin on his daughter's recovery. Meanwhile, Yuuto adjusts his pace to walk ahead of a newly enlisted soldier. With a subtle flick of his hand, he lets the same item from earlier slip from his pocket, making it look like he dropped it by accident. It lands near the newbie's feet.

The newbie picks up the item and holds it out to Yuuto. "Uh…sir, you dropped this."

Justin sees what happens out of the corner of his eye, but continues walking like he saw nothing. "Here we go again."

However, William catches the shift in the air and immediately spins around. "Yuuto. Are you really doing this again?" He reaches into his uniform and pulls out a similar item, holding it up for Yuuto to see. "How many times do we have to go through this?" He walks up to Yuuto, forcing the item into his face. "For the last time, my granddaughter is way cuter than your son."

"Not so," says Yuuto, taking the item from the newbie while scoffing. "Have another look at my son. I know your eyes don't work like they used to, but even you should see my son is better looking. He just turned seven last month."

The item Yuuto has been casually tossing around is a picture of his son. For the past three years, Yuuto and William have been debating whose child is superior. They have been trying to get Justin involved with his daughter, but he always ignores them. They both stay outside, debating with each other as Justin begins his inspection inside the warehouse. The newbie stands awkwardly between them, surprised by the insistence. Yuuto and William pressure him about who has the better child. Feeling the pressure, he points at Yuuto.

William shakes his head at the newbie. "I'm disappointed in you." He walks away while slipping his photo back into his pocket.

Yuuto watches William walk away. He puts his hand on his hips and shakes his head. "You think you know someone?" He lets out a dramatic sigh before turning to the newbie. "What's your name?"

"The name is Omi, sir."

Yuuto smiles and puts his arm around Omi's shoulders, pulling him into a friendly embrace. "Nice to meet you, Omi. I'm Yuuto. As you can tell, we are very eccentric here. I hope you can fit in with all the games we play."

"Can you get me up to speed with everyone here? Everyone is tight-lipped," says Omi.

"Under normal conditions, I would also keep my mouth shut. However, since you praised my child in front of William, I'll get you caught up on the important people," says Yuuto, pulling Omi closer. "Let's start with me and Justin. He is my best friend. His full name is Justin Myers. I joined the military seven years ago, back when I was twenty and he was thirty-one. We met and had an instant connection. He was born in America, or more specifically, he was born and raised in the Dallas-Fort Worth area in Texas. You know where that is, right? It doesn't matter. There, he joined the army when he was eighteen. He went to college and got his degree in engineering in Austin. Then, he was stationed at a place called Fort Cavazos until he was moved here to Okinawa. He met his beautiful wife and had a child when he was twenty-six. Unfortunately, his wife lost her life a few years ago in a terrible accident."

"I think you are giving me too much information," says Omi.

"It's fine," says Yuuto. "Next, we have the guy I was arguing with. His name is William Woods. He's also American. I'm not sure where he was born, though. He's tight-lipped about his past. All I know is that military life was forced on him. He's from a broken home, so he had to get out of there, and the military was the only way he could. He went all over the world but never could find a place he could call home until he came here to Okinawa fifty years ago. When he was stationed here, he loved it here so much he asked to stay. He told me he never plans on retiring because he has nowhere in America to go back to. He cut off everyone back home a long time ago. Now he's a mentor to everyone. If you ever have any tough questions, he's the one to ask. He helped Justin get through the passing of his wife and the sickness of his child." He releases Omi, pats him on the back, then raises his index finger to his lips and winks. "If anyone asks where you heard any of this from, you didn't hear it from me."

Justin finishes his inspection, putting away his to-do list as William stands silently beside him. "That completes the inspection. Everything's in order."

"What else do you have planned for today?" asks William.

"That's all for today," says Justin.

"Well, how about indulging this old man by getting lunch with me?" asks William.

"Sure. What do you have in mind?" asks Justin.

"There's a nice little restaurant not too far from here I've heard people talking about. Want to give it a go?" asks William.

Before Justin can answer, Yuuto eagerly cut in. "If you guys are going out for food, I want to come along."

Word of the lunch plans spreads quickly, and soon a dozen more soldiers quietly gather, eager for a break. By the time William and Justin head out, the group has grown to fifteen. They all jump into the military Humvees in the front, and William and Justin get into Yuuto's vehicle. The restaurant is only a five-minute drive from the warehouse. It does not have many customers because of the festival. When the group enters, the staff exchange surprised glances at one another, then quickly spring into action. The manager helps guide them to tables. The soldiers settle in and claim nearly half of the dining room space. It does not take long for the chatter to get loud. Justin, William, and Yuuto sit together at the first table near the entrance.

William lets out a heavy sigh as he lowers himself into the seat, rubbing the back of his neck. "Ah, feels good to get off these old legs."

"Weren't you just sitting in the car?" asks Yuuto.

"You'll understand once you get my age," says William. "That is, if you can make it to my age."

"Are you still going to buy me that beer, Will?" asks Justin, flipping through the menu.

"And watch only you drink?" asks William. "Hell no. You might be done for the day, but I'm still on the clock. I also want to have a beer so I can share the moment with you."

The waitress comes up to their table with a notepad in her hand. "What can I get you, gentlemen, to eat?"

Yuuto holds up the menu and orders first. "Let's see. I'll start off with the miso soup, then I'll take the udon special. After that, I'll have a full plate of Takoyaki, finishing with two onigiri and the house sushi."

William chimes in, "To make it easier, just say what you don't want."

The waitress chuckles while writing it all down, then she looks at Justin. "And for you?"

"I'll take the udon," says Justin.

"Same here," says William.

"I'll put that in," says the waitress, closing her notepad. She takes the menus and walks to the kitchen.

"So, Justin, what are your plans after lunch?" asks William.

"I'm going back to the hospital to spend some time with Lilly. Yuuto's going to drop me off," says Justin.

Before William can respond, he receives a message on his phone. He looks it over, narrowing his gaze. "Unfortunately, I just got orders from the higher-ups. They want all soldiers to be ready for an attack." William stands, clearing his throat to capture the attention of the entire group. "You hear that, everyone? As your commander, be on guard. The next few days could be rocky." He sits back down.

"Let them try something," says Yuuto, slamming his hands on the table. "This is my home. I'll go down fighting if I have to."

"Let's hope it doesn't get that escalated," says William as he turns to Justin. "You can stay at the warehouse for the time being. I'm sorry you can't see your daughter right now."

"That's fine," says Justin, shaking his head. "I'll make it up to her tomorrow at the festival." He takes out his phone and sends Lilly a text saying he will be back late tonight.

The three friends chat and share jokes to pass the time until their food comes out. They know the kitchen is busy, and the wait will be long with so many orders coming in at once. When the food finally arrives, the rich aromas fill the air. By the time they finish and make their way back to the warehouse, it is one o'clock. The group disperses and looks for ways to fill the time. Some gather in small clusters, playing card games. Others lounge against crates or walls to chat with each other. The atmosphere is calm but filled with a restless energy, ready for anything. After an hour of moving around the warehouse, Justin slips outside for some fresh air. He sits in the shade of a tree and listens to the breeze. Not too long after, he falls asleep.

On the cruise ship   1205 Japan Standard Time

Lunch wraps up, and Ayane, Miyu, and Kazuo prepare to meet with their fans. Yuko joins them, eager to be part of it. The event hall sits near the top, at the ship's center. When they arrive, a long line has already formed. As they walk by, Miyu and Ayane apologize for the wait. The staff shows them to the table in the back of the room. Once they settle in, fans flood into the room. For three hours, they shook hands, signed autographs, and exchanged heartfelt words. When the last fan leaves and the door closes behind them, Ayane, Miyu, Kazuo, and Yuko lean back in their chairs, letting out a collective sigh of relief, grateful for the moment to breathe and recharge.

"That was so much fun," says Yuko. "I haven't done one of these in years."

Ayane rolls her shoulders, then lifts her hands to release the tension from her neck. "I think I'm going to head back to my room and rest for a bit."

Kazuo leans forward and glances at her. "We'll come get you thirty minutes before five."

Miyu and Yuko wave goodbye to Ayane. They continue to talk as she walks out of the room.

As Ayane walks down the hall, she whispers to herself, "Okay. An hour and a half until I need to get ready."

She makes it to her room and goes straight for the mini-fridge for a bottle of water. When she turns around, the TV is already on, but she does not remember turning it on. She looks around the room for the remote, but cannot find it anywhere. She gives up and sits on the edge of the bed, twisting the cap off her drink.

An eerie voice speaks from the TV. "Are you having fun forgetting about us, Ayane?"

Ayane wakes abruptly on the bed as a jolt of confusion floods her senses. Her heart pounds in her chest, and her palms tremble as she pushes herself upright. She glances around the room, not remembering when she fell asleep. An unsettling fear creeps over her, distorting the boundary between dream and reality until everything feels uncertain.

She notices the unopened water bottle in her hand, and the TV is off. She grabs her phone to look at the time. "It's only 3:36. I must have fallen asleep without knowing. I might need therapy." She gathers her things as her heart still races and hurries out of the room, meeting back up with Miyu, Kazuo, and Yuko.

"You're back soon," says Miyu, waving at her.

"I felt uncomfortable being alone," says Ayane.

"You look pale," says Yuko. "Did something happen?"

Ayane hesitates, and her words get caught in her throat as she struggles to find the right response. "I've been having recurring nightmares these past few nights."

"About what?" asks Yuko.

"My idol group," says Ayane, under her breath.

"It might be PTSD," says Yuko. "Have you talked to a doctor?"

Ayane shakes her head. "I was planning to go sometime next week. After this festival is over."

Yuko stands and walks over, wrapping her arms around Ayane from behind. "Don't push yourself too hard. I remember reading somewhere that dreams are a gateway to one's heart. It's okay to ask for help. You don't need to do any of this alone."

At 4:30, the bridge is busy with the crew coordinating the final preparations to move the ship into port. Suddenly, Captain Louis' voice rings over the intercom, grabbing everyone's attention with an announcement. "Good afternoon, everyone. This is your captain speaking. At five, we will begin docking at the port. It will take us about thirty minutes to complete the process. Luckily for us, we have our performers back on stage tonight. Be sure to get to the theater room early for seating. You don't want to miss Miyu Yoshioka and Ayane Sugita's last performance of the day. If you're unable to make it, don't worry. The show will play over the speakers and on the TVs around the ship. We hope you're enjoying your cruise with us." Captain Louis turns off the intercom. "Let's get everything ready for the docking."

Captain Louis moves around the bridge. He checks with the crew to confirm that everything is functioning properly before they head into port. Through the large windows, the open sea lies in front of them, with no other ships between them and the harbor. Tonight, no other vessels will dock, leaving the path ahead free for them to move with ease. Once satisfied, Captain Louis gives confirmation and signals the crew to be on standby until it is time for the ship to approach.

Ten minutes before five, Ayane and Miyu are backstage, freshening up their makeup in the mirror as they calmly prepare for the second performance.

Yuko is nearby, watching Miyu dab her face. "Hey, Miyu, would it be fine if I sing the first song with you? After the meet-and-greet, I have an urge to sing."

Miyu stops for a moment to think. "I think we can arrange that. What do you say, Ayane? Is it fine if Yuko and I sing first?"

"Go right ahead. We can sing the next song," says Ayane.

Yuko hurries to sit in front of a mirror, and Miyu leans in, carefully helping her freshen her makeup. At 4:55, Miyu and Yuko walk on stage. Their unexpected appearance leaves the audience confused and whispering among themselves.

"We have a slight change for the first song," says Miyu. "Since Yuko Kusumoto came all this way to be with us, we decided, why not let her sing? So we are starting a little earlier than we planned, and we'll be performing this first song together."

The crowd cheers loudly.

Miyu and Yuko perform one of Yuko's most popular songs. Its lyrics are a declaration of strength and perseverance to overcome impossible odds. The melody swells with hope, with each verse painting a vivid image of struggle and triumph. While their voices do not harmonize, their emotion carries them through with ease. Their passionate delivery fills the theater, inspiring the audience to feel every word.

After they finish, Yuko leaves the stage with a bright smile, then her eyes catch Ayane. She passes and pats her on the back. "I warmed them up for you. Give it your all."

Ayane rushes onto the stage, energy radiating from every movement. The crowd erupts into a frenzy of cheers and applause. The stage lights dim and focus on Miyu stepping forward to begin the next song. This song is one of Miyu's most popular songs. The upbeat melody pulses through the theater. It is a vibrant anthem about shaking off fear and embracing the moment. The lyrics urge everyone to forget their worries and dance freely. Ayane's voice soars confidently, inviting the audience to join in; their hands raise and feet tap in unison. The entire room seems to pulse with the beat, alive with a shared sense of liberation and celebration.

Right as the opening notes echo over a TV in the bridge, Captain Louis gives out his orders. "Let's move her to port." Around him, the crew moves quickly. He keeps his eyes on the horizon through the windows to ensure every step of the approach to port goes as planned.

On the port side of the ship, another cruise ship is close by and anchored. Then, without warning, a streak of light cuts across the horizon, followed by a deafening explosion. A missile slams into the ship's midsection, and in an instant, a blinding fireball erupts, sending a shockwave that rattles the windows of the bridge. Shards of twisted metal and burning debris rains down. Flames race along the other ship's decks, destroying everything in its path.

Before the crew can process what they see, another fireball appears. Then, one by one, each of the seven other cruise ships are struck, the missiles tearing into their hulls, causing a massive amount of water to enter. Within minutes, the once-crowded waters become a graveyard as the ships list heavily before vanishing beneath the oil-lit ocean. The captain and crew stand frozen in place, not sure how to react. Flames create an unbroken wall of fire across the ocean's surface as the smoke rises into the sky, darkening out the sun.

Captain Louis regains his composure, straightening his posture. "Get us out of here."

A crewman turns around. "We still need time for the propellers to fully start."

"How long?" asks Captain Louis.

"About a minute or two," says another crew member, frantically checking the controls.

"Once we move, head north while slightly turning starboard," says Captain Louis.

"Yes, Captain," says the crew.

Captain Louis grips the railing so hard it creaks under his hands as his eyes fixate on the burning horizon. Sweat forms on his forehead despite the cool air in the bridge. His mind races with scenarios of his ship being the next hit. Then, out of nowhere, military jets appear overhead. The sudden sonic booms shake the windows. Within seconds, they unleash a rain of missiles on the enemy warships. They are powerless against the speed and precision of the jets.

Through the chaos, the cruise ship's propellers come to life and launch the ship forward. Of all the warships, one is barely holding on as it lists hard to port. Its hull is blackened and its deck twisted, yet the crew aboard moves with purpose. The warship targeting system locks onto the cruise ship. Inside the enemy bridge, a hand hovers over the launch button. The warship shudders violently, rolling farther to port. Just before the button is pressed, the warship tips, launching the torpedo off-course.

The torpedo slices through the water, leaving a silver trail of foam behind. As the weapon curves, it detonates directly beneath the front of the ship, sending a massive column of water skyward. The front of the ship jumps up for a moment then splashes back down. Alarms instantly shriek across the bridge, flashing red as the ship takes on water. The tilt is already noticeable.

"What's the damage report?" asks Captain Louis.

"Compartments three through eight are reporting water. No, make that nine," says a crew member.

Captain Louis wastes no time. He sounds the alarm over the ship's intercom and brings the microphone to his mouth. "This is not a drill. The ship has been hit, and we are sinking by the head, fast.

I'm ordering a full evacuation of the ship. Everyone needs to abandon ship." Before he can say another word, the ship's power shuts off and communication stops. "May God have mercy on us all."

6

On the island   **1710 Japan Standard Time**

"Justin, wake up," says Yuuto, shaking him awake.

Justin jolts awake at the distant gunfire and explosions of the cruise ships in the distance. "Have they started their attack, Yuuto?"

"Yes, Kun finally made his move," says Yuuto. "We're under attack."

"Where's Will?" asks Justin, jumping to his feet.

"He and the other soldiers are inside, getting ready to move out," says Yuuto.

They rush inside the warehouse and see a group of soldiers gathering around William.

He notices Justin and Yuuto and waves them over. "Good morning, Sleeping Beauty. Hope you got your rest in because we're not sleeping tonight."

"Will, what's the situation?" asks Justin.

"Moments ago, we received a message about Kun's warships sinking cruise liners near Naha Port. Now we have enemy paratroopers flying their happy asses onto us," says William.

A backpack radio crackles with overlapping voices from the urgent reports. Akihiro, a radio operator, sits with his headphones pressed tightly to his ear as he listens to all the crucial information. "William, enemy boats are landing on the island near where we are. They're about two kilometers west."

"All right boys, we're going to be the first line of defense. Get your gear and let's head out," says William, pressing a rifle and helmet into Justin's hands. Without delay, the team moves outside to where the military Humvees are. He points to the largest Humvee that can hold at least ten people. "Justin, you're driving this one. Yuuto will be your spotter."

"You're coming with us, newbie," says Yuuto, grabbing Omi's arm. "Get in the back."

Justin climbs in and shuts the door with a heavy thud. His hands shake as he quickly unlocks his phone and searches for Lilly's contact. He presses the call button only to be met with a repeating beep. "Damn, it's no use. Connections are already down."

"The hospital staff is trained for things like this. Lilly will be fine," says Yuuto.

Justin shoves his phone in his pocket as his expression tightens under the tension. "You're right. Everything should be fine." He turns the key in the ignition, and the Humvee rumbles to life.

The lead Humvee takes off with William in the passenger seat while Akihiro listens to the radio in the back. Justin is next in line and follows behind. One after another, the six Humvees leave the warehouse and enter the main road, and rush westward to intercept the enemy at the beach. In the distance, loud sirens cut through the island, accompanied by the distant roar of jets. Gunfire cracks like sudden thunder, followed by sharp explosions that light the dusk sky. Along the roadside, frantic people dash in the opposite direction William's platoon is going. Their faces are pale and eyes wide with confusion and fear as they flee to safety.

William takes the Humvee's mic from its holder and presses the side button to talk to everyone in the convoy. "Once we make contact, we shoot on sight. I repeat, shoot on sight."

Justin eases his Humvee back a few meters from the Humvee ahead, keeping his eyes sharp for any sign of the enemy. The convoy moves with purposeful urgency, with each soldier aware of the imminent danger that awaits them. After two minutes of tense driving, the team arrives near the beach.

William locks his eyes onto the first enemy ahead, then he catches his breath. "Oh, good Lord." Up ahead, hundreds of dead civilians who tried to flee from the invaders cover the ground. "How could they have massacred this many people in this short amount of time?"

A lone enemy soldier stands over the dead, scanning the surrounding area. He spots William's Humvee approaching and lifts a pistol, aiming straight at the Humvee.

"You can't penetrate us with that small weapon. Why even try?" asks William.

Without warning, the driver drops dead with the windshield still intact. William's mind goes blank with disbelief, freezing him for a moment. Then his instincts take over, and he grabs the steering wheel, jerking it hard to the right. The tires screech sharply across the asphalt.

Justin watches the sharp turn and narrows his gaze in confusion.

Over the radio, Akihiro's voice crackles with static. "Retreat, retreat. Do not engage. They have a weapon we know nothing about."

"Oh shit," says Justin. He turns the wheel hard to the right as the enemy shoots another shot that barely misses him.

The other four vehicles are not so lucky. Twenty enemy soldiers arrive and begin shooting at them, killing them all. The military vehicles swerve with screeching tires and crash into the surrounding buildings.

"What the fuck?" says Yuuto. He leans out the window, watching the chaos unfold behind them.

"Get back in here, Yuuto, and contact William," says Justin, pulling at Yuuto's clothes.

Inside William's Humvee, he fights the steering wheel as he tries to keep control. "Give me a hand, Akihiro. I can't hold on much longer."

The dead soldier slumps against the steering wheel, making the Humvee hard to control. It veers wildly, fishtailing more erratically until William loses his grip and crashes into a ditch. A towering cloud of dust erupts, hiding the Humvee in a thick plume.

Justin slams on the brakes, bringing the Humvee to a screeching halt beside the thick dust plume. Yuuto jumps out as the dust clears, gradually revealing the crashed Humvee. The doors burst open, and William and Akihiro climb out, shaken but unharmed.

"We need to move," says William. "We don't want them getting us."

"You're not hurt, are you?" asks Yuuto, standing next to the passenger door.

"I'm fine, get in," says William, jumping into the passenger seat.

"I'm fine too," says Akihiro, holding a backpack radio to his chest. He tries to open the back door but cannot get a grip on the handle. Yuuto steps forward and opens it. Out falls Omi's dead body, hitting the ground with a thud.

"Shit, they got Omi," says Yuuto.

"We can mourn over the dead later," says William. "Pull him out. Once this is over, we'll come back for him."

Yuuto picks up the dead body and gently places it on the ground beside the wrecked Humvee. Akihiro climbs inside, and Yuuto follows in after him. The door slams shut, and Justin hits the gas, pulling away from the crash.

Akihiro lifts the radio mic to his mouth, forcing his voice to keep calm despite the horrors still fresh on his mind. "To all who can hear this, be advised, the enemy has a new weapon that can pierce through the armor of military vehicles. I repeat, the enemy has a weapon that can pierce through the armor of military vehicles." He then repeats the message in Japanese, trying to keep his tone the same.

"We just lost a full platoon in an instant," says Justin, hitting his hands on the wheel. "How are we supposed to fight against that?"

"We need to take them by surprise, but even that could be a fool's errand," says William.

Akihiro listens closely to the incoming chatter, then leans forward toward William. "I'm getting word that our forces are converging at the airport. They're in desperate need of reinforcements. They also say the enemy has a shield that protects them from danger. Not even bullets can pierce through."

"A shield that bullets can't pierce? Give me a break," says William.

"I wouldn't have believed it if our entire team just didn't get wiped out," says Justin. "We need to do something. I cannot let them get to Lilly."

"Step on it, Justin," says William. "Go to the airport. Maybe someone can find a way to overcome that shield before we arrive."

Justin presses the gas and comes across more dead people lying across the road ahead. His stomach knots as he eases his foot off the pedal, letting the Humvee slow as they approach the grim scene.

"Why are you slowing down? Keep driving," says William.

"There could be survivors," says Justin.

William reaches over and rests his hand on Justin's shoulder. "Son, I assure you, whatever weapon they're using killed them all instantly. Now drive over them."

Justin clenches his jaw and grinds his teeth with the weight of what he is about to do. His hands grip the wheel tightly as he presses forward. The tires roll relentlessly over the fallen bodies. Yuuto covers his ears, fighting to block out the sickening crunch that grows louder the longer they go. Akihiro presses the headphones to his ears, letting the static and distant voices drown out the noise. For Justin and William, they have no choice but to harden themselves, forcing their minds away from the horror beneath their wheels, refusing to give it a second thought.

On the cruise ship   1710 Japan Standard Time

The cruise ship trembles violently as the torpedo hits. In the theater room, the explosion hits the hardest, sending a tremor through the floor and rattling every row of seats. The lights flicker, and people fall from their seats, tumbling into the aisles and over one another. Some clutch their arms or heads where blood is seeping through fresh wounds. Cries of pain mixed with panic echo off the walls.

Onstage, Miyu and Ayane collapse mid-performance. The music stops in an instant, replaced by screams. When they regain their senses, they push themselves upright. The sight of the audience horrifies them and freezes them in place.

Kazuo wastes no time rushing onto the stage, grabbing them and pulling them close. "We need to go now."

As they leave the stage, Ayane glances back at the audience, feeling helpless.

Once backstage, Miyu turns around to look at Kazuo with anxious eyes. "What's going on?"

"We need to get to a lifeboat now," says Kazuo as his breath becomes erratic. "I overheard a call from a worker saying the ship is being attacked by the warships."

Yuko stands by the elevator, waving frantically at them. "This way's the only way out of here. We need to leave now."

The intercom turns on, filling the room with Captain Louis' voice. "This is not a drill. The ship has been hit, and we are sinking by the head, fast. I'm ordering a full evacuation of the ship. Everyone needs to abandon ship." The power shuts off, plunging the room into complete darkness.

Ayane stands frozen, listening to her surroundings. The piercing screams echo from the auditorium, mingling with the low groan of the ship as it shifts unevenly in the water. Moments later, the lights flicker back on, and without hesitation, they race toward the elevator. It shoots upward, letting them out onto the deck with the lifeboats.

All around, passengers panic and shout over each other, unsure of what has happened. Five minutes after the torpedo hit, the ship's condition took a sharp turn for the worse. The vessel lists noticeably to starboard. The bow normally sits fifty feet above the waterline, but now is thirty feet and plunging rapidly.

They step off the elevator, and suddenly, the power dies again, plunging them into total darkness. The emergency lights stay off, and cries of confusion and fear fill the air. Kazuo grips Miyu's hand desperately, keeping her close as the chaos unfolds around them. In the confusion, Ayane and Yuko separate from them.

Kazuo and Miyu force their way through the panicking crowd, fighting to reach the outside deck on the port side of the ship with the wind whipping against their faces. They look around frantically for Ayane and Yuko, only to realize they got split up. Miyu is not thinking clearly, and tries to go back in.

Before Miyu can run back inside, Kazuo catches her and wraps his arms tightly around her waist. She struggles for a moment, but his grip is firm. "There's nothing we can do, Miyu. I'm sorry."

Miyu stops struggling and looks up at him with tears welling in her eyes. "But we can't just leave them. They're our friends."

"I know, but I can't lose you," says Kazuo, holding Miyu even more tightly.

A crowd of passengers gather around the nearby lifeboats, their voices rising in anxious chatter. Two crew members struggle with the pulleys.

"It's jammed," says a crew member. "We can't launch this one."

Panic surges through the crowd as passengers push and shove, desperate to reach the stern to find an available lifeboat. Farther down the deck, the lifeboats are already full and swing over the side, ready to launch into the water.

Kazuo grabs Miyu's hand and pushes forward with the surging crowd, but she struggles to keep up. "I can't run in this dress. It's too tight."

They move to the side as the crowd rushes past. Kazuo looks around, noticing a knife sitting on a nearby table. He runs over and picks it up. "Let's try this. Hold still." He grabs Miyu's dress and slices it up to her knees. Tossing the knife aside, he grabs her hand again, pulling her through the chaos. "We need to move."

Miyu nods and runs alongside him. They continue pushing toward the stern, driven by the hope that there might still be room in a lifeboat. The chaos intensifies around them. People take their chances by leaping off the ship into the waters below. Their screams pierce the air and fade as they disappear into the dark water. Despite their urgency, Kazuo and Miyu quickly realize that the last remaining lifeboat on this side has already launched, leaving them and others stranded on the tilting deck with no way to safety.

Ayane blindly stumbles through the ship's darkened interior with her arms outstretched as she navigates. After several tense moments, she finally emerges on the starboard side. Compared to the chaos on the port side, this side is calm with a few people scattered about. She makes her way to the nearest lifeboat, where nine others have gathered. The bow looms just feet above the waterline.

A crew member works desperately to get the lifeboat launched. "The damned thing is jammed. I need help."

Others from the group rush to help him free the lifeboat. With one final push, they get it swung over the side just as the bow dips into the water. Suddenly, the ship lists more heavily toward starboard, causing a violent jolt that shakes everyone on deck. Ayane stumbles because of her dress. She reaches out, trying to catch herself, but there is nothing to grab. Her forehead slams against the deck with a sickening crack, and blood spews everywhere. She collapses on the floor, motionless. The small group stops and stare at her lifeless body as shock and disbelief ripple through them, unsure what to do next.

Yuko feels her way around the interior of the ship. Having been on board for only a short time, she has no sense of where the exits might be. Unlike the others, she wanders through the corridors. Eventually, she reaches an open area where the emergency lights glow yellow-orange at her feet. Shadows stretch ahead, and she can barely make out what lies in front of her.

The ship's tilt forces her to fight to stay upright. Each step is an uphill struggle for her as she tries to keep her balance. At the far end of the room, she runs into a bar with a handful of people clinging to whatever they can. Her legs give out, and she grasps a fixture bolted to the floor. Chairs and tables slam into the wall behind her. Glass shatters, and all unsecured objects tumble around her. She holds on desperately so that she will not be the next to fall.

Kazuo and Miyu reach the stern, gasping for air, unable to find a lifeboat. The deck tilts sharply as the stern rises out of the water and slowly rolls over. The wind whips their hair and clothes as they desperately clutch onto the railing.

"I'm scared, Kazuo," says Miyu, trembling.

Kazuo wraps himself around her, pressing her against the railing. "It's going to be all right. As long as I'm here, nothing will happen to you."

The stern towers fifty feet above the water, exposing its propellers that are still in motion. It rises faster and faster, nearly coming to a complete rollover. However, with a large section of the hull already submerged, the ship abruptly halts its rolling. Instead, it stands upright, lifting the stern farther into the sky while the bow sinks deeper into the ocean below.

"You need to climb over the railing, Miyu," says Kazuo.

Tears stream down her face as she shakes her head. "I can't."

Without a second thought, Kazuo picks up Miyu with one arm. She screams as the terror rips from her throat. He pushes her to the other side of the railing. Once she is over, he follows but loses his footing, and clings to the railing with one hand. After a few moments of helplessly holding on, he pulls himself over with all his might. When he is on the other side, he pins Miyu down so she does not fall.

He lifts his gaze to the scorched island in the distance. Thick black plumes of smoke spiral into the sky, transforming Okinawa into a chaotic battlefield. Military jets streak across the horizon, locked in deadly dogfights above the chaos. Beneath him, the ship comes to a complete stop, standing vertically three hundred feet above the water below.

"Are you okay, Miyu?" asks Kazuo.

Miyu nods, despite her body trembling as fear courses through her.

Off in the distance, a massive explosion erupts at the airport. Quiet at first, then the shock wave slams into the boat with extreme force. The blast is so intense that passengers get stripped from the ship and hurled toward the churning propellers below. Kazuo and Miyu barely hang on to the railing as the violent blast threatens to push them off.

Miyu squeezes her eyes shut and lets out a piercing scream. "I want to go home. I can't take this anymore. What happened to Ayane and Yuko?"

"Once this is over, we are going on a nice vacation wherever you want," says Kazuo.

Moments later, the ship begins its final plunge into the ocean. Within the ship, Yuko desperately holds on for dear life. Water surges in, rising rapidly around her. Silhouettes of strangers hold on beside her, speaking a language she cannot understand. When she feels the water touch her, she takes one final deep breath, hoping she can find a way out. The emergency lights dim and shut off. There is nothing she can do as she loses consciousness, ultimately succumbing to the water.

Kazuo and Miyu brace themselves for the worst to happen. Within seconds, the ship vanishes beneath the waves. Kazuo tightens his grip on Miyu, determined not to let her go as they get pulled under water. With one last glance, Kazuo sees the massive ship fade into the deep abyss below, not knowing what happened to Ayane or Yuko. They both resurface, gasping for air. Around them, there are lots of people floating nearby, some dead and others injured. In the distance, five of the ship's lifeboats come toward the crowd, offering a bit of hope amid the devastation.

On the island   1725 Japan Standard Time

Justin speeds toward the airport as adrenaline surges through him. He is nearly there when the colossal explosion happens, sending a massive fireball upwards, lighting up the dusk sky. "Shit, was that at the airport?"

"Communications just abruptly ended," says Akihiro, adjusting the radio to find a signal.

"What now, Will?" asks Justin.

"I don't know," says William, staring at the fireball. "Our only hope just got blown up."

"Hold on, guys, I might have something," says Akihiro, finding a signal.

"Don't keep us in suspense," says William.

Akihiro listens closely and repeats what he hears. "Fire. Explosions. That's what they are saying. That's how we beat them."

"How the hell does fire and explosions work?" asks William.

"I'm not sure," says Akihiro. "Hurry and turn us back around. There's another group nearby that we can meet up with."

Justin does not hesitate. He immediately turns around and goes back the way they came. "Where are we going?"

"They're not too far from here," says Akihiro. "There's a group of soldiers at a gas station making Molotov cocktails."

"Well, isn't that convenient?" says William.

Five minutes later, Justin arrives at the gas station, steering the Humvee up to the curb. Five lookouts scan the streets for any threat. At the pumps, the others work frantically, filling bottles with gasoline and stuffing in rags as they prepare the Molotov.

A lookout walks up to the Humvee as Justin rolls down the window. "Looks like someone got our message."

William exits the Humvee and walks around to greet him. "When we got your message, we rushed over here as fast as we could. What can we do to help?"

"We don't have a way to transport the Molotov," says the soldier. "We need to load your Humvee so we can ambush the enemy."

William immediately shakes his head. "I'd advise against that plan. They have weapons that can penetrate the armor of this vehicle. I lost a lot of good men in our encounter with the enemy. We'll be going into the slaughterhouse if we don't know where the enemy is."

"As luck would have it, we have three drones with us. We can easily find and ambush them," says the soldier.

"We need a better plan," says William.

"This is the best plan we have," says the soldier, irritated by William. "If we take any longer, we risk losing everything."

"He might be onto something, William," says Yuuto, chiming in. "It's a better plan than just driving around hoping for something else. We need to just polish up this plan, and we're all set."

William lets out a sigh. "Fine. Load us up. However, I want visuals of the enemy before we leave. I want to know all the details if I plan on putting the lives of my men on the line. You got that?"

The soldier salutes William. "Loud and clear." Then he turns around and yells at the other soldiers at the pumps. "All right, boys, you heard the man. Start filling them up."

The soldiers pick up baskets full of bottles; each one has twelve. Simultaneously, the drones fly around the area, looking for their targets. The Humvee fills up fast, fitting fifteen baskets in the back.

"We killed a group before you arrived. Come with me," says the soldier. He guides them around the building.

At the back of the gas station, they find the charred remains of eight enemy soldiers. The air is thick with smoke and the stench of burnt flesh as the blackened corpses lie among scorched debris.

"How were you able to kill them?" asks William.

"The drones spotted them when we were in the building. We got on the roof and, as they passed under, we threw the Molotov to see it would do anything. Luckily, it did," says the soldier, pointing his finger. "There are six more bodies farther away."

William moves closer to inspect the dead bodies. "What about their weapons?"

"Unobtainable," says the soldier. "When they die, so does their gun and helmet. They crumble into pieces and become worthless." He walks over and picks up a gun, but the moment he touches it, the weapon falls apart in his hands.

"So, even if we kill them, we can't use their gear. That's just great," says William.

Justin bends over and carefully tries to pick up a gun, but the moment his fingers brush it, the weapon crumbles into pieces. "They really don't want these weapons getting into the hands of their enemies. They thought of everything."

"Almost everything," says Yuuto. "If they thought of everything, fire wouldn't kill them so easily."

Justin stands back up, brushing the dust off his hands. "I guess even an alien civilization can overlook basic things like that."

They return to the front of the store. Their faces display a mixture of disappointment and grim relief, knowing that fire kills them.

Another soldier walks up to the group, carrying a map that he unfolds carefully. He spreads it out before them, tracing several key points of interest. "We spotted an enemy unit about fifteen klicks south of here. This is where we are." He slides his finger across the map. "And this is where you need to go. You'll be able to intercept them along this street. Let them pass and get them from behind."

William looks around at the soldiers. "We can fit three more people in the Humvee. The more hands I have, the better chance this will succeed."

The soldier looks at who he thinks will be the best to send with them. "These three will assist you. We'll keep in touch with the enemy's movements. I wish you all the best of luck."

As everyone hurries to the Humvee, Yuuto turns to Justin. "Have you been able to reach Lilly?"

"Not yet. The network's still down. I don't think I'll be able to until this battle is over," says Justin.

William gets in the passenger seat, pulling out his map. "I would say we could go to the hospital and protect it ourselves, but that would take good manpower from this mission."

Justin jumps into the driver's seat and shakes his head. "If the enemy is only coming from the north and west, they shouldn't be there yet. The hospital should be fine as long as we can hold our ground. I'm going to fight like hell to protect everyone on this island."

"That's the spirit," says William. "Let's be off."

Once everyone is in the Humvee, Justin hits the gas, kicking up dust as they speed off.

William runs his finger over the map, double-checking their route. "We need to catch them by surprise. One wrong move, and it's over for us. We hit them hard and fast before they can react." He looks around at the back of the Humvee. "I want no mistakes. If anyone messes up, that's it. No second chances. You got that?"

They give stiff nods at William's harsh words.

Across the island, word spreads fast about how to defeat the enemy. Forty minutes into the battle, the surviving soldiers have gathered every explosive they can find. Jets have already destroyed the enemy's warships and planes, though at a heavy cost. The battle has been brutal, with hundreds of thousands of civilians already dead. But once the crucial intelligence circulates among the troops, the tide of war shifts. Only the enemy ground forces remain. Confident that their helmets will shield them, the foot soldiers stand their ground as jets sweep in, only to be annihilated by their bombs.

"We are almost there," says William. "We should stop here and walk the rest of the way. No need to alert them."

Justin pulls the Humvee to the side of the road. The tires crunch on the gravel as the group climbs out. Akihiro takes a moment to secure the radio on his back so he can carry it with him.

"Make sure you silence that radio," says William. "I don't want that to be what gets us killed."

"I did, but let me check again," says Akihiro.

"Always good to check multiple times just to be safe," says William. He walks to the back and opens the trunk to grab the Molotov. He points at the three others who came with them. "You three, get a basket each. I want you to check over each one of them and make sure they are ready to be thrown. Once you're done, we can start heading over."

They each grab a basket and carefully look each Molotov over.

Yuuto walks up to William. "Will three baskets be enough? Shouldn't we bring more just in case?"

"If we bring anymore, we could risk the enemy hearing us," says William as he quietly closes the trunk. "From this moment on, everyone is to remain silent except Akihiro. He will keep us informed of where the enemy is."

Justin takes the lead, guiding the group toward the last spot the enemy was seen. William, Akihiro, and Yuuto are in the middle of the formation, and the three carrying the baskets are behind them because of the bottles clinking together as they walk.

Akihiro listens to the others on his radio. He whispers, "They're close; be on guard and stay quiet."

They move in a tight line along a wall, brushing their left shoulders on the rough concrete. The uneven crunch of the gravel beneath their boots feels deafening, like anyone can hear their approach. As they near an intersection, Justin comes to a stop and presses his chest against the wall's edge. He leans just far enough to see around the corner.

Nine enemy soldiers appear ahead, walking down a narrow path with their backs to the group. Their formation is loose, and their guns casually hang at their sides. They move at a slow pace; their voices loud and careless, believing fully in their helmets to protect them. Word has not gotten to them about their vulnerability to fire.

Without looking back, Justin raises his left hand and makes a series of precise gestures, directing them into positions. His eyes stay locked on the enemy's movements. Behind him, William's hand touches his shoulder with a firm pat, silently confirming they understood.

The team works quickly. The three soldiers set the baskets on the ground with care. William takes out a lighter and begins lighting the Molotov. When twelve in one basket are lit, each one of them takes two bottles, except Justin. He stays at the corner, never looking back. William leans forward and gives Justin a nudge with his elbow, signaling they are ready. Justin lifts his left arm into the air, giving them the signal. The six men round the corner together and line the street in silence. They simultaneously toss the twelve Molotov, hitting their targets with pinpoint accuracy.

The bottles shatter in a massive fire that spreads across the narrow path. The flames engulf the soldiers before they can even register what is happening. They scream sharply, clawing at their burning uniforms, but the fire has already melted it into their skin. Two of them drop to the ground but roll in the burning gas, causing the flames to burn even hotter. The screams gradually die out as the men collapse and their skin sags off the bone. By the time the last scream fades, the only sound left is the faint crackle of fire that consumes what remains. The group watches in horror as the fire lights their stricken faces.

Yuuto staggers to the side with one hand covering his mouth to hold it in, but it is no use. He leans over and vomits violently as his body convulses. When he finishes, he stands upright, wiping what remains off his mouth. He is the first to turn toward Justin, ready to say something, but his expression drops in an instant. Behind them, a lone enemy soldier stands motionless. Everyone turns around in a heartbeat. The air feels heavy, as though time stretches until every second feels like an eternity.

Justin catches their shifting expressions and quickly spins around. The soldier stands just yards away, holding his gun at chest level. His thoughts race as he thinks of the impossible. *What can I do? I could get a Molotov. No, that won't work. I wouldn't even make it halfway before I'm shot dead.* He looks back at the enemy as they walk closer. *What if I rush him? No, that won't work either. Shit, think. Come on, think. I don't want to die. I need to get back to Lilly.* Justin's life flashes before his eyes as the soldier closes the distance with the gun pointing at his chest. Every step feels heavier, dragging out the inevitable. His breath becomes shallow as the cold weight of reality settles in. *It's over.*

Then, the enemy lowers the weapon and tosses it to the ground at Justin's feet. "I surrender. I'm sick of all of this needless death. You can have these." He takes off his helmet and breaks down in tears.

Still reeling, Justin stares at the man, unsure if his mind is playing tricks on him. The soldier holds out his helmet, and Justin takes it without thinking. He then glances down at the gun lying between them. Moving slowly, he bends and picks it up.

William is the first to snap back to reality, scanning the scene to make sense of all this. He stares sharply at the soldier. "This isn't a joke, right? You're really surrendering to us?" His hand drops to his waist and grips his sidearm just in case.

"Yes, I give up," says the soldier, raising both hands.

The group pulls themselves together, shaking off the lingering shock. Eyes dart between one another as questions arise.

"What's your name?" asks Justin.

"My name is Ming, and after those things arrived, our leader let the power go to his head. He wanted to try these weapons, and the Americans gave him the reason he needed. Anyone who didn't follow his orders to invade was told our families would be killed." His voice cracks as tears fall down his face. "We didn't have any other choice but to come here and fight."

"Don't give me that crap," says William. "Everyone has a choice. Just like how I'm choosing not to kill you where you stand."

"Easy for you to say. I don't want my family to be killed because of me," says Ming.

"Let's give it a rest," says Justin, putting his hand up to William. "When this is over, we can interrogate him further. Now we need to regroup." He takes off his helmet and hesitates for a moment before putting on the other one.

"How does it feel?" asks Yuuto.

Justin shifts the helmet slightly, tugging at the straps until it sits just right, then gives a small shrug. "It feels like a normal, run-of-the-mill helmet. Not special at all." He takes the other helmet and puts it on Ming's head.

"Maybe you're using it wrong," says Yuuto. "Let me try."

William puts his hand on top of Justin's helmet, interrupting their conversation. "Justin will not be taking this off. He will keep these safe until we can hand them over to the higher-ups. For now, let's get back to the Humvee and continue the mission. Having this helmet should make our job easier." He looks at Justin and pats him on the back. "I'm counting on you to kill off the enemy, seeing how you're the only one of us protected."

William takes the lead to the Humvee, and everyone follows.

Akihiro lifts the radio to his ear, scanning for any hint of what is happening on the island. "Everyone, I'm getting word the enemy's losing their ground. We're winning."

Everyone lets out a burst of relief and excitement, but William remains calm, anchoring their celebration. "Let's not get ahead of ourselves. We still need to rendezvous with the others."

Akihiro's grin fades and the color drains from his face as the words on the radio change to despair. "No, this can't be. You need to hear this." He slings the radio off his back and sets it on the ground. He turns the dial, cranking the volume so they can hear the grim news that darkens everyone's expressions.

"Shoot it down," says a man over the radio. "They just dropped the Deatomizer over Kin. Anyone in the area, shoot it down now."

Miles away, near the center of the island, the Deatomizer hovers menacingly over Kin. People scatter in every direction as they try to get as far away as possible. Soldiers weave through the chaos with their weapons drawn. They fire upon it, but it seems to do nothing. Sweat drips down their faces as their eyes widen with terror and disbelief.

"Do not stop firing," says a soldier. "We can't let this thing kill us."

"I'm out of ammo. I need more," says another soldier.

At a nearby military base, targeting systems lock onto the Deatomizer. Launchers spit missiles and rockets in a hailstorm, but each strike goes through, causing no damage. Panic grips the crews as every weapon and tactic they have trained for seems useless against this unstoppable foe. All the remaining jets race toward Kin, but only one is close enough to reach it before it detonates. The pilot makes a split-second decision and dives straight into the Deatomizer. But the Deatomizer is merciless. The jet slams into the inner blue light and vanishes in an instant, leaving only its wings crashing down to Earth.

Seconds later, the outer light expands, swallowing the island. Soldiers on the ground continue to fire blindly, but the weapons have no effect. After all hope is gone, the panicking soldiers drop their guns and run away in search of a safe place. Every desperate attempt to fight back crumbles under the undeniable truth that they are powerless, and nowhere is safe.

After a minute passes, the inner light follows the first, ending everything in its path. Around the island, streets erupt into chaos as screams pierce the air. Crowds run desperately, but the light relentlessly catches up. By now, the news of the battle in Okinawa is known throughout the world. Satellites broadcast the terrifying expansion. Millions watch in horror as the massive dome covers the island, knowing the scale of the disaster that is about to unfold.

Amid the chaos, a mother clutches her child's hand, running down the street for their lives. The little boy gasps for breath, then trips on the asphalt, stumbling onto the road, and cries. The mother turns around, and panic spikes in her chest when she sees the enormous blue wall approaching fast. Instead of picking her son up and running, she drops to her knees and wraps him in her arms as people rush past, desperately trying to save themselves. She holds him tight, rocking back and forth as the light engulfs them.

At the hospital, Lilly lies in bed, pale and fragile, oblivious to the horrors erupting outside. In the hallway, nurses and doctors moved in a frenzy, their faces tightened with fear and confusion when the first light engulfed them. Dr. Ogawa bursts through the doors and rushes inside Lilly's room.

Tears form in Lilly's eyes. "What's going on? What happened?"

From the window, they notice the light growing as it pushes closer with terrifying speed.

Dr. Ogawa rushes over to Lilly and gives her a reassuring hug. "It's going to be all right." She rests her face in her beanie. "I'm here with you, Lilly."

Terror grips Lilly. Her body trembles as she screams. Tears streak down her cheeks as her gaze locks outside the window. Her small hands clutch the sheets, as if holding on could somehow keep the unstoppable force at bay. "Daddy. Where are you?" Their figures blur and vanish as they fade away.

Kazuo and Miyu drift helplessly in the water, clinging to each other while chaos erupts all around them. The desperate crowd surges toward the five lifeboats, shoving and clawing aboard, but Kazuo pulls Miyu close, anchoring her to him. Their eyes meet, drowning out the screams and turmoil. Miyu closes her eyes, parting her lips slightly, and Kazuo moves in. They share one last kiss as their hearts pound in unison before the relentless light takes them away.

7

November 14th, 2026   0415 Eastern Standard Time

Xavier pounds his fist against the president's bedroom door. Not waiting for a response, he bursts through the door and wakes Angus. "Sir, you need to see this."

Angus jolts awake, jerking upright as his body stiffens with sudden alertness. He rubs his eyes, blinking rapidly as he comes to his senses. "What's going on?"

"Kun's military launched their attack," says Xavier. "They're fighting the Japanese in Okinawa."

Angus throws the covers aside and leaps out of bed. He slips his feet into his slippers and rushes down the hallway toward the situation room. "What's the situation?"

Paula stands at the front of the room, her nightgown slightly slipping at her shoulders, yet her presence commands the space. Military officials and intelligence officers follow every order she issues. The moment Angus bursts onto the scene, she locks eyes with him. "Sorry for waking you this early, sir, but you need to see what's going on. Fifteen minutes ago, Kun began a full-scale invasion of the Japanese island of Okinawa. I took the liberty of getting everything ready for you."

At the front of the room, multiple TVs display live satellite footage of the battle from different angles.

"Good call," says Angus, stepping closer to get a better look at one of the TVs. "I see smoke coming from the ocean. What's that?"

"That would be the first casualties of this invasion," says Paula. "Kun's warships sank nine ocean liners about a mile from the harbor. Our military made swift work of the warships, but it looks like they couldn't save any of the ships."

The door swings open with a sudden force, and Robert stomps into the room. Heads instinctively turn his way as his presence fills the room. "Reinforcements. Where are they?"

"Reinforcements are going to take some time," says Xavier. "They're on their way, but it will take two hours for them to arrive. It's an island in the middle of the Pacific, of course."

"Why didn't we have any ships close by?" asks Robert, slamming his hand on the table. "We've known about their warships around Okinawa since last night."

From across the room, Angus meets Robert's gaze. "You need to calm down and assess the situation."

Robert forcefully pulls out a chair with a sharp scrape against the floor and sits. He glares at Angus, his eyes burning with anger, and points at him. "No, you need to assess the situation. People are dying because we didn't prepare for this when we should have. We had enough time and resources to avoid this. If anything, it was foolish to host that event. What did they expect to happen?"

"We did what we could with the time we had. We sent extra troops and weapons to Okinawa," says Angus.

"Obviously that wasn't enough to deter an attack," says Robert, shifting his finger toward the TV. "Look at the screen. The island's on fire. We needed our own warships around the island to prevent a situation like this." He slams his hand on the table again.

Before the tension can escalate any further, an advisor speaks with a phone pressed to her ear. "You both need to hear this. We're getting word that the enemy has a new type of weapon."

"What kind of weapon?" asks Angus.

"Something like a force field is protecting them. Bullets don't have any effect," says the advisor. "Also, have a look at these pictures we just received." She puts a few pictures on the TV. They show thousands of dead bodies scattered across the island.

Robert leans forward in his chair with his eyes wide and jaw tight as the grim images flash across the screen. "Paula, how long has it been since the attack began?"

"It's been thirty minutes since the warship started the attack," says Paula.

"How is that possible?" asks Robert, falling back into his seat. "So many people died in that short time." His mind races, trying to understand what could have caused them to die. "Are there any reports of gas being used?"

"No, but we're getting reports the enemy has another weapon that can kill on the spot," says the advisor.

"Another weapon, huh? What did these aliens give them? There's no way we could have prepared for any of this," says Robert.

Twenty minutes pass, with updates coming regularly. "We're getting reports they found a way to defeat the enemy," says the advisor. "Their shields don't protect against explosions. They're winning now."

A grin appears on Angus' face, then he glances at Robert. "Looks like the extra missiles we provided are being used to their fullest."

Xavier peers at his computer screen, his expression marked by deep concern. "Angus, we have an unidentified flying object heading toward the island." He transfers the footage to the TV for everyone to see. The object streaks across the sky from the southwest, cutting through the clouds toward the island.

"Can we get a clearer image of what that is?" asks Angus. He then looks at Paula. "How fast is that thing going?"

Paula grabs a pencil and paper, then fills it with numbers as she calculates the speed. "From what I can tell, it's traveling between twenty-eight hundred to three thousand miles per hour."

Robert narrows his focus on the TV, his brow furrowing in confusion. "It doesn't look like any jet I've seen before. Is it a new weapon? What could be going that fast?"

The object decelerates after it reaches the island, and then comes to a stop, hovering in place.

"Why did it stop? What's it doing?" asks Xavier.

Angus feels his stomach drop. He gasps, realizing what it is. "Oh God, it's the Deatomizer. Give me a closer view now."

The Deatomizer expands over the island as the advisors frantically look for a close-up video.

"Here, sir, I found one," says Paula.

The outer light expands rapidly across the screen, engulfing everything in its path. Once it stops, the second light expands over it. The faces in the situation room turn pale as they watch, realizing the unimaginable scale of lives being lost. A minute later, the light finishes covering the island. The dome slowly dissipates, revealing a massive hole as ocean water surges in.

Angus clenches his hand into a fist, heat floods his face, and his jaw grinds so hard it aches. The rage boils inside him. He reaches for whatever is within arm's length, ready to hurl it at the TV.

Paula steps beside him, placing her hand firmly on his shoulder. She gives a small shake of her head. Her eyes met his with a steady gaze. "Remember what happened the last time you lost your temper? You promised me you'd never let anger consume you."

Angus takes a deep, shaky breath, forcing the fire in his chest to cool. His shoulders ease slightly as he lifts his hand and rests it over hers. "Thank you." He collects himself and rubs his face. "What's the estimated loss of life?"

Paula looks away, trying to hold back tears. "A million and a half, sir. I would expect it to be higher because of the festival."

Robert sits quietly in the background as the room fills with tense voices. His eyes drift to a pack of cigarettes on the table with a lighter resting beside it. After letting out a sigh, he caves and grabs them both, and slips out of the room unnoticed. Outside, the night is calm. Sunrise is still two hours away. He pulls a cigarette from the pack and puts it in his mouth. The lighter flickers, and the flame illuminates his worn face before the tip glows red. He inhales deeply, holding the smoke in his lungs for a few seconds, then exhales slowly. The haze drifts upward, then fades away, revealing the full moon overhead. His shoulders sag. The weight on him is visible in every line of his face. He feels defeated, ready to go back to sleep, but he knows there will be no rest. Today is going to be hell.

Three hours later   November 14th, 2026   0800 Eastern Standard Time

Brittney sits in front of a camera as the glow of the studio lights gleams across her face. Her expression is grave as the story weighs on her. Behind her, a screen shows looping satellite images of Okinawa before and after the Deatomizer went off. "We begin this Saturday morning with breaking news out of Japan. Four hours ago, Kun's military attacked the small island of Okinawa as a festival was taking place. The Deatomizer was used, and everyone on the island is presumed dead."

The broadcast cuts to shaky, grainy footage captured from the ground moments before the Deatomizer takes the island. The camera jerks wildly as the person filming sprints and breathes loudly into the microphone. They stumble, and the view shows the inner light approaching, then the video abruptly ends.

Brittney continues her report while holding back tears. "It's currently nine at night over there, so there isn't any live footage of what was left behind. The videos we have were taken hours ago as the sun was setting. The president is expected to give a speech in an hour. He recently talked with the Canadian prime minister about how to proceed with this situation. Let's turn now to our war correspondent, Luke Hurst, who has been watching this situation unfold outside the capital building in Philadelphia." Brittney turns her chair to view a screen with another reporter on it. "Good morning, Luke. Can you give us an update on the situation at the capital?"

"Good morning, Brittney," says Luke. "If I had to sum up what's happening in one word, that word would be chaos. Everyone ranging from the president to lawmakers are trying to figure out how to respond to this horrendous attack on unarmed civilians. Angus has already spoken with NATO, but the talks fell through. They will not be sending any aid or reinforcements. The Salvation Army and the Red Cross have also declined a request for aid. I wouldn't have expected much from them anyway because of their headquarters being taken out by the Deatomizers earlier this month."

"Have you seen the president?" asks Brittney.

"No, I have not," says Luke, shaking his head. "From what I'm hearing, he's currently in a meeting with Japan's newly appointed prime minister. I wouldn't be surprised if they're discussing the possibility of surrendering. Kun has shown he possess more of these Deatomizers, and he is not afraid to use them. What we need right now—"

"Hold on, Luke," says Brittney, interrupting Luke. "We have breaking news that Kun is about to speak."

The camera cuts to a live broadcast showing Kun standing behind a podium with a menacing gaze. For a few tense moments, he says nothing, only scanning the room as cameras flash. Finally, he addresses the audience with a bitter tone. "To all that still oppose me, I'm talking to you: Japan, Canada, and the United States. Tonight's attack on Japan is not the only attack we have planned for you. It's the first of many. This is my declaration of destruction. A full annihilation of those who oppose me. I gave you your chance to surrender, but you just didn't listen. If you only stopped and gave yourselves up to me, I wouldn't have to resort to wiping your existence from history. Future generations will never know you ever existed; I will make sure of it. Okinawa was just the beginning." He pauses, allowing his gaze to sweep across the room again, hoping someone dares to challenge him. "To show I mean business, I am sending the full force of my military to the United States in the coming weeks to kill every last one of you. The time to surrender has passed. You had your chance, and you blew it. Don't make this harder than it needs to be. Just lay down and let my forces end your pathetic existence." The feed abruptly cuts out.

After the cameras shut off, Kun violently slams the podium to the ground. "How did we lose in Okinawa?" He breathes hard and looks at the faces of those around him, then he locks his gaze over to where Taf is sitting. "Where's Ignin? I told him to be here an hour ago."

Taf remains unshaken, her posture remains steady and her expression unreadable. She calmly meets his gaze, not an ounce of fear or doubt shown in her eyes. "Ignin is still making preparations to meet with you. Have a little more patience. He'll be here in a moment."

Before Kun can respond, the doors swing open, and Zhen enters with Ignin following behind. "I brought Ignin like you asked."

Zhen steps aside as Kun hurries to confront Ignin. "What the hell was that? Your weapons only worked to surprise them, but once they collected themselves, they started killing my men."

Kun's harsh tone catches Ignin off guard. He stumbles slightly, not expecting this side of Kun. "We didn't know the weapons your planet has. We believed what we gave you would be enough, but we were wrong."

"Yeah, you think," says Kun. "From this point on, I'm taking over the weapons manufacturing. I want every piece of my equipment protected with the same force field that protected us from the Russian attack."

"That will take some time to make. It would take three of your months to make all that is required," says Ignin.

Kun tightens his fist, wanting to punch Ignin for talking back. Instead of letting his fist do the talking, he channels the intensity into words as he lays down an ultimatum. "You have two days, and nothing more. I expect you to work with that."

Ignin desperately steps forward. "But, sir, that's not nearly enough—"

"I'm tired of all the excuses," says Kun, slamming his hand down on the nearest table. "Figure out how to do what I'm telling you. Do I make myself clear? I don't want a repeat of what just happened. Now get out of my sight."

Ignin seizes the chance to leave the room. Without another word, he turns around and hurries to the exit.

Another advisor enters the room as Ignin leaves. "Sir, we have reports that some of your soldiers have made it back from Okinawa."

Kun straightens his posture and darkens his expression. "Round up all that came back. We need to show everyone we mean business."

Twelve hours later, towering platforms rise just outside the capitol building. Immense crowds gather close, waiting in anxious anticipation. On the platforms, hundreds of people are bound and immobilized with black sacks covering their heads. Many are children; their small forms tremble under the ropes as tension and fear radiate through their silent, helpless bodies. The air is thick with dread as every onlooker is aware of the horrifying outcome about to happen.

At the podium, Kun stands tall as the cameras focus on him. His expression shows no sympathy for what he is about to do. "Last night, we faced a humiliating defeat in Okinawa. To set an example, I have gathered all the returning soldiers who fled the battlefield with their tails between their legs. Let it be known, I do not have the patience anymore to deal with deserters and traitors, and I'm taking action against them now." Kun's cold eyes sweep over the crowd before he looks over at his soldiers. "Bring the first family to me."

The soldiers drag eight captives forward and force them to their knees in front of Kun, silencing the crowd's murmurs. The soldiers remove the black bags from their heads, exposing their faces to the world. Gags press tight against their mouths, muffling their sobs. The spectators freeze when confronted with the reality of the captives' suffering.

Kun points to an unmasked man on the other end of the platform. "These eight people are the family members of that man over there. He betrayed his country and must pay the ultimate price."

The man's voice cracks as he screams for Kun to stop, but his desperate pleas are nothing more than background noise to Kun. The eight people in front of Kun are the man's wife, both parents, two siblings, and three children, who are all under ten years old.

Kun withdraws a pistol from his waist and cocks it. "This is what happens to traitors." Without hesitation, he presses the gun against the forehead of the youngest child and pulls the trigger. He moves down the line, deliberately killing them slowly so the tied-up man can feel more pain. When the last shot rings out, he gives the gun to a nearby soldier and pulls a handkerchief from his pocket. He wipes away the stray blood from his face, then turns to face the cameras with his expression eerily calm and composed. "From this day forward, I will no longer tolerate anyone surrendering."

Behind Kun, his soldiers aim their guns at all the remaining people and open fire, killing them all. The platforms become a scene of carnage as bodies collapse one after another, with blood splattering across the wood and ground below. The crowd recoils in horror as the scene descends into a nightmarish bloodbath.

November 15th, 2026   0100 Japan Standard Time

"Shiro, I don't think we should go outside. The voices could belong to them," says Kiyomi, gripping Shiro's arm.

"We can't stay locked in here forever," says Shiro, pulling away from her. "Seven hours have already passed. And besides, they're speaking English. This might be our only chance to contact the outside world before our resources run out." He slowly opens the door, the hinges creak softly, and he peers out into the darkness beyond. Every one of his senses tenses as he takes in the silent void.

"Do you see anything?" asks Kiyomi, moving her head to see outside.

"I can't see a thing," says Shiro, fully opening the door and walking out of the building. "I'm used to seeing the city lights in the distance, but it's completely dark. Not even the bugs are making noise."

Kiyomi turns around with a concerned look on her face. "Shigeko, stop him."

Shigeko shakes her head. "You know him. Once he gets an idea, he won't stop. Just let him be."

From the back room, a man emerges, holding a flashlight. "I'll go with him. We can't risk anything happening to the smartest person here," says Ryuunosuke, rushing out the door to catch up with Shiro.

"The voices we heard should be in this direction," says Shiro, moving through the dense undergrowth.

"Let's be careful," says Ryuunosuke, handing Shiro the flashlight. "We don't know who's out there. For all we know, they might not be friends."

Shiro smirks as his hand casually slips into his lab coat, revealing a pistol resting in his pocket. "Don't worry, I have us covered."

"How did you get that?" says Ryuunosuke.

"I have my ways," says Shiro, turning off the flashlight. "Now stay quiet. We're getting close."

They quietly crouch through the bushes, careful to avoid making any noise. The voices ahead grow clearer with each step as laughter breaks through the night. Once they make it to the edge of the tree line, they stay hidden in the shadows. On the beach, a fire burns, flickering its light across six figures hunched over, playing cards next to a marooned boat.

"Let's stay hidden for the time being," says Shiro. "We need to decide if they are friend or foe."

Ryuunosuke gives a silent nod before turning his gaze to the figures.

The fire crackles, casting their shadows across the sand. The six figures laugh and tell stories, completely unaware they are being watched. "What I wouldn't give to be in a bed right now," says a figure. The other five groan in unison as they continue their card game.

"Well, boys, looks like I win again," says a man.

They all moan and groan again, tossing down their cards for the deck to be reshuffled.

"This is the fifth game in a row. How are you so good?" asks a different man.

The voice from before speaks, "Before our ship sank, I was a dealer in the casino."

From the darkness, Shiro suddenly bursts from the bushes, turning on his flashlight. The light lands on the sand at the strangers' feet. He slowly steps forward, making no sudden movements. "Warships don't have casinos. So, can I assume each of you were on one of the sunken cruise ships earlier?"

The men jump to their feet, and their cards scatter on the sand. Each one instinctively drops into a defensive stance, bracing themselves for a confrontation with whoever is ambushing them.

Shiro quickly raises his hands to chest level while keeping the light at their feet. "Relax. I mean no harm. I overheard you talking and wanted to see whether you were friend or foe."

One of them speaks up, "How do we know you're not sided with Kun, and when we let our guards down, you'll kill us?"

"Fair point," says Shiro. "But wouldn't it have been easier for me to kill you when you didn't know I was here?"

A brief silence follows before another man speaks up. "Yes, we were on one of the cruise ships. Our lifeboat got caught in the currents, and we got marooned here an hour ago."

A woman's voice calls from within the shadows of the marooned boat. "Is that someone here to help us?"

"Yes, I'm here to help," says Shiro.

"Oh, thank God. We need a doctor. We have someone injured in here."

Before Shiro can respond, a man interrupts her. "I still don't know if we can trust him."

The woman shoots back, "What other choice do we have? Look around. We're stranded here, and there's nothing we can do. I don't know about you, but I'm not from Okinawa. I'll take my chances with that guy."

The men relax a bit as they exchange uncertain glances. Her words make them realize the situation they are in.

Shiro turns his head back toward the tree line. "You can come out now, Ryuunosuke."

"How many of you are there?" asks a man.

"Enough," says Shiro, walking inside the boat. He sweeps the flashlight across the interior, revealing three women beside someone lying across the seats. "What type of injury do they have?"

The same person who spoke before responds, "They have a head injury. We've been watching them closely. I'm Alice, by the way."

"Shiro. Nice to meet you." He points his flashlight at the unconscious person. A bloody cloth covers their face. "Let's get them to my lab. My wife's a doctor. She can look them over and hopefully fix them up." He sticks his head out the window. Below, the group gathers around Ryuunosuke to talk. "I need three people to help carry the injured to my lab."

They all hurry over to help. Three men hurry inside, and Shiro instructs them what to do. Together, they carefully lift the injured person, shifting their weight in unison to keep the injured person steady.

Shiro moves towards the exit, keeping the flashlight at their feet. "Be very careful with their head."

They carefully climb down from the boat, sinking into the sand below. The group moves slowly through the beach and make it to the dense foliage. Shiro lights the bushes as everyone else moves branches and limbs out of the way. Above them, the thick canopy filters the moonlight, allowing only the faintest glimmers to reach the ground. They finally reach the clearing where Shiro's lab waits, its windows gently glowing by candlelight.

Kiyomi leans against the doorframe, crossing her arms tightly over her chest. "I see a light."

"Don't worry, it's just us," says Ryuunosuke.

The group steps inside the building, and the door closes behind them. The two people who were already waiting in the room stand and watch them.

"Shigeko, we have a patient for you to look at," says Shiro. "They have a head injury."

Shigeko hurries over to have a look at the patient. After assessing their condition, she throws everything off of a nearby desk. "This will have to do for now. Lay them here."

As they gently lay them down, another person rushes from the back of the building. "Here Shigeko. I brought a face mask, gloves, your lab coat, and medicine I thought would be useful," says Yoshiko.

Shigeko pulls the mask over her face and slips into her lab coat. Yoshiko helps secure the gloves over her hands. Ryuunosuke takes the flashlight from Shiro and shines it on the patient's head, keeping it steady for Shigeko and Yoshiko to get to work. The others step back, giving them space while watching closely.

"Does this person have a name?" asks Shigeko as she removes the blood-soaked cloth around the patient's head.

"No one here knows who they are. We just came across them," says Alice.

Shigeko stays quiet, her focus unwavering as she carefully peels back the bloodied cloth. The moment it comes undone, blood spews out. "Whoever applied this cloth did a fantastic job."

Yoshiko grips the patient's head, applying pressure to stop the flow of blood. The sight is too much for the others. They look away, unable to stomach it. Only Shigeko remains focused on her task. Her gaze remains sharp as she assesses the damage and prepares for the next move.

Shiro steps forward, positioning himself between the group and the patient. His voice is steady as he talks, drawing everyone's attention away from the gruesome scene. "So, what's everyone's name? I'll go first. My name's Shiro. This is Kiyomi. The guy holding the flashlight is Ryuunosuke. The beautiful doctor is my wife, Shigeko, and her assistant is Yoshiko."

The tension in the room eases slightly. One by one, the group introduces themselves. They exchange their names and shake Shiro's hand. The introductions create a sense of normalcy, and give Shigeko and Yoshiko the space they need to focus on the patient without distractions.

After they finish, Shiro repeats their names to remember them. "Starting with the ladies, we have Alice, Scarlet, and Freya. Then, with the guys, we have Leo, Russell, Sebastian, Tristan, Adam, and Ed. Is that correct?" Everyone nods. "And everyone's from America?" They all nod again.

They all calm down and talk to each other before Yoshiko interrupts them by making a loud gasp. "Hey, no one knows who this is? Really? After fixing her up, it's clear who this is. This is the idol who has been rising to fame recently, Ayane Sugita."

Six hours later   November 15th, 2026   0700 Japan Standard Time

A knock at the door startles everyone awake. Tension hangs in the air as everyone exchanges nervous glances, unsure whether to answer.

Shiro takes out his gun as he approaches the door. "Are you friend or foe?"

A voice responds from the other side. "It depends. Are you with the Japanese or Kun?"

"We're with the Japanese," says Shiro, tightening his grip on the gun.

"Then I'm a friend," says the voice. "I'm looking for a man named Shiro. Is he here? I was told a while ago that if anything were to happen to me and I needed help, I was to come here to look for that person."

Shiro hesitates for a moment before unlocking the door. He opens it just enough to see the man standing before him. "Yes, I'm Shiro. How can I help you?"

In front of Shiro stands Justin. Tears stream down his face as his emotions get the best of him. "I didn't think there would be more survivors." He wipes off the tears with his sleeve and collects himself. "I'm Justin."

"An American soldier?" asks Shiro, recognizing his uniform. "Please come inside."

Justin slowly walks inside, still wiping his face with the back of his sleeve. The others stay silent, watching to see what he will do next.

Shiro shuts and locks the door before turning to him. "Can I get you anything?"

Justin regains his composure and shakes his head. "I need to talk to you in private. This is very important."

"Sure, follow me," says Shiro, leading Justin to the back of the building. They enter a small room, and he closes the door behind them. "Do you need anything before we begin? Food or water?"

Justin pulls out a chair and slumps into it. "No, I'm fine." He sits up, focusing on his task. "Have you seen the aftermath the Deatomizer left behind?"

"I've seen the photos," says Shiro as he pours himself a cup of coffee. "I can't say I've seen the recent one."

"That's fine. I need you to look at these," says Justin. He unfastens his helmet and places it on the table. He then grabs his gun from his pants pocket and sets it beside the helmet.

"What am I supposed to be looking for? Is there something special about them?" asks Shiro.

"An enemy soldier gave me these before the Deatomizer took everything away," says Justin. "These are the weapons they were using."

Shiro spits out his coffee and sets down the cup. He narrows his eyes as he picks up the gun for a closer inspection. "You're kidding. These are the infamous weapons they tried to take over Okinawa with? I was hoping I would get the chance to see them, but I didn't expect I'd see them so soon. Where is the soldier who gave you these? I have some questions for them."

"The Deatomizer took them. Along with my family and friends," says Justin, fighting back tears.

"I'm sorry to hear that. At least you weren't caught in it," says Shiro.

"That's the thing. I was in the middle of it. Just like everyone else," says Justin.

Shiro stops looking at the weapons and glares at him. "How? Tell me everything leading up to the moment you and everyone around you were consumed." He takes out a piece of paper and a pen from his desk to document everything he is told.

Justin takes a slow breath. His chest tightens as he tries to remember what happened thirteen hours ago.

A frantic voice crackles over the radio. "Shoot it down. They just dropped the Deatomizer over Kin. Anyone in the area, shoot it down now."

"Move, move, move," says William. "Get back to the Humvee."

Everyone runs to the Humvee as fast as they can, without a second thought.

Justin hurries into the driver's seat and turns it on. "What's the plan, Will?"

"Drive southwest as fast as you can. If the location of the Deatomizer is true, we should barely be on the edge of where it will end," says William.

Justin slams his foot on the gas pedal, then his tires screech, leaving behind black streaks on the asphalt as the Humvee speeds away. The engine roars, but it is not enough. The blue light catches up and engulfs them.

"Step on it, Justin," says Yuuto.

Justin presses the gas pedal to the floor, forcing the Humvee to pick up speed quickly. He glances at the side mirror and sees the darkened light gaining on them. Panic grips as the world around the Humvee blurs and fades into the void. For an instant, everything goes silent. The darkness swallows light and sound, tearing the world apart all around him.

"Next thing I know, I'm lying on the ground looking up at the stars," says Justin, narrating his experience. "The sun was already gone. I could barely see anything. But what I could see was a large body of water rushing toward me to fill the hole."

Justin gazes out at the massive hole that stretches for miles, then he jumps to his feet. "Lilly, where are you? Talk to me. Lilly?" He lets out a desperate scream. His lungs burn, and each inhale comes shallow as he nears hyperventilation. "I need to calm down. I need to get out of here before the sunlight is gone."

Justin continues his narration. "I looked up and saw this huge mountain in my way. If I didn't start moving when I did, the water would have killed me. I think it took two hours to climb out of the hole and reach the top. All I could hear was water crashing behind me. Next thing I knew, I woke up, and it was already six in the morning. The water had already risen to its normal level. What was once a thriving island was reduced to nothing but this small chunk of land."

Justin puts his hand over his face, peeking through his fingers to look out to where Okinawa once stood. "How did I survive? What happened to the others?" He removes his helmet and looks it over. "Was it the helmet that saved me? It doesn't matter. What's my next move?" He puts the helmet back on and takes out a map from his pants pocket. "I should be around here, I think. Damn it, there aren't any notable landmarks, but I for sure was driving down this road." He folds the map and puts it away. "The place Will told me about shouldn't be too far from here. Let's hope someone's there."

"And then I arrived here," says Justin, finishing his story.

"This guy, Will, wouldn't happen to be William Woods, would he?" asks Shiro.

"Yes, that's the guy," says Justin. "He told me about six places across the island to look out for if I was ever in a bad situation, but told me to make this place my first priority and look for you because you would know what to do."

Shiro looks at the floor, giving a small grin. "William always did put a lot of faith in me. Did he ever tell you why to look for me?"

"He never talked about who he knew," says Justin.

"That sounds just like him. He was a very reserved man. That makes sense. He told you to find me because I'm a problem solver. If a problem has a solution, I can find it," says Shiro. He stands and opens a drawer, pulling some papers out. "Five years ago, when I was twenty, I won a Nobel Prize in physics for a thesis I wrote about antimatter. These papers are what the Japanese government tasked me with. Have a look."

"I can't understand any of this. What am I looking at?" asks Justin, scanning through the pages.

"I have to find out all I can about the Deatomizer and the properties of the Disappearance. I was always so close to finding the answers, but I was missing one thing," says Shiro, tapping on the helmet. "These weapons might hold the key to finding all the answers I'm looking for. I'm going to need some time to study these weapons, and hopefully I can turn this war around. In the meantime, let me introduce you to everyone."

Shiro and Justin step out of the room together. Justin takes a shaky breath before introducing himself to the others. His voice wavers as he recounts the events of what happened in Okinawa. The group listens in tense silence as the weight of his words press down on the room.

Each person struggles to process Justin's story. Alice is the only one not at a loss for words. "When are we going to contact someone about this?"

"I have a radio in my office, but all I am picking up is static," says Shiro. "The Deatomizer took out every communication tower. We're alone out here, in the middle of the Pacific. Stranded on what remains of Okinawa."

"But we can't stay here forever," says Alice. "How are we supposed to get out of here?"

"Just north of here, there's a storage facility with a small plane," says Shiro. "As long as the Deatomizer didn't take it out, we can use it to get off this island. We can split into groups and search the island for supplies in the meantime. One group can go look for the hangar." He puts his hand on Ryuunosuke's shoulder. "He has a pilot license, so he'll be in charge of finding the hangar."

"I'll come with you," says Justin. "I'm an engineer, so I can help if the plane needs any repairs."

Russell nods and stands. "The lifeboat I was controlling should have enough food and water for us to survive for about two weeks. We can move the supplies here before searching the island."

Shiro claps his hands together, getting everyone's attention. "That sounds like a great plan to me. So, group one will be Ryuunosuke and Justin looking for a plane. Group two will be me and Kiyomi, analyzing the weapons. Group three will be Shigeko and Yoshiko, taking care of Ayane. And group four will be everybody else gathering the supplies out of the lifeboat. This sounds easy enough. Let's get to work."

No one complains, and the group splits into their groups. Shiro and Kiyomi immediately dive into researching the items, working with urgency and making fast progress.

Kiyomi carefully documents their findings, recording every detail while Shiro continues his work beside her. "Fascinating. This helmet can prevent the wearer from succumbing to the effects of the Deatomizer."

"I was astonished too when Justin told me he was in the middle of the Deatomizer," says Shiro. "It makes sense the wearer would be protected. You can't have your entire team wiped out because of your own weapon."

"This is what we've been looking for," says Kiyomi, giggling with joy. "The missing piece of the puzzle."

Shiro sets a thick stack of papers on the table beside the helmet. "Let's cross-reference all the info we know about the Deatomizer and see if there are any points that align with the helmet. Then we can do the same with the gun. I wouldn't be surprised if they're made of the same thing."

Meanwhile, up north, Justin and Ryuunosuke arrive at the hangar.

"This must be the place Shiro was talking about. Let's go inside," says Justin.

Ryuunosuke looks around the hangar and sees the hole stopped just fifteen feet away from the entrance. "We're very lucky. Any closer, and this hangar would have been swept into the ocean. However, I don't see a runway. This could be a problem."

"I guess we'll worry about that later," says Justin. "We still need to see if the plane's here and if it's operational. Let's be careful when we open the hangar doors. I don't know how stable the ground is."

They push the metal doors open, letting the sunlight brighten up the interior.

"Well, this isn't a plane, but it will do," says Ryuunosuke. "It's a bit small, though. I was hoping for something bigger."

"Are you able to fly a helicopter?" asks Justin.

"Yes, I am," says Ryuunosuke, opening the helicopter's door and climbing inside. "I can fly any small aircraft. I'm going to see if it's in good condition to fly." He presses a button, and the control panel lights up. He studies the instruments carefully, checking each gauge and dial, making sure the plane is in running condition. "Everything looks good. However, we have no gas in the tank. We need to find diesel fuel."

"The tanks should be around the side. Let's take a walk," says Justin.

They spend several minutes walking around the hangar, inspecting every corner and searching for anything that can hold fuel, but despite their efforts, they come up empty-handed.

"If I had to guess, the Deatomizer took the tanks," says Justin.

"You might be right," says Ryuunosuke. "Let's go back to the lab. We can tell everyone what we found."

Throughout the day, people come in and out, bringing back any resources they can find.

Yoshiko keeps a tally of the food and drinks brought in. "If we include what we already had, we should be able to last ten days."

Ryuunosuke walks into the lab. "We're back and have great news."

"You found the plane?" asks Shigeko.

"It was a helicopter," says Ryuunosuke. "Unfortunately, it can only fit five people and has no fuel. If we find fuel and get it running, I should be able to fly it."

Alice slumps down in a chair, rubbing her eyes. "Now it's just a matter of who gets to leave this island."

Shiro walks out of his office after hearing how lively the main room has gotten. "We'll worry about that when we need to."

"Anything you want to share with us, Shiro?" asks Justin.

"These items are so amazing," says Shiro, as his eyes beam with excitement. "They were the last pieces I needed to put all the information together."

Kiyomi follows behind him, looking through her notes. "If the data is correct, we should be able to make a replica, no problem."

"How can you replicate alien technology? Shouldn't that be impossible?" asks Justin.

Shiro shakes his head. "If we have a sample, we can recreate anything, provided we have the materials. Making these weapons should be simple enough." He notices a look of confusion spreading across everyone's faces. "Let me put it in simpler terms. Imagine we went back in time and wanted to make a gun using the technology from this era. We could. The materials exist; we just need to gather them and make whatever we want. It's the same with these alien weapons. We have the materials needed to make them. We just need to figure out how to assemble it. I'll start by using the gun and helmet I already have as the base for the replicas."

"While you figure that out, we need to figure out how to get diesel," says Ryuunosuke.

"I think I can help with that," says Russell. "The lifeboat we were on has a full tank of diesel."

Before anyone can respond, Shiro interrupts them. "We can figure out how to transfer the fuel to the helicopter tomorrow. Night will be in a few hours. We don't need anyone getting lost."

For the rest of the day, the group chats about small things to distract themselves from the uncertainty ahead. When night falls, exhaustion takes hold, and one by one, they fall asleep.

Justin's eyelids grow heavy, and he drifts into a deep sleep. The dream unfolds around him with startling clarity. He sees Lilly walking beside him down a path through a forest. A gentle wind pushes through the towering trees, filtering sunlight across the forest floor. Flowers bloom along the path's edge, and birds chirp between the branches, bringing life to the forest. Every sound and detail feels alive. He smiles, feeling at peace as he watches Lilly skip ahead, her laughter mingling with the rhythm of the forest, and he wishes the moment could stretch on forever.

Lilly turns around with her arms behind her back. A gentle smile spreads across her face. "You need to start taking better care of yourself, Dad."

"What do you mean? Your dad is in tip-top shape. Just look at me," says Justin, flexing his arm muscles.

Lilly laughs, shaking her head. "You're so funny, Dad."

"Your mother loved my humor," says Justin, softening his voice. "You take after her, after all"

"I am her daughter. It makes sense," says Lilly, skipping farther ahead of him.

Justin watches her as a bittersweet warmth settles in his chest. "She was my best friend. She always knew how to make me happy."

"Well, I can say the same thing about you," says Lilly. "You know how to always make me happy."

Suddenly, a bright white light forms behind her.

The light blinds Justin, and he puts his arm up to block it. "What's that behind you, Lilly?"

"This is where we must part ways, Dad," says Lilly. "You have to go on this journey by yourself. We'll be waiting for you when you get here." She turns around and walks into the light.

"No, I'm not ready to lose you. Please don't go," says Justin. He runs to catch up to her, but no matter how fast he runs, she keeps getting farther away.

"This parting will only be for a little while," says Lilly. "It's up to you to save this world and to save me. I love you, Dad."

"Lilly, come back. Come back." The bright light overtakes Justin, and he wakes up with tears running down his face. After a moment of collecting himself, he sits up and wipes the tears away. The air inside feels suffocating, so he gets up and steps outside for some fresh air. The night remains still as a gentle fog clings to the island. He stands for a while, gazing upward at the stars and the Milky Way galaxy stretching across the sky. "Of all the places in the vast universe, why did you have to come here?"

Meanwhile, Ayane is fighting her own battle. Ever since she got knocked out on the ship, a relentless nightmare has trapped her. Her idol group now haunts her at every turn. Each step she takes feels orchestrated, as if she is a puppet manipulated by invisible strings, forcing her body to move against her will. To the people on the outside, she appears peacefully sleeping, but on the inside, her mind screams for help, pleading for someone to pull her out of this torment. Her subconscious claws at the edges of the nightmare, trying to escape, but the nightmare drags her deeper into the everlasting darkness.

She runs through endless streets in the middle of the night. Her footsteps echo against the pavement. Buildings loom on either side, with their blackened windows staring down at her. The city is unnervingly silent, yet from somewhere just beyond the edges of her vision, whispers drift toward her, unintelligible but sharp enough to make her skin crawl. She clutches her hands over her ears, desperate to block them out, but the voices continue, impossible to escape. "You're not real. None of this is real. Stay away from me."

Ayane rushes into the nearest building as her heart hammers in her chest. She presses her back against a cold concrete wall, trying to catch her breath. From the shadows behind her, arms wrap around her, pulling her into the wall. Panic surges through her as she struggles, kicking and twisting as she tries to break free. With a desperate shove, she tears herself from the wall and stumbles out of the building, back into the empty street. Her screams slice through the night. She spins in a frantic circle, scanning the endless street for safety. "Where do I go? What should I do? Someone, please help me."

A voice echoes from the building she was in. "No one's going to save you, Ayane. Accept your fate."

As Ayane runs, the world around her twists and turns. The streets warp into narrow alleyways, pressing around her. Ayane continues to run away. The shadows behind her get bigger as they catch up to her. Their eerie laughs send shivers down her spine. She turns a corner only to be greeted by a dead end. "No, no, no, no, no. Get me out of here." She runs up to the wall and bangs her hands on it with all her might. "This is only a dream. I should be able to control this." But the nightmare does not bend to her will.

Ayane turns around and all eight members stand in her way, not giving her a chance to escape. Their bodies are broken, bloodied faces torn beyond recognition. Where their eyes should be, there are only gaping black voids. She looks at them, frozen in fear. She tries to move, but her legs lock in place. They give out, and she falls to the ground, not once taking her eyes off of them.

They slowly walk up to her, their voices overlapping each other. "Did you forget about us, Ayane?"

"How can you live with yourself?"

"You killed us."

"This is your fault."

"You must pay for what you did."

The whispers grow louder, pressing into her mind. Ayane curls up and buries her face between her knees as her breaths come in short bursts. Every instinct screams to run, but her body refuses to obey.

Their stiff fingers slowly run through her hair, then yank her head up. "Don't look away."

"Look at us."

"Open your eyes."

"Look at what you did."

"Are you trying to forget, Ayane?"

"Of course not," says Ayane. "How could I ever forget my friends? You all mean everything to me. I would give anything to get you back. Every single day, all I do is wonder why it wasn't me who died. Why was I left behind? It should have been me. I miss you all. I miss you so much."

The screams suddenly stop. When Ayane slowly opens her eyes, she is no longer in the alleyway. Instead, she stands in a vast field of flowers that stretches endlessly in every direction, sunlight bathing it in a warm glow. Standing in front of her are her friends, appearing just as she remembered them from happier days. She blinks, unsure if she is awake or dreaming. The oppressive fear from before seems to vanish, replaced by a sense of peace. She rises to her feet, her legs unsteady but driven by newfound determination.

Sachi steps forward, wrapping Ayane in a comforting embrace. "Coming to terms with what happened was the first step you needed to take. You need to find the strength to push through this. You need to find the will to live. Don't drown in your sorrows anymore. Regret is a thing of the past. Look forward to a bright future. It's up to you how to live your life. Just remember to always be true to yourself. Never forget that, Ayane."

"I will," says Ayane. She wipes the tears from her cheeks and gazes at everyone.

Sachi pulls away, giving Ayane a warm smile. "You have grown so much these past few days. If there was another way, I would have stopped these nightmares long ago, but we needed you to come to terms with our deaths. This is where we say our goodbyes. Never forget us."

One by one, a white light engulfs them, and they fade away. Each of them turns to Ayane, gently waving and offering comforting goodbyes. Their voices linger for a moment before fading completely.

A sharp ache spreads through Ayane's chest as she watches them go. She feels the weight of their absence pressing down. Her hands tremble slightly, and she struggles to hold back her tears, longing for just one more moment with her friends. "How do I know if what I'm doing is the right thing?"

Sachi's voice echoes as her form fades into the light. "Give it time. That's for you to decide. You'll have to figure that out for yourself. Live your life looking forward. Don't regret the past as you have been. We are all counting on you to save this world, Ayane."

Ayane whispers one last goodbye. As the words leave her lips, the world around her dissolves and fades into the bright light.

November 16th, 2026   0715 Japan Standard Time

Justin could not fall back asleep. He lies awake, lost in his thoughts. *That dream seemed very realistic. What did Lilly mean by I will save her and the world? Oh, get it together, man. It's only a dream. There's more pressing matters to deal with.* With a sigh, he gets up and goes toward the room where Shiro is working. As he makes his way over, he passes Ayane, who is still lying down. He looks at her and notices she is awake. "Can you hear me?"

She looks at him, and without saying a word, gently nods.

"Let me get the doctor," says Justin. He raises his voice to call out. "Shigeko, I need you."

"Is everything all right?" asks Shigeko, coming from the room where Shiro is.

"Your patient is awake," says Justin.

Shigeko hurries over to Ayane. "How are you feeling? Can you talk?"

Justin watches for a moment before continuing to Shiro. He knocks on the door before stepping inside. "Up early, I see."

"I'm so close to finishing these replicas. I want to hurry so we can leave," says Shiro.

Justin crosses his arms and leans on the door frame. "We need to decide who's leaving in the helicopter."

"When everyone is awake, we can have a talk about that," says Shiro. "Do you want a coffee while we wait?"

"Coffee sounds great," says Justin.

An hour later, everyone is up and sitting in the main room.

Justin begins the discussion, addressing the group with a serious tone. "Our two biggest concerns are who's going in the helicopter and where we're going."

Shiro chimes in. "The only person who can pilot the helicopter is Ryuunosuke. So, we have four more spots."

Russell raises his hand. "I think the both of you should go. Justin, you've been in the middle of the Deatomizer. That information should be given to whoever needs it. Then you, Shiro; you're making a replica of the weapons used during the attack. You can change the war we're in. The fourth person should be Ayane. She needs medical treatment. If she stays here, she will most likely die. These are my three picks. I don't know who should be the last one."

After Russell shares his recommendations, the group talks with each other and agree with his proposal.

"If we can't figure out who else should go, I think doing a drawing would be the best way. Leave it up to chance," says Justin.

No one objects, and Shiro cuts a piece of paper into slips to write their names on.

Before he can write the first name down, Shigeko interrupts him. "You don't need to write my name. I'll stay behind and make sure everyone's in good health."

"Same with me," says Russell. "I have a lot of outdoor skills I can use just in case we need them."

One by one, they tell Shiro not to write their names except Alice. "I don't know about you, but I want to get out of here. Write my name down."

Shiro shakes his head, tossing the paper in the trash. "There's no need. Everyone said they didn't want to go, so by default you'll go. Is everyone okay with that?"

No one disagrees, and Alice is the last person.

"I still need time for my research," says Shiro, standing from the table. "Get everything ready. I should finish this later today."

With a renewed sense of purpose, the group moves quickly to fuel the helicopter. They make their way to the lifeboat to prepare to transfer fuel.

Ryuunosuke stands on the steps of the lifeboat to gather everyone's attention. "To make it easier to transfer the fuel, we can fill the helicopter enough so I can fly it over here, then we can put the rest in."

"How much fuel do we need to take to the helicopter so you can fly it over here?" asks Russell.

"It's about a kilometer away, and I need to run the engine for a while to warm it up," says Ryuunosuke. He mentally calculates the distance to fly and how much fuel it needs. "We need at least ten gallons, but to make sure I get here with no problems, let's go with twenty."

Russell steps past Ryuunosuke, and climbs inside the lifeboat. He walks to the back, searching for a suitable container for the fuel. Upon finding one, he holds it up for the group to see. "This holds only three gallons. We're going to be making multiple trips." He also grabs a hose to siphon fuel from the tank.

"I'll come with you again, just in case you need help with the helicopter," says Justin.

"I'll also come with you," says Leo. "You need someone to bring the container back and forth."

When the fuel container is full, Ryuunosuke, Justin, and Leo begin the fifteen-minute walk to the hangar. They do not want to run and risk dropping the only container they have.

Halfway there, Tristar shows up. "I figured it would be better for two people to walk back together so they don't get lost."

Once at the hangar, Ryuunosuke refuels the helicopter. "Six more trips and we'll be good to go."

The process is slow, taking three hours to transfer twenty-one gallons to the helicopter. In that time, Ryuunosuke puts nine gallons in and starts the helicopter to see if it runs. The engine turns on with no problems. After looking it over again, he shuts it off. To pass the time, he and Justin play cards. Once the twenty-one gallons are in, Ryuunosuke now has to fly it out of the hangar.

"How are you going to get the helicopter out?" asks Tristian, eyeing the tight space inside the hangar.

"Normally, we would attach wheels to the bottom and tow it out, but we don't have the device to do that, so I'm going to fly it out," says Ryuunosuke.

"Isn't that dangerous?" asks Leo.

"It's very dangerous," says Ryuunosuke. "One wrong move, and the helicopter hits the hangar. If that happens, we can say goodbye to leaving the island."

A tense silence settles over the group as Ryuunosuke climbs into the pilot's seat. He runs through a mental checklist before turning it on. Meanwhile, Justin, Leo, and Tristan hurry out of the hangar, moving far away to a safe distance.

Ryuunosuke exhales slowly, forcing his nerves to stay calm. Once the rotors get to full speed, he carefully lifts the helicopter off the floor and inches forward toward the exit. The helicopter is just a foot off the ground. Any higher, and the blades risk hitting the hangar as he exits. Slowly, he makes it out of the narrow opening and eases down onto the grass outside.

The group erupts in cheers, running over with relieved smiles. They get inside and compliment him on his maneuvering skills. The short flight to the beach is smooth, taking less than three minutes. Ryuunosuke sets the helicopter beside the lifeboat and powers it down.

Russell exits the lifeboat as everyone disembarks the helicopter and meets with Ryuunosuke. "The boat's still holding three hundred and fifty-six gallons of fuel. Is that going to be enough?"

"Lucky for us, the helicopter holds a hundred and eighty-five gallons. It should be able to fly over four hundred and fifty miles on a full tank," says Ryuunosuke.

Russell takes the container from Tristan. "I'll start refilling this bad boy, then."

"Wait," says Justin. "Do we have a longer hose so we don't have to keep using the container?"

Russell shakes his head. "The lifeboat only has the small one. Does Shiro have a hose?"

"You can start filling it up. I'll ask him," says Ryuunosuke. He returns five minutes later with a water hose. "Will this work?"

Russell takes the end of the hose. "It looks long enough. The only problem I see is if the helicopter tank is higher than the lifeboat's tank. Go put your side next to the helicopter tank, but don't put it in yet. Justin, come with me to hold the hose in the gas. When I tell you to, you're going to pull the hose up, but make sure you keep it in the gas. That should start the siphoning process." He puts the hose in the lifeboat's tank and leaves Justin to hold it. "Leo, Ed, and Tristian, I need you three to hold the hose at an even decline."

The trio move into position, carefully keeping the hose steady.

Russell takes the other side from Ryuunosuke and covers the end with his hand. "All right, Justin, you can bring it up from the gas."

Justin lifts the hose, keeping it submerged in the tank.

Russell removes his hand, and a steady stream of fuel flows into the helicopter's tank. "Works like a charm."

They cheer and compliment Russell.

Justin peers out the window of the lifeboat. "How did you know that would work? I thought you would have to suck it for the fuel to come out."

"It's a trick I learned from being outdoors all the time. No need to work hard if there's an easier solution. I'll tell you when to remove the hose from your end," says Russell.

It takes twenty minutes to fill the helicopter. Once the tank is full, Ryuunosuke moves the helicopter to the building, so they can easily get in it when they leave tomorrow morning.

When they arrive, Shiro greets everyone while showing off what he recreated. "I did it. The replicas are done. Have a look at them."

Justin takes the replicas from Shiro and looks them over. "Amazing. I can't believe it worked."

"Even though they are replicas, these are the real deal. Be extremely careful with them," says Shiro.

"Good job," says Justin, giving them back to Shiro. "Now, our next task is finding out where to go."

They head inside, and Ayane is sitting down talking with Shigeko. As soon as she sees everyone enter, she stands up, bows her head, and in English says, "Thank you all for saving me."

The girls immediately gather around her, offering comfort and reassurance.

Alice places her hand gently on Ayane's shoulder. "Adam is the one who picked you up and put you on the lifeboat, and Russell bandaged you up."

Ayane walks up to Adam and Russell, and takes their hands. "Thank you so much for saving me."

Shiro comes from his office and lays out a large map of Japan across the table. "Let's figure out where we can go."

The group gathers around the map and begin saying places too far for the helicopter to fly to.

"Those are good places to go," says Ryuunosuke. "I'd also like to fly to Hawaii, but the helicopter can only fly about seven hundred kilometers."

Justin puts a ruler on the map. "With that range, I don't think there are any military bases we can get to."

It goes quiet for a few moments as they think of what to do. Then, Shiro points to a city. "How about the airport in Kagoshima? It should be in range."

Ryuunosuke measures the distance using the ruler. "Roughly seven hundred kilometers. I think this will work. We can make it there and contact the military."

After some more suggestions, they all agree on Shiro's plan of going to Kagoshima.

Night arrives, and everyone goes to sleep, ready for tomorrow.

November 17th, 2026   0600 Japan Standard Time

The group awakens before sunrise on day three of being stranded on the island, only to be greeted by a relentless downpour. Sheets of rain pound against the windows, causing the glass to rattle with each gust of wind. Anticipation turns to frustration, knowing that their plans have to be put on hold until the skies clear.

Justin stands by a window, pressing his hand against the cool glass as he watches the rain. "Damn it, we were so close to leaving."

Shiro steps beside him, putting his hand on Justin's shoulder. "There's nothing we can do about it. All we can do is wait for the storm to pass."

But the storm is merciless. For two days, the rain pours without a pause. The group grows restless, waiting for the rain to end.

November 19th, 2026   0700 Japan Standard Time

On the fifth morning of being stranded on the island, the group awakens to a welcoming sight: the skies are finally clear. Without hesitation, they waste no time gathering their things as Ryuunosuke checks the helicopter; everything is in working order.

Inside his lab, Shiro gathers his notes, ensuring he has everything he needs to reproduce the replicas. He carefully places the weapons and documents into a duffle bag before heading outside. He is the last to step through the doors, pausing for a moment to take in the place he has been sheltering at.

Nearby, Shigeko is talking with Justin and Alice. "I need you both to have Ayane sit between you. Keep an eye on her and make sure she's okay. If her head starts hurting, have her take these pills. This is going to be a long trip."

Justin takes the pills and puts them in his pocket. "I'll keep a close eye on her."

Alice helps Ayane into the helicopter. She leans in, carefully pulls the seatbelt across Ayane's lap and fastens it with a firm click, before sitting beside her. On the other side, Justin climbs in and glances at Ayane to make sure she is secure.

Shiro hands Justin the bag of weapons. "Since you're in the military, I trust you can keep these safe." He closes the door with a thud and turns around to his wife.

"I'm going to be fine, Shiro. You don't need to worry about me," says Shigeko, assuring him with a gentle smile. "When you make it to the mainland, we'll be rescued in no time."

Shiro places his hand on her face with his thumb lightly brushing against her cheek. They stand there for a long moment, neither willing to say goodbye. No one dares interrupt them. "I'll see you soon, Shigeko." She nods, her eyes shining as he leans in and they kiss each other. After their touching moment, he exhales and climbs into the passenger seat, securing himself as Ryuunosuke starts the engine. The helicopter lifts off the ground as everyone below waves goodbye.

The journey to the mainland is smooth. The sky remains clear, with hardly any cloud cover and no turbulence. Three hours later, they reach the coast, and after another thirty minutes they arrive at the Kagoshima airport at 10:30 in the morning.

Ryuunosuke radios the tower at the airport. "Kagoshima Tower, this is Cango Eighty-Six-Sixty, requesting permission to land." No one responds to his request. He repeats himself and again, no one responds.

Justin leans in from the back. "They could be on lockdown. Give me the mic." Ryuunosuke hands him the mic. "Kagoshima Tower, this is Sergeant Myers from the United States Army, stationed in Okinawa. We are requesting clearance to land. Do you copy?"

After waiting a while, there is no response. They reach the airport and see inside the control tower.

"It's empty. That's odd. Has anyone ever seen that before?" asks Shiro.

"Something must be going on. Stay alert," says Justin.

Ryuunosuke lands the helicopter on the tarmac. When the rotors stop spinning, everyone unbuckles and steps out, stretching their legs and scanning their surroundings. The airport is quiet. Planes and vehicles are scattered all over, and a jumbo jet sits abandoned on the runway.

"Let's go inside and see what's going on," says Justin.

"I've never been to an airport where no one has greeted me. Something must be going on," says Ryuunosuke.

They make it inside the airport, and an eerie silence greets them. Not a single person there.

Justin passes a water fountain and presses the button, but no water comes out. "Looks like the power's off."

They continue walking cautiously toward the entrance, each step echoing against the floor. In the center of the lobby, there is a large portable changeable message sign that is shut off.

"Looks like this had a message. Let's see if we can turn it on," says Shiro.

They examine the sign until they find a button and press it. The screen turns on, and a message pops up.

Justin reads the message out loud. "This is a mandatory evacuation. Everyone is expected to evacuate to the north. Looters will be shot on site."

"Are we going to die?" asks Alice.

"I don't think so," says Justin. "Judging by the state of this place, it looks like it's been abandoned for at least two days. Whoever was stationed here is already long gone."

"Oh, this is just great. What are we going to do now?" asks Alice.

Justin collects his thoughts and thinks out loud. "We could head farther north. No, we don't know what's going on. What if we refuel the helicopter and leave? Where could we go?"

Ryuunosuke chimes in, "I have an idea. It's a little crazy, though."

"Anything's crazy at this point," says Justin.

Ryuunosuke points toward the runway. "There's a large passenger jet on the runway. If I can get it running, we can take it to Hawaii."

Alice's face lights up. "I want to go to Hawaii. I like that plan."

"What if it's the same as here?" asks Shiro.

"That shouldn't be a problem," says Justin. "If we can make it to the Hawaiian military base, I should be able to use my credentials to override any system to get in touch with someone. That is, if there's power. If I can't, we can refuel in Hawaii and head to mainland US." He looks at Ryuunosuke. "Are you able to fly a commercial jet?"

"I've tested in simulators before, but not in real life," says Ryuunosuke. "If it puts everyone's mind at ease, I always aced the simulations."

"If you trust your ability to fly it, I'll put my trust in you as well," says Justin.

They turn back toward the runway and head to the plane. The boarding stairs are already in place, allowing for easy access. Ryuunosuke climbs the steps and opens the door.

Justin steps past him. "Let me go first. I want to make sure it's safe." He enters and sweeps the interior. After a few seconds, he comes back. "It's safe to board."

Ryuunosuke goes to the cockpit, flip a few switches, and runs a diagnostic on the plane. "Looks like we're in luck. We have a full tank." He glances back at the others. "I'm going to let the engines warm up. Go back into the airport and get some food and other supplies you think we might need. This flight's going to be about eight hours."

The four of them step back off the plane and head back into the airport.

"Let's split into two groups so we can cover more ground," says Shiro.

"I'll go with you, Shiro," says Alice, sticking close to him.

Justin and Ayane are alone together. He points in the opposite direction. "We can go this way, Ayane." They walk through the empty terminal. Each step echoing, sounding louder than the last. Justin spots a small convenience store and grabs two baskets from a nearby rack, then hands one to Ayane. As they move down the aisles, Justin speaks softly. "My daughter's a huge fan of you and your idol group. She was devastated when she learned what had happened to them. I'm sorry if I'm bringing back bad memories."

Ayane shakes her head. "No, it's fine. I've come to terms with what happened. I will never forget the smiles they … No, the smiles we brought to everyone. Where's your daughter now? Was she one of the girls back in Okinawa?"

Justin stays quiet for a while, putting items into his basket. "No, she was caught up in the disaster."

Ayane looks at her trembling fingers when she picks up a snack. "I'm sorry. I know that pain very well. Only recently was I able to overcome my torment of losing those who were close to me. When I was on the cruise ship, I was with three friends. We had lunch together, sang together, and now they're gone." Her voice wavers, and she wipes away her tears.

"Sorry for bringing the mood down," says Justin.

As Ayane wipes away her tears, she shakes her head. "It's fine. It helped me remember those I lost." She slaps her cheeks and begins filling up the basket.

Justin looks at his hand and clutches it into a fist. Sorrow weighs heavily on him, but he stays strong. "The last thing I did was give her a pinky promise. I promised her I would take her to the festival where she could see you perform."

Ayane stops in place. Then, without hesitation, she steps forward and wraps her free arm around him from behind. "What you're doing now is the best thing you can do. If I could do more, I would." She lets go and touches the bandages around her head.

"Is your head hurting?" asks Justin.

Ayane quickly moves her hand. "No, I'm fine. Let's hurry before the other two finish."

After talking for a bit more, they continue moving through the aisles, filling up basket after basket. After six baskets fill up, they prepare to leave.

Justin picks up four of the baskets. "This should be enough. Let's head back."

Ayane nods and gives Justin a smile that could light up the world.

They make it back to the plane, and Justin moves to the side to let Ayane through. "You go up the stairs first. I'll catch you if you fall."

Ayane smiles and takes the lead, carefully walking up the stairs.

"We're back," says Justin as he enters the plane.

Shiro and Alice already made it back.

Alice takes the basket from Ayane and digs through it. "Wow, you guys found a lot. We found only a few supplies."

Justin sets the baskets down and wipes the sweat off his forehead. "I figured since we haven't eaten since yesterday, we'd all be hungry. I wanted to make sure we had enough. We also got drinks. Let me see if there's ice somewhere in here."

Ryuunosuke comes out of the cockpit and takes a few items out of the basket for himself. "Are we ready to go?"

"Yes," says Shiro.

Ryuunosuke closes the cabin door and locks it. "Okay, sit down and buckle up. We're about to take off." He sits in the left pilot's seat while Shiro sits in the right.

Shiro smiles at Ryuunosuke. "I figured you would need some company for this long journey."

"You're right," says Ryuunosuke.

Alice peeks her head inside. "Don't forget about us. We're here too." She moves back and sits in the front row, with Ayane sitting in the aisle seat. Justin takes the seat directly across the aisle.

Ryuunosuke skillfully guides the plane around the runway and lines it up for takeoff. He presses a few buttons and pushes the throttle forward to gain speed. The engines are at full power as the plane drives down the tarmac. Within moments, they are soaring through the open skies at noon, heading for Hawaii.

To pass the time, they reminisce about the time before the aliens came, remembering the simple joys they took for granted. Despite her injuries, Ayane gives a heartfelt performance. She does not push herself, careful not to strain her head injury. Her voice, full of emotion, fills the cabin. For a moment, it feels like hope comes back to the world.

November 19th, 2026   0100 Hawaii Standard Time

Eight hours pass. The weight of exhaustion dulls the passage of time. As they near Hawaii, reality comes rushing back.

A military jet is quick to intercept them when they enter the Hawaiian airspace. "You're flying in restricted airspace. What is your reason for coming here?"

Justin goes to the cockpit and grabs the microphone. "This is Sergeant Myers from the United States Army, stationed in Okinawa. We have highly classified materials on board and request permission to land."

A minute later, the jet pilot responds. "You are to land at the Kalaeloa Airport in Oahu. I'll guide you there." The jet gets into position ahead of them, guiding them to the airport.

Ryuunosuke follows its lead, maneuvering the plane smoothly through the approach. As they descend through the clouds, the coastline of Hawaii comes into view, untouched by the horrors they fled from, but as they near the airport, they remember the world that awaits them. Military vehicles line the runway. Soldiers stand around, setting up a perimeter. The moment the plane touches down and comes to a stop, armed personnel surrounds it.

"Do not make any sudden movements," says Justin. "They will not hesitate to kill you. I'll go out first and explain what's going on." He opens the door as stairs come up to the plane. A spotlight shines on him from a helicopter as he walks down and meets with some soldiers. "I need to talk to the person in charge. I have something very important in my possession."

A military truck pulls up, and everyone is told to get in. Justin turns back toward the others, raising his hand to signal they should follow. He reaches the truck first and pulls open the door, glancing back to make sure everyone is following. One by one, they step off the plane. Shiro clutches the bag with the weapons tightly to his chest. Alice and Ayane hurry down the stairs, feeling anxious. Ryuunosuke is the last to exit. After a few moments, they all enter the truck.

Inside the truck, an older man sits. He greets them as they enter. "I'll get straight to the point. How did you get here, aside from the obvious?"

"We're survivors from Okinawa," says Justin.

"Survivors? We were told the Deatomizer killed everyone from Okinawa," says the man.

The military transports them to a secure location, where armed guards escort each member into individual rooms. For the next hour, they are each questioned by military personnel, who carefully probe for details about their identities and their journey from Okinawa.

Justin slumps in a chair, alone in a well-lit room. He fades in and out as exhaustion weighs over him. A knock on the door wakes him up.

A man in a military uniform enters. "Come with me." Justin gets up and walks with the man. "I'm Phil, and we reviewed everything you and your friends told us. They're waiting for you this way." He guides Justin down the hall and they enter a break room where Shiro, Ryuunosuke, and Alice are eating.

"Where's Ayane?" asks Justin.

"She's undergoing surgery," says Phil. "Her head injury's really bad. She must have been pushing herself through the pain."

Justin breathes a sigh of relief. "That's good to hear. I was worried about her. She looked like she was pushing herself."

Phil pulls out a chair for Justin. "Have a seat. We need to talk with everyone together." As Justin sits down beside Shiro, Phil puts the bag with the weapons on the table. "We had these tested, and they are the real deal. How exactly did you come to possess these?"

Justin recalls the events that took place in Okinawa, and Phil writes his story. "And that's why we need to get to the US. We need to get these weapons mass-produced."

Phil puts down the pen and paper. "Don't you know? Of course, you wouldn't know; you've been out of contact with the world. Kun has launched a ground invasion of the United States. The whole western seaboard has fallen. Yesterday morning, there was a large massacre of soldiers in San Francisco."

8

Five days ago　　　　November 14th, 2026　　　　1900 Eastern Standard Time

　　James stands before a roaring crowd gathered at his home in Pennsylvania. He brought his supporters together hoping to spark a revolution in the hearts of the American people. He addresses them with unwavering conviction. His words carry the weight of their shared frustrations. "I know what you're feeling, and I'm here to relieve that stress. If I had only been given the presidency a few days ago, none of this would be happening. I call on everyone who feels the same way I do. We need to get America back to the way it was. And to do that, I need to become president of the United States." Cameras' flash, and his words are broadcast to the entire nation. The crowd cheers in agreement, but James lifts his right hand high into the air, signaling for silence. "Everyone's seen the video of what Kun said. I believe he's a reasonable man, and I can talk him into calling off the invasion. I will end this war before more lives are lost. No more needless bloodshed, and no more American lives will be lost when I am president. The only obstacles standing in my way are Angus and Robert. They must hand over the presidency so I can correct their failures for the good of the American people. If they don't hand me the presidency, I cannot hold the full power of the United States and cannot negotiate a deal with Kun. I hope we can all be reasonable adults about this and know what's at stake for the American people." The crowd erupts in cheers once more. James' eyes burn with conviction as he pumps his fist into the air. "Thank you all for your time and support. You'll be hearing from me soon. Don't stop fighting, or else you'll regret it."

　　In the Philadelphia capitol building, Angus and Robert sit in the situation room alongside their advisors. Initially, their strategy was to wait for James to lose momentum and fade away, but he grew stronger, becoming an ever-present obstacle. With each speech he delivers, he sways more and more Americans to his side, intensifying the opposition toward Angus and Robert's leadership.

　　Robert slams his hands on the table. His frustration is reaching its breaking point. "I knew that son of a bitch was going to give us problems."

　　Angus remains silent, deep in thought. He has bigger things to worry about, so he thinks of James as a nuisance, but not enough of a threat to do anything about.

　　Across from them, Xavier calmly flips through his notes, wondering what to do. The room is quiet for a few minutes before he finally speaks. "I think our best course of action is to abandon this location and move to somewhere more secure. Your speech this morning didn't do us any good, Angus. I've looked over a few social media sites, and people saw it as a weak response. That speech only turned more people against us. As things are, the vast majority of Americans could be James' sympathizers by the end of the day."

　　"What about martial law? Could that calm the upheaval?" asks Angus.

　　"Martial law should only be used in dire situations," says Xavier.

　　"And what would you say this situation is?" asks Robert, scoffing. "We have the full force of Kun's military knocking on our door. Who knows what new weapon they have."

　　"If they wanted to destroy the US, they would have just used the Deatomizer again. There must be a reason they're not," says Xavier.

　　"It's because Kun is a madman," says Angus. "He gets pleasure from killing. What good is the US to him if he can just kill us off quickly? Oh no, he wants us to suffer. Run like rats in a cage looking for a way to escape."

　　"It can't be that simple," says Xavier.

"Well, it is," says Angus. "The previous administration watched Kun like a hawk during his military occupation of Southern Asia last year. He could have finished quickly, but he prolonged it so that hundreds of thousands of civilians would get caught up in the fighting. He calculates everything he does. For him to just send his full military at us means he has already won."

Robert slams his hand on the table again. "Don't give me that crap. He's the only one who thinks he has won. The US has fought harder battles in the past. We've faced impossible odds before, and this won't be any different."

"I'm not giving up. Far from it," says Angus. "Answer me this; what weapon was used during World War Two that was so advanced, no one saw it coming?"

"The atomic bomb," says Robert, rolling his eyes. "But we saw firsthand that those weapons are obsolete now."

"If our scientists can enhance an atomic bomb to match the parameters of the alien's weapons, in theory, we should have a fighting chance," says Angus.

"It sounds good on paper, but what about in practice?" asks Robert, exhaling sharply. "Have you even started on such a weapon? I'll ignore the fact that we don't know the full extent of their weapons."

Paula taps her finger on the table, grabbing Robert's attention. "Angus already made the preparations with the military to research such a weapon. We have a lot of manpower looking over all the footage of the aliens and their weapons. We know their weak points and how to combat them. All we can do is hope it works."

"Where is that weapon now?" asks Robert.

"Somewhere in Japan," says Paula. "We only have one, so we need to pick the right time to use it. If it works, we can produce another one or two in undisclosed locations somewhere in the world."

Robert lies back in his seat, rubbing his eyes. "I'm going to be honest with you all. This plan is shit. It feels like you're throwing everything at the wall and praying something sticks."

"Do you have a better plan? I'm all ears," says Angus.

Robert sighs and slowly leans forward, interlocking his fingers. "Just because I don't have a plan doesn't mean I'm not taking this seriously. We're the United States, goddamnit. We have a plan for anything and everything. I know we have more than just one contingency plan to rely on. Let's go through what we have and use it to its fullest. Get me a team of the best and brightest people we have, and I'll put something together."

"If you're serious, I know of some people who fit that bill," says Paula.

"Then what are we doing just sitting here?" asks Robert, pushing back from the table. "Kun's forces will be here in two weeks."

November 16th, 2026   1630 Indochina Time

Nearly two days pass since Kun ordered Ignin to develop more advanced weapons for his military. Now, the moment has arrived for Ignin to fulfill his promise and present Kun with whatever he made.

Kun paces back and forth in his office. His patience is wearing thin with every passing minute. The anticipation for the news from Ignin continues to test his resolve.

Across the room, Taf silently observes him pacing. Although she finds a certain amusement in watching him struggle, she keeps her expression unreadable, not allowing a hint of her thoughts to show. "Don't you have anything better to do?"

Kun stops in his tracks and fixes his angry gaze on her. "I wouldn't be in this situation if I got what I was promised from the start."

Taf meets his gaze, unshaken, keeping her words calm. "Like I said before, Ignin is remorseful about the outcome of that island. However, we didn't know the opposing force was well versed in their own tactics. Of all the other planets we've been to, once the first settlement's gone, no one opposes us anymore. This is a first for us."

"You come to our planet, claiming to bring peace, and yet you've never done your research on how to accomplish your goal," says Kun. He pauses, realizing what he just said. He thinks to himself. *If they had done their research, they would have sided with the United States and everyone else, and I would be the one on the defensive.* Without another word, he pulls out his chair and sits, lost in thought.

"What's the matter?" asks Taf.

Kun exhales. "You know what? I think I'm being too hard on you. Mistakes happen. I should have informed you of the opposing forces' capabilities from the beginning. I had a lapse in judgment."

His sudden change of heart surprises Taf, but does not give it a second thought. Moments later, she receives a message from Ignin. "The items are ready. Ignin's waiting outside for you."

Kun shoots up from his seat. "It's about time."

Both of them head for the door. Taf moves to leave the room first, but Kun grabs her shoulder, pulling her back so he can step out ahead of her.

Outside, Ignin stands next to a large crate that towers over him. The container is full of dime-sized gadgets. As Kun approaches, Ignin reaches inside, pulls one out, and holds it up. "With the time I had, I designed these. We used a similar mechanism in the helmet we gave you. I figured it would be far more efficient to make these than focus on a few larger ones. Allow me to show you." He pulls another gadget from the crate. "One of these create a shield that protects a one-meter radius. Putting two of these together protects a little less than two meters. And putting ten of them together protects five meters. The more you put together, the less distance they cover." He puts his hand up to the crate. "Inside, there are nearly thirty-one million of these for you to use however you see fit."

Zhen walks up to Kun, holding a tablet. "If the number Ignin gave us is true, combining all these together can generate a shield covering nearly seventeen kilometers."

"Figure out the number needed to protect each of my warships. I want to set sail by tomorrow morning," says Kun.

November 16th, 2026   0800 Eastern Standard Time

"We are on day two of this," says Robert, rubbing his eyes. "How is it that the enhanced nuke is still our best option?"

Paula hands him a cup of coffee, then pulls out the chair beside him and sits. "I told you, I already looked through everything days ago. I was hopeful you could find something I may have missed."

Robert sips his coffee, trying to savor every drop. "We've lost so much. Is this really how the US falls?"

"I just got word not too long ago that the enhanced nuke is complete," says Paula.

"When are we planning on launching it?" asks Robert.

"Kun's fleet has to cross the Pacific. That's our best shot," says Paula, laying her head on the table. "And if we're lucky, that alien ship will go down with them."

Robert stays quiet, lost in thought, continuing to sip his coffee. After a while, he lets out an inaudible sigh. "You should leave the US. Any country in Europe would be safer than here."

Paula quickly sits up, shooting her gaze at him. "And leave everything behind? Don't be ridiculous. I'm involved with this just as much as you and Angus are. I will see this through to the end."

"Even if this ends with our deaths?" asks Robert.

"I know what I signed up for," says Paula. "If I fled now, I'd spend the rest of my life wondering what I could have done differently. You know I'm not the type of person to just stop something, especially if it's this important."

"Have you talked to Angus about this? I don't think he would approve," says Robert.

"If it puts your mind at ease, I'll consider the option of fleeing the country. But for now, I will do everything in my power to help you and Angus succeed. Now, if you'll excuse me, I need to be checking on other things," says Paula. She pushes up from the chair and hurries out of the room, frustrated by what Robert told her.

Robert sits alone, still sipping his coffee. He lets out another sigh and stands. "Wait up, Paula. I'm coming too."

Together, they enter the situation room, where Angus is watching a screen displaying a map of the Pacific Ocean.

"Any new information?" asks Robert.

"We expect Kun to launch his fleet at any moment," says Angus, leaning against a table. "It would be nice if we still had people on the inside to tell us what Kun is up to, but it seems like they are all missing. Most likely killed."

"So we're still helpless," says Robert. "Anyway, what happened to James? I haven't heard from him these past two days."

"Biding his time," says Paula. "Looks like he's waiting for Kun to make his move before he makes his. Last I heard, he plans on marching through Philadelphia with his supporters."

"What does he hope to accomplish by doing that?" asks Robert.

Angus chimes in, "Most likely, he's going to the capitol building to ask me personally to step down. While I don't like what he plans on doing, I will say he has some courage in doing that." He leans over and opens a mini-fridge, pulling out a Coke. "Do either of you want one?"

Paula shakes her head. "I need to watch what I drink. I've already had a coffee, and I don't want to crash later."

"Fair enough," says Angus, turning to Robert. "What about you?"

Robert hesitates, then sighs. "Oh, what the hell. Give me one." Angus tosses him the can. Robert cracks it open and downs it in one gulp. "You know, normally I'd say no, but since I feel like I'm knocking on death's door, I feel more inclined to eat unhealthy foods than I normally would."

Paula slaps Robert on the back. "Don't know about you two, but I plan on surviving this. I don't need to consume all those needless calories. I still want to look good after this."

The three of them share a laugh, the weight of the moment lifting for a moment. For the next few hours, they sit together, reminiscing about better days.

Four hours later   November 17th, 2026   0000 Indochina Time

Zhen steps into Kun's office with a report in his hand. "Our fleet of five hundred ships carries at least seven thousand of these tiny devices. We used three and a half million so far, leaving twenty-seven and a half million left over. We distributed a few among our soldiers. This mission is going to have half a million soldiers, and each one got one, leaving us with twenty-seven million left. The remaining devices we put in our equipment that will remain here in Vietnam, using nearly all of them. The trip is eight thousand miles, so it will take us about two weeks to arrive. We're ready for your orders to head to the United States."

Kun leans forward, placing his hands on his desk. "Then what are we waiting for? Let the mission begin. Time to take over the United States."

November 16th, 2026   1300 Eastern Standard Time

Angus and Robert sit in the situation room with high-ranking military officials and advisors, all fixated on the latest intelligence reports as the fleet leaves Kun's territories.

"Angus, what's our plan?" asks Robert.

"I really hoped we could have avoided it, but we have to use the nuclear warhead when the fleet enters open waters," says Angus

Paula sits at a table, reviewing calculations on her tablet. "I've calculated the normal speed of a fleet that big. They should be in the middle of the South China Sea by midnight. That's when we should launch the attack."

"Then we don't have time to waste. Tonight is going to be hell," says Angus.

Eight hours later, Paula looks over satellite imagery of the fleet, her eyes widening in shock. "It's only been eight hours. How are they already near the southern tip of Japan?"

"What's going on?" asks Angus.

"Kun's fleet's moving fast, too fast. Faster than they should be," says Paula. "They're about to enter the waters near the southern tip of Japan. We missed our window of attack. If we launch the nuke now, the fallout in Japan would be catastrophic. We'll have to wait a few hours for them to move past Japan."

An advisor in the room speaks up. "We're getting reports the Japanese government has ordered a full evacuation of all its residents up to a hundred miles inland from the southern tip."

"We can't waste our time worrying about what the Japanese are doing. We have a military force heading our way," says Robert, turning to Paula. "How long until they get here?"

Paula writes numbers on a piece of paper. She looks at Angus as her face turns pale. "At this rate, a day and a half. They'll arrive on the morning of the eighteenth."

"What's making them move so fast?" asks Angus. The room goes quiet. No one answers him. "Give me something. I need suggestions."

The advisor finishes writing equations on a piece of paper. "I think I might know the reason. I jotted down a few math problems and came to this one. For them to be going that fast, only a few things came to mind. They're ignoring air resistance and hydrodynamic drag. So instead of the air and water slowing them down, they have something that moves them effortlessly."

"Another piece of alien tech, I'm assuming," says Robert.

"I think at this point anything we don't understand can be explained away by the alien technology," says the advisor.

Angus takes a deep breath and looks at Paula. "You said a day and a half, right?"

"That's the best-case scenario," says Paula. "At this point, I'd assume they have something that can make them go faster once they're in open water."

"Okay, Paula, I need you to get in touch with the media," says Angus. "Tell them to issue an emergency broadcast to all the states west of the Rocky Mountains to evacuate."

"Let's hold off on the evacuation orders until we drop the nuke," says Robert. "We still have three hours till midnight."

At the same time, James sits in his office, watching the news report on the fleet's movements. Around him are individuals who will be part of his administration if he becomes president. "It's about time we spread the word around that I'll be in Philadelphia tomorrow morning. The window is closing faster than I expected it to. I need to take over so I can stop the inevitable." He is met with applause and admiration. His team is quick to get the word out about his rally at the Capitol. Thousands are going to be in attendance.

Two hours pass, and Paula is still hard at work watching the screens. "Kun's fleet is far enough from Japan. Now's the time for our attack."

"I authorize the attack," says Angus.

A general picks up a phone, issuing the order.

Robert places his hand on Angus' shoulder. "Even if this works, we still need to worry about what happens next. Kun will be furious, and who knows what the aliens will send our way."

"Right now, we need to focus on the threat in front of us. We'll worry about that later," says Angus.

The general hangs up the phone. "It's done. The nuke's about to be launched."

Everyone sits in silence while watching the live footage of Kun's fleet. Twenty jets rush from a hidden military base in Japan. Nineteen of the jets fan out, surrounding the one carrying the warhead. They fly toward the fleet at three times the speed of sound, cutting through the clouds, but get nowhere close to the fleet. The jets slam into the force field and blow up, sending a massive mushroom cloud erupting into the sky. Angus and Robert watch in horror, knowing their last line of defense is going to be soldiers giving up their lives for an unwinnable war.

Angus slumps in his chair, running his hands down his face. "Paula, get the word out. Tell the news: every state west of the Rockies needs to evacuate." He pushes himself to his feet. His movements become sluggish and drained. "Also, I need to address the nation about what just transpired. Give me a minute to collect my thoughts." He stumbles out of the room, looking broken and defeated.

Brittney is behind the news desk, expressing a grim look. "We are getting news that President Turner is about to address the nation regarding Kun's fleet. We now go live to the president."

The broadcast cuts to Angus walking up to a podium. His movements are heavy with the weight of the impending war. He grips the edges of the podium and looks directly at the camera. "I'm going to be frank with each and every one of you. The nuclear strike we launched was useless. The fleet is advancing, and now we expect them to arrive on the West Coast by the morning of the eighteenth. I urge every man, woman, and child in every state west of the Rocky Mountains to evacuate and head east immediately. Do not wait. Do not hesitate. Time has run out. This is the end. I'm calling on all military personnel, whether you are currently serving now or have served in the past, to contact the people you need to reach out to so we can prepare for a land invasion of the United States. We must prepare for the largest land invasion in our nation's history. I understand these are difficult times. If we work together, we can overcome this threat." He walks away, and the feed cuts.

November 17th, 2026   0000 Eastern Standard Time

"Dallas is the latest city to confirm rioting," says Paula. "That makes eight cities so far. I think our best course of action is to invoke martial law."

Angus sharply exhales while rubbing his eyes. "Are we really out of options? There has to be another way."

"There isn't," says Paula. "We need to force an evacuation of the entire West Coast. If this keeps up, people won't leave in time. It will be a slaughter once the fleet arrives."

Angus shuts his eyes for a moment, then nods. "Fine. Get your phone out. Record me. I'll tell the American people what I want them to do."

Paula takes out her phone and stands. "You're live. You can start when you're ready."

Angus straightens his posture. "I'll get straight to the point. Effective immediately, the United States is under martial law. Everyone needs to go home except for the residents of the following states: Washington, Oregon, California, Nevada, Idaho, Utah, and Arizona. These seven states must evacuate immediately and either make their way east or leave the country to Canada or Mexico. I have talked with both presidents, and they agreed to let anyone through regardless if they have proper documentation. Also, these seven states will no longer receive federal help from here on out. All government officials are to evacuate as well. I strongly urge all local police forces to do the same. Your family's safety is more important than stopping the rioters. I am activating all military personnel to defend the country from the opposing forces. We're about to be in the war of our lifetime. To everyone who's not in the military, this will be the last time I address the nation until this is over. The only updates I will giving are to the military. I hope our citizens can handle their own matters and understand the situation we're in." Angus looks beyond the camera at Paula. "You can stop recording."

She ends the stream, staring at the screen for a moment before looking up at him. "That didn't go the way I was expecting it to."

"I said what I had to," says Angus. "Enough is enough. As much as I hate to say it, it's time for them to worry about themselves. If they want to continue rioting, let them. The West Coast will most likely fall anyway. I just hope the good people heed my warning and leave as soon as possible."

Paula steps forward and wraps her arms around Angus. "I fear people will only flee once it's too late."

"You might be right," says Angus, returning the gesture.

Throughout the night, the country descends into chaos. In cities east of the Rockies, the streets fill with protesters and rioters. Riot police flood the streets in full gear, attempting to contain the growing unrest. Tear gas swirls, but the crowds only swell. Fires ignite in alleyways and abandoned cars. People scream, clash, and flee, leading to many deaths.

On the West Coast, the lawlessness is even more relentless. Rioters go wild through the empty streets. They smash windows, overturn vehicles, and set buildings ablaze. Flames engulf the sides of skyscrapers while sirens wail in the distance, though no one comes to stop them.

The borders of Mexico and Canada surge with people fleeing. Border Patrol on both sides allow everyone through, barely glancing at what is being brought across. In Canada, everything is running smoothly. The story is different in Mexico. As the Americans cross, the cartel lies in wait, seizing anyone they can and dragging them into their compounds, holding them as hostages.

By sunrise, the US is unrecognizable. The country that once was hailed as a symbol of stability is now standing on the brink of collapse. The familiar frameworks of order and normality fade away, leaving only a shell of what the nation once was.

November 17th, 2026   0800 Eastern Standard Time

News spreads like wildfire that James is organizing a march on the capitol.

Brittney is determined to witness and report on the unfolding event firsthand. She and Frank make quick arrangements, chartering a private flight to Philadelphia. Their flight touches down at eight in the morning, and as they step through the airport, they find it deserted. Wasting no time in going to the city, they hail a taxi to take them to downtown Philadelphia. They head straight to the capitol building where James is to lead his rally. When they arrive in front of the capitol building, they are the only ones around.

Frank takes his camera out of his bag and swiftly sets it up. "Are you ready?"

"Ready as I'll ever be," says Britteny, fastening her mic securely to her shirt. "I just hope things don't get out of hand."

"If things get dicey, we need to get out of here as soon as possible," says Frank.

Brittney steps in front of the camera, ready to start the news.

By ten o'clock, James stands in the bed of a truck, holding a microphone to his mouth as he addresses a crowd of five thousand marching behind him. "They are trying to take our freedom. They are trying to take our rights. They are trying to take our land. We can no longer stand for any of this."

His followers roar in agreement; their footsteps echoing through the streets as they surge toward the capitol building.

James raises his hand high in the air. "Follow me to the capitol building. Today, I will take over as president. I'll allow Angus to hand me the presidency, and if he refuses, then things may get a little nasty." He sits in the back of the truck and looks at the driver. "You can take us now. Make sure you drive slowly. I don't want my supporters to be left behind."

The truck drives slowly, allowing the massive crowd to keep pace. No military personnel or police officers stand in their way; they abandoned the city hours ago when everything fell apart.

Brittney stands on the sidewalk, watching James as he pulls up to the capitol building. "If you are just tuning in, we're outside the capitol building here in Philadelphia. As of right now, everything is calm, but we could see that change once the president comes out."

Once the truck comes to a stop in front of the building, James jumps out, ready to make his last move. Before he says anything, he notices Britney and Frank filming him. He smiles and gives them a friendly wave. "When I'm finished here, I want you to have the first interview with the new president."

Brittney nods at James and continues her live coverage. James stands firmly on the sidewalk as the crowd yells behind him, chanting for Angus to come out and surrender.

James brings the microphone to his mouth. "Angus, all you have to do is forfeit the presidency to me, and this will all be over. I promise nothing will happen to you or anyone else with you. You don't even need to come out here. I can happily come inside to conduct business. This can be over as quickly as it started."

Inside the capitol, Xavier clutches his phone to his ear as he talks with Angus. "I'm going out to talk with him. James seems like a reasonable man."

"That's too risky," says Angus. "You should have already left town."

"It's fine," says Xavier. "I'll talk to you when this is over. I'll meet up with you later tonight. Give Paula and Robert my best wishes."

Before Angus can respond, Xavier hangs up and goes outside.

Brittney stands close by, reporting on the unfolding crisis. "The door's opening. I think they are going to let James in."

The crowd quiets down as Xavier steps out. As he walks to James, he raises his hands high above his head, forcing himself to stand tall despite the urgent fear overtaking him. "Angus and Robert aren't here. They left this location two days ago."

James lowers the microphone to his side. "Really? Did he say he's stepping down and handing me the presidency?"

"We want you to stop this," says Xavier. "They have better things to worry about than you causing a scene. We need to peacefully—"

"Enough of this farce." says James. He turns around and brings his microphone up to his mouth. "All right, ladies and gentlemen, I have given Angus and Robert many opportunities, but they just don't know when to give in. It looks like it's open season." He directs his attention back at Xavier, turning with a nasty look. "Have at him." James steps back as the crowd surrounds Xavier.

"You don't have to do this," says Xavier. The mob forces him to the ground and smashes his head in, blood splattering on the lawn.

"Oh God, Frank, we need to get out of here now," says Brittney.

Before Brittney and Frank can move away, the mob surrounds them.

Brittney falls to the ground, scraping her right palm on the asphalt. "Please let us go. We're only reporters. We had nothing to do with this."

James pushes his way through the crowd, his expression unreadable. He walks up to Brittney and extends his hand down to her. "I know you have nothing to do with this. Please stand up. I still want you to interview me, even though Angus didn't relinquish his power."

Brittney is unsure how to respond. Her hands are trembling uncontrollably, and blood rushes down her forearm. Her mind races from what she just witnessed, but she takes James' hand regardless.

As he helps her to her feet, he studies her face. "Oh, you poor thing. I can tell you're uncomfortable. We can do this interview some other time after you have that wound looked at."

Frank immediately steps between them, grabbing Brittney's bloodied arm. "I think that would be for the best. She looks a bit shaken up after seeing what happened."

"That's understandable," says James. "Let me give you my number and sometime within the next day or two, we can have that interview. What do you say?"

"That would be a good idea. Let me get your number," says Frank, taking out his phone.

James tells Frank his number, then smiles at him. "I look forward to our interview." He puts the microphone back up to his mouth. "Let these two people through. No one touches them. Do I make myself clear?"

The crowd parts, forming a path for Brittney and Frank to pass through. They waste no time and hurry past everyone as quickly as possible without drawing more attention to themselves. Neither of them pause or look back as they distance themselves from the chaos, only stopping once they are well away from that mob.

Brittney clenches her hand tightly, trying to stop the bleeding. "I thought we were goners."

"We very much could have," says Frank, helping her cover the wound. "We got lucky he intervened when he did. I could see the crowd was out for blood. We need to leave the city now. There's no doubt in my mind it will be a bloodbath soon."

"Then let's hurry out of here," says Brittney.

Across the country, Frank's live broadcast is shown on every screen, capturing the attention of viewers everywhere. People watch in horror as James commanded his supporters to kill Xavier. This act marks a turning point, signaling that conditions in Philadelphia are about to deteriorate even further. Throughout the city, James' supporters storm the homes of residents, dragging them onto the streets, and executing anyone who opposes them in cold blood. James does nothing to stop them. He believes that if they are not with him, they are against him.

Angus, Robert, and several other high-ranking officials watch the events unfold on TV. The room is silent, the only sound coming from the broadcast.

"Why did Xavier stay behind?" asks Robert, clenching his fist. "He should have left hours ago."

"I told him to come with us, but he said no. Dammit all to hell," says Angus.

The door swings open, and Scott steps inside. "Angus, Robert. Now is not the time to grieve for the dead. We need to think of something."

Robert blinks in surprise, taken aback by Scott's sudden appearance. "Scott? When did you get here? I thought you stayed in Philadelphia."

"I just arrived. I got out while I could," says Scott, walking past Robert to stand beside Angus. "After thinking it over for a bit, I know the perfect solution to all our problems."

"What do you have in mind?" asks Angus.

"Oh, nothing much. Just how to wrap things up." In one swift motion, Scott pulls out a gun from his pocket and shoots Angus in the chest. He turns around and points the gun at Robert, but with all the training Robert has had throughout his military career, he draws his gun faster and shoots Scott in the head, killing him instantly.

Robert rushes to Angus, dropping to his knees. "Angus, speak to me." He pushes his hands against Angus' chest, trying to plug the wound. Despite his efforts, blood seeps between his fingers.

The room erupts in chaos. Some officials run for the door, shouting for help, while others rush to Angus' side, their faces pale with shock.

Angus gasps for air, trying to keep his eyes open. "It's up to you, Robert. Finish what I couldn't. Protect...America." He goes limp and his eyes close.

Medics rush into the room, moving swiftly to tend to Angus' injuries. Robert steps aside, looking at the blood on his hands. "Scott was a James sympathizer. He was a damn sympathizer." He takes a deep breath and looks at Angus. "If James wants to play this way, I'll show him no mercy."

James made the capitol building his new home. He tries to give orders to the military, but no one listens to him. Outside, the streets fill with his restless supporters, waiting for a command. The bodies of those who resisted him lay in gruesome piles in front of the capitol building. He stands looking out the window at the bodies. "All of this and I still don't have any power. I think I'm going to have to take even more drastic measures." He turns from the window, facing a few of his people. "Get me on TV. I'm going to tell my supporters across the nation they need to stand up to their oppressors. They're going to die anyway. They might as well die for me." A TV blares in the background as James focuses on his plans. He looks up when he hears a familiar voice and sees Robert.

"A few hours ago, Angus was shot in the chest by the speaker of Congress, Scott Hage," says Robert, keeping his tone stern. "We thought Scott could be trusted, so we kept him informed about everything we were doing, letting him come and go as he pleased, but we were wrong for doing that. Effective immediately, I am now the president of the United States."

James smirks. "So Angus is dead. Good riddance."

Robert steps forward, locking his gaze directly onto the camera. "James, I hope you're watching. You might have gotten to Angus, but I'm still here. Just so you know, Angus was holding me back. If it was up to me, I would have put you down back at the park when we took office. Now that he's gone, there's no one standing in my way for what I do next. In a few minutes, you'll receive a small gift from me and everyone else you hurt today. I hope you burn for what you did."

Someone rushes into the room. "James, you need to see this."

James rushes into the hall and presses himself against a window. A military jet heads their way, approaching fast. "You son of a bitch. I can't believe you're going to end the lives of all these people."

The bomb detonates over the city. A shockwave ripples outward, vaporizing everything within a mile radius.

Robert remains in the spot where he delivered his message, trying to come to terms with all that just happened. The sound of the door interrupts the silence of the room, and Angus enters quietly behind him. "Was that the right thing to do, Robert?"

"I don't know if it was the right thing, Angus, but it was something I had to do," says Robert. He turns around, but no one is behind him. He straightens his posture, holding himself together in any way he can. "Time to get ready for this war. No more loose ends."

Paula enters the room, wiping away her tears. "We know where the fleet's heading. They're going to the San Francisco Bay Area. They're trying to end the lives of millions in one attack. Thousands of soldiers are heading there as we speak to wait for their arrival."

"On second thought, get me a plane," says Robert. "I'm going to San Francisco."

"Like hell you are. You're needed here," says Paula.

"I want to go there and give my support in any way I can," says Robert. "When I'm done, I'll come back here."

Paula crosses her arms and furrows her brow. "I forbid it."

"Either you do it or I'll get someone else to do it," says Robert.

"You're a stubborn man. No matter what I say, you'll go," says Paula, stomping her foot. "Fine. I'll get you on a plane. Give me some time to set things up."

An hour passes, and everything is ready. Paula walks alongside Robert toward the plane. At the bottom of the staircase, she comes to a halt, turning to face Robert. "Well, Robert, this is where we part ways. I still want to advise you against going. If you end up getting stuck there, you will die."

Robert pats Paula on her shoulder. "I have to go. I need to show up in San Francisco to give my support. If I can convince even one person to leave before it's too late, it'll be worth it."

Paula wipes away tears. She wraps her arms around Robert, reluctant to let him go. "Just stay safe. I don't want to lose you. Today has already been hard for me."

Robert places his hand on the back of her head. "You have grown up to be a fine adult. You're a big girl now. I know you can handle this." He steps back from her embrace. "What are you planning to do? Will you flee to Canada or Europe?"

Paula wipes the tears from her eyes while forcing a weak smile. "I've given it some thought. I'll make my decision when you get back."

"I'll be back tomorrow, early in the morning. Stay safe until then," says Robert. He turns to walk up the stairs and vanishes into the plane.

Six hours later   November 17th, 2026   1600 Pacific Standard Time

Robert lands at the Oakland International Airport. He steps off the plane into the dimly lit terminal, where a large group of soldiers greet him.

A soldier stands tall in front of Robert and salutes him. "Welcome to Oakland, sir. I'm Sergeant Roland Heed. Though we wish your arrival was under better circumstances, we're glad you could make it."

"What's the situation here?" asks Robert, returning the salute.

"Let's get you to a more secure location first," says Sergeant Heed. "We have a car waiting outside to take you to our campsite."

They hurry through the terminal, escorting Robert outside where an armored vehicle is waiting for them. As soon as they climb into the car, the doors lock, and the driver pulls away.

"Here's the situation," says Sergeant Heed, handing Robert a picture of the area. "This is a photo of the location of the 2,854 soldiers we currently have stationed around the Bay Area."

"And what about the residents of the area? Have they all evacuated?" asks Robert.

"Most of the highways leading out of the area are still packed with people fleeing," says Sergeant Heed. "Even though the former president ordered a full evacuation yesterday, some people are waiting to leave at the last minute or not leaving at all."

"Don't they know this place is about to be a war zone?" asks Robert.

"There's nothing more we can do," says Sergeant Heed, shaking his head. "Our resources are all being used in getting ready for war. It's up to the people if they want to leave."

As they head north on Interstate 580, Robert gazes out the window, noticing the city of San Francisco and the Golden Gate Bridge off in the distance. "Why are we so far from the ocean? Are we not going to San Francisco?"

Sergeant Heed takes the picture from Robert. "We're keeping our main campsite out of the city. We don't want to clog the streets as the civilians evacuate. This base camp here is where we're heading." He taps on the location south of Richmond. "The higher-ups are already there, and they want to talk with you and get your thoughts."

Twenty minutes later, the vehicle comes to a stop at the makeshift camp. As Robert steps out, a large group of soldiers quickly approaches, praising his actions in Philadelphia as necessary. From a distance, his critics watch him in disgust. Most of the soldiers stand firmly by his side, having witnessed the horrors James' sympathizers unleashed on the city. After exchanging brief greetings with those around him, Robert moves into a nearby tent where the higher-ups are. Inside, maps stretch across a table with pins marking troops' positions and strategic points. For the next two hours, they review every detail of the battle for the following morning.

"And that wraps up what we needed to tell you," says a general.

Robert's eyes remain fixed on the map on the other side of the table, marked with red and yellow-colored areas. "What about this map? Shouldn't we broadcast this information to the public?"

"There's no point," says the general. "These people are already dead. Telling them won't change anything."

"It may be worthless to you, but to me, it's very important," says Robert. "Get me on the air. I'm releasing this information to the public."

Whispers ripple through the room, but no one challenges him. They get in touch with a news company willing to play Robert's message. Thirty minutes later, Robert is live for the nation to see. He pins the map he was talking about to a bulletin board. "I'm going to be blunt with everyone here on the

West Coast. It's too late for many of you to evacuate. Anyone in this red area, your window has closed. Everyone from the entire state of California up to Seattle, Washington, your best bet is to shelter in place. Stay as quiet as possible. But know that even if you get lucky and survive, rescue will not come. I repeat, rescue will not come. The yellow area is up for debate whether you can make it out. This area is from Seattle, Washington, up to the Canadian border. If you're here, you might stand a chance of escaping, but you need to leave now." Robert looks at the camera to address the viewers. "Do with this information what you will. I pray for the best outcome." The camera shuts off.

Sergeant Heed walks up to Robert and hands him a water bottle. "You did a good job. Follow me."

Robert follows Sergeant Heed to the chow hall for dinner. The scents of the finest meats and sweets hang in the air. He walks into the building, and when people see him, they stand and cheer in unison. He freezes in place, looking at the faces of the men and women around him. They smile and clap, but all he sees are the faces of people who will most likely be dead by dinnertime tomorrow. As he gets his food, an idea pops into his head. *I can't do much for these poor souls, but what I can do is give them the encouragement they need to fight.* He sets his tray down and sees a small stage for him to stand on. He gets on the stage, and everyone slowly turns his way. The room goes quiet, waiting for him to speak.

"I don't know what I'm doing. Something told me to get up here and talk to each of you. So here we go." He takes a deep breath and scans the crowd. "I know you all are feeling nervous about tomorrow. The American people are watching, knowing the outcome will not be pretty. I'm sick to my stomach, knowing what's coming our way. I wouldn't blame anyone for running away. No one would ever know. However, sticking around could be the deciding factor whether a family can make it to safety in time. You may or may not have family in this area, but wouldn't it be nice if you could make that difference? Speaking of family, let me talk about mine. I've been quiet on the subject for all my time serving in the military. Now, I think it's a good time to go back down memory lane. But first, can someone bring me a glass of water? I'm parched."

Someone gives him a glass of water and takes a drink, then continues. "I was born in New York City. The Big Apple, they call it. Back in my teenage years, four friends and I would roam the city, trying to find the next best hangout spot. We would find a place, then get forced out when people found us. We went to the craziest places. There was one time we found a way into the subway. Anyway, in the summer of '94, we were walking around the World Trade Center during the early morning before sunrise. We walked through the lobby expecting to be stopped, but never were. We got to the elevator and rode it up to like the eightieth floor, where we found another set of elevators to take us to the top of the towers. We were about to make it outside when we were stopped by a worker. We knew we were in for it. We all were sweating, thinking about how our parents were going to react when they found out we snuck into the World Trade Center. The man, whose name was Bill, walked up to us and said, 'How did you kids get in here?' We were extremely nervous. No one said a word. The idea of turning around and running back the way we came didn't even cross our minds. We were too busy thinking about the ass-beating once we got back home. And let me tell you, women from New York don't mess around. Anyway, Bill came up to us and said, 'Hey, nothing to be worried about. I won't tell anyone. Since each of you came all this way, you want to see something cool? Follow me.' Without question, we followed him. He opened the door to the outside, and it was such an amazing view of the city. Nothing I've ever seen before in my life. After a few moments of looking around, the sun started to rise. It was the best feeling I've ever felt. All of my friends had the same feeling I did. So, every chance we got, we would make our way to the top of the towers and watch the sunrise. Bill would meet us in the lobby and take us up. No one who worked there would ever ask questions because Bill was the man in charge. In '96, my friend Steve applied to work at the towers and got hired to work with Bill. Every morning, Bill and Steve would meet the four of us and let us in. Then, in the summer of '98, I met her, my future wife, Jenny. She was a year younger than me. Her mom started working at the Windows on the World as a waitress and would bring her to work with her every morning. At this point, everyone knew who we were. It was only natural that Jenny would be joining us every morning. Two years later, we started dating and a year after that, we got married in the summer of '01."

Robert takes another sip of water and a moment to collect his thoughts. "Then the unthinkable happened. Only two hours after we watched the sunrise, the towers were hit. It was just like any other day. We were talking, watching the sunrise. If I'd have known it was going to be my last, I would have spent it appreciating that amazing view. I was in disbelief at what I was seeing. My second home was being destroyed, and I couldn't do anything about it. My hometown was being attacked. After those events, I was able to get in touch with all but one of my friends. Steve never made it home. Jenny's mom was also working that day. She didn't make it either. I learned days later that neither Steve nor Bill made it out. We held a funeral for them; the caskets were all empty. After that day, I made a vow to protect the people and things I hold dear. I, like many other people in their youth, joined the military to fight to protect our homes. Never again would I allow an event like that to happen. I shot through the ranks fast. I didn't care how others felt about me. My only goal was to get into a position of power, so that's what I did. Years later, Jenny gave birth to our two children. We bought a nice home just outside of New York City, and we planned to spend our retirement there. But as you all know, fate had different plans. My wife and two children were taken from me when the Deatomizer wiped New York City off the face of the Earth. The despair I felt when I was watching what was happening was unimaginable. Not only did I fail that city, I failed myself. Since then, I have dedicated myself to bringing revenge to the people who took everything from me. And that's my story. A helpless man who couldn't even save the people he loved." Robert finishes his speech, and everyone claps.

Unbeknownst to Robert, someone recorded his speech and shared it online. Within a few hours, the video circulates across social media, quickly gaining traction. As the video spreads, Robert becomes a trending topic, and countless Americans find themselves moved by his courage and honesty.

After his speech, Robert spends the next hour engaged in conversations with the soldiers. He moves among them, listening to their concerns, sharing in their hopes and fears, and offering words of encouragement. Eventually, Robert steps outside for some fresh air. Sergeant Heed tags along.

He lights a cigarette, inhaling deeply as he tilts his head back to gaze up at the stars. "How can I ask these people to end their lives while I'm about to leave for safety?"

Beside him, Sergeant Heed lights his own cigarette, slowly exhaling the smoke. "I believe you are thinking about it the wrong way. Being in charge is just as important as what we all have to do tomorrow. I saw the way they looked at you when we first walked in. Their eyes were hollow. But after your speech, they looked like they could take on the whole world. What you said inspired so many people. We need people like you to guide us in the right direction. We want to believe our sacrifice tomorrow will help America rise again. But only time will tell if I'm right."

They both stand in silence as they finish their cigarettes. Robert thinks deeply about what he was just told. "I know my answer." He tosses the cigarette butt onto the ground and steps on it. "I'm going to be staying and fighting alongside everyone tomorrow."

Sergeant Heed tosses his cigarette as well, and a look of surprise flickers across his face. "But, sir, we need someone with your power to help not only us, but the United States as a whole."

"Everyone here needs me," says Robert. "Don't worry about my position. I know someone who is more qualified than me." He pulls out his phone and makes a call. "I've decided to stay." He pauses for a moment. "Yes, yes, I know. I need one more chance to show myself who I really am. I hope you can understand, Angus. Make sure that tomorrow you announce to the world you're still alive. Well, this is goodbye, old friend. Tell Paula I wasn't able to keep my promise."

On the other side of the call is Angus, resting in a hospital bed. "Goodbye to you too, friend." Angus hangs up the phone and sits quietly, lost in thought. He reflects on the weight of his friend's decision and the uncertain future ahead.

Beside him, Paula holds his hand as tears well in her eyes. She overheard the conversation and did not say a word.

Angus looks at Paula and wipes away the tears on her cheeks. "This is what Robert wants. You know him just as well as I do. He's still heartbroken about losing Jenny and his kids to the Deatomizer. This is his way of finding peace. I can only hope he can be with his family after all this is over."

"I hope you're right," says Paula.

Back at the military camp, Robert puts his phone in his pocket and throws his arm around Sergeant Heed. "Come on, friend, let's head back inside. We need to party it up like it's the end of the world."

Sergeant Heed lets out a small chuckle. "Yes. Let's do that."

"What about your family? Have they gotten out?" asks Robert.

"They left two days ago," says Sergeant Heed. "I'm going to be calling them in the morning to say my final goodbyes."

Robert nods, tightening his hold around his friend's shoulder. "We all need to say our goodbyes before it's too late."

They both head back inside, joining the rest of the soldiers for what will be their last night together. A sense of calmness fills the air as everyone is determined to make the most of the time they have left. Laughter and conversations echo throughout the camp as the soldiers choose not to sleep, preferring instead to savor every remaining moment. Robert embraces the evening wholeheartedly; indulging in food and drink without restraint. Most of the time he spends on stage leading the group in karaoke until the first light of morning appears.

As the sun rises on the morning of the eighteenth, a heavy silence hangs over the camp. Every soldier stands at the ready, with their eyes locked on the ocean, waiting for the fleet's arrival. At 9:10, the first ship appears on the horizon. The soldiers get into battle positions, waiting for what seems like an eternity. As the fleet gets closer, something shoots from a ship. The soldiers try to shoot it down, but a force field protects the object. It gets over San Francisco Bay and detonates, frying all electronic devices.

Robert stands frozen at the camp with a determined look on his face. "They fired a EMP." He looks at his cracked phone, only to see his reflection. He clutches it to his chest and closes his eyes. "The time has finally come, honey. I'll be with you soon." He opens his eyes, crying out to everyone around him, "All right, men. Our time has come. Let's lay down our lives together in hopes we can stop the enemy for only a moment so we can give people any chance they can get to escape from this hell." The soldiers near him erupt in cheers. Robert moves through the crowd, exchanging countless handshakes and heartfelt pats on the back with his fellow soldiers.

The invasion begins.

The city of San Francisco falls within three hours. Buildings blow up, toppling like dominos. The enemy ground forces sustain no injuries. The gadgets protect them from anything that would have harmed them; fire and explosions have no effect. Tens of thousands of enemy troops march throughout the surrounding area, killing everyone in sight instantly, with the same guns used during the battle of Okinawa. No one stands a chance against them, not even Robert.

Robert proudly stands his ground when the enemy shoots him in the chest. He lifelessly collapses on the ground, and a bright white light overtakes his vision. He regains consciousness on the ground at his house outside of New York City as a familiar voice calls out to him.

"Hey honey, it's time to come home." It's his wife, Jenny.

Robert takes Jenny's hand and slowly rises to his feet. He looks around with his mouth open in astonishment. The sunlight bathes his face, and a gentle breeze carries the scent of his home. Robert is greeted by the sight of his children running toward him, their faces bright with happiness as they wrap their small arms around his legs. "Daddy, we missed you."

Overwhelmed with emotion, Robert gazes down at his children as tears well in his eyes. He drops to his knees, pulling them close. "No need to worry anymore. Daddy's home for good."

As Robert takes his children by the hand, a bright white light envelops the area. Together, he, Jenny, and the children move toward the light, eventually disappearing within its radiant glow.

9

November 19th, 2026   0300 Hawaii Standard Time

    After the battle in San Francisco ends, the five hundred warships move along the coast. The Golden Gate Bridge stands untouched, having sustained no damage during the fighting. This allows the warships to enter the bay and offload soldiers and equipment. Each ship carries a thousand soldiers, all armed and ready for combat. The men march down the ramps with the alien pistols clutched tightly to their chests. Any trace of fear has long vanished, driven out by Kun's brutal display of what happens to deserters and traitors. For these men, the consequences of failure does not just cost them their lives but condemns their families to death. The weight of that truth keeps them unwavering, obedient, and ruthless. None of them flinch when killing the Americans. Civilians and soldiers alike collapse where they stand. To the invaders, the killing is necessary for their survival. The bodies are left to rot, untouched unless they block the enemy's advancement. This is not a war. This is an extermination.

    Phil takes a breath, wrapping up his story to Justin and the others. "By the end of the day, all equipment had been unloaded. Their army of nearly half a million began traveling in all three directions. The largest group of three hundred thousand soldiers are heading east toward the Rocky Mountains. And that's what has happened until tonight."

    Everyone's mouths are wide open from shock. No one speaks, letting the weight of Phil's words sink in.

    "Damnit, if only it didn't rain," says Justin. "We could have made it here two days ago and had a fighting chance with these weapons."

    "Where exactly is the enemy now?" asks Shiro.

    Phil lays out a map of the US on the table and runs his finger across it. "They're spread out west of the Rockies. From our last report, the largest group is heading toward Salt Lake City. They will be there by morning at the rate they're going. Unfortunately, we've lost contact with anyone from the continental US a few hours ago."

    "We need to leave now," says Justin, jumping from his seat. "The Rockies can buy us only a day or two."

    Phil leans back, narrowing his eyes. "And where do you want to go? The US is in disarray and falling apart. It's only a death wish if you go."

    Justin quickly considers his next move. He looks over the map and puts his finger in the middle of Texas. "If the largest group hasn't made it to the Rockies yet, we can still make it to Fort Cavazos here in Texas. That's our best shot at getting these mass-produced and pushing the invaders back."

    "But these would take weeks, if not months, to study and reproduce," says Phil, scoffing.

    Shiro cuts in before Justin responds. "These replicas took me only three days to study, and should only take a day or two to reproduce."

    "What do you think we were doing for the five days we were stuck in Okinawa?" asks Justin. "Shiro was hard at work, finding the best way to study and reproduce these weapons."

    "From what you told us, the enemy isn't moving fast," says Shiro. "We can make it to this fort and reproduce the weapons before they even make it halfway through the mountains. But we need to leave now if we want a fighting chance."

    Phil throws his hands into the air, conceding to the determination of Justin and Shiro. "All right, you've convinced me. What do we have to lose? I can see you are both hellbent on getting the job done. I'll get on the phone with the higher-ups and see what I can do. Just know that this may be a one-way trip for you both. We don't know what remains of the US military. But for now, I'll show you to your rooms for you to get some rest."

After a grueling journey that lasted fifteen hours since leaving Okinawa, fatigue overtakes the group. The exhaustion weighs heavily on them. Once their heads hit the pillow, they fall asleep in no time.

Seven hours later   November 19th, 2026   1000 Hawaii Standard Time

Justin and Shiro wake up early to meet with the higher-ups. They have the bag of weapons and meet back up with Phil. Phil already spoke with his superiors about Justin's demands, and they agreed to meet with them. Together, the three enter a conference room where five generals are waiting. Justin stands in front of the room with his hands by his sides and his chin up, while Shiro casually stands beside him.

Phil clears his throat. "I trust everyone has been briefed on the current situation, so I'll skip that. This is Justin Myers. He was stationed in Okinawa as Kun's military invaded. He was also caught in the Deatomizer and lived thanks to the tools he had." Then he gestures toward Shiro. "And this is Shiro, the researcher responsible for replicating the enemy's weapons."

Justin steps forward, unzipping the bag and laying out the items on the table for the generals to see. They lean in, and the room fills with murmurs as they whisper among themselves.

The general in the center leans back and looks at Justin. "I've read what you want, Sergeant Myers. Let me introduce myself. I'm Kealoha Pua, commander of the military forces here in Hawaii. I'll get straight to the point. You want two jets to take you and your friends to mainland America as an unstoppable force rips through."

Justin meets his gaze without hesitation. "Yes. That's correct."

Kealoha taps his fingers on the table while looking Justin over. After a long pause, he sits back in his chair and nods. "Then you can have them. I see what you have in your possession are the real deal, and I do not want to get in your way. The jets are already being inspected as we speak. It will take a few hours for them to be ready for the flight and for us to find two capable pilots willing to fly you to Texas. I assume you find that acceptable?"

"Yes, that's acceptable. Thank you. I appreciate this," says Justin.

"No need to thank me. I'm only doing what's best for my country," says Kealoha. "Now, in the meantime, would you two tell us what happened in Okinawa and how you came into possession of these?"

For the next three hours, Justin and Shiro remain in the room with the generals, recounting their experiences in Okinawa. At first, the generals exchange doubtful glances, their questions sharp and skeptical. But as time passes, their attitudes change. By noon, the retelling wraps up, but word comes that the jets are not ready. Lunch comes out to them on trays. The conversation softens as they eat, shifting to small talk to get familiar with each other. By one o'clock, an aide steps in to report the jets are ready. Justin and Shiro thank the generals and leave the room, then meet with Ryuunosuke and Alice at the hospital.

"There you two are. How did everything go?" asks Ryuunosuke.

Justin smiles, giving a thumbs-up. "It took a while, but we secured two jets. Only Shiro and I are going from here on."

"That's fine," says Ryuunosuke. "I doubt I'd be much help. All I needed was to get everyone here."

Alice, peeking out from behind Ryuunosuke with a broad grin, cheerfully chimes in. "I guarantee I wouldn't be any help. So I'm happy to stay here in Hawaii."

"While you were fighting to get a plane, we spoke with some people about our friends back in Okinawa. They said they'll send a rescue team out to get them," says Ryuunosuke.

"That's terrific news," says Justin as his face lights up. "I hope they're all doing okay. It's been a while since we left. I didn't think it would take this long to send help."

Shiro stands beside him, giving a confident smile. "My wife's with them, so I'm not worried."

Alice folds her arms and glares at Justin and Shiro. "Aren't either of you going to ask how Ayane is doing?"

"You're right," says Justin. "Where is she? How is she doing?"

Alice exchanges a glance with Ryuunosuke. "Me and Ryuunosuke have already seen her. I'll take you to her so you can see her as well." She leads the way down the hallway and stops in front of a door. She knocks lightly. "Are you awake, Ayane?" She opens the door and steps inside. "Shiro and Justin are here to see you."

Ayane sits up in bed with bandages covering her head. The glow of the TV illuminates her face as she looks toward the doorway. The moment she sees Justin and Shiro, she smiles. "It took you guys a while to visit me. Where have you two been?"

Justin approaches the bed. "We've been trying to negotiate with the people in charge to get us a plane to the US."

"You all are leaving?" asks Ayane with a sad look on her face.

Justin runs his hand across the blanket. "No, only Shiro and I are leaving. Alice and Ryuunosuke are staying behind. They need to find the others."

"I overheard the nurses talking," says Ayane, lowering her gaze. "They said the US is being invaded. Will you make it in time?"

"We can only hope for the best," says Justin. "With any luck, we'll make it and take back what we've lost."

Ayane tears up, but tries her best to smile. "I hope you're right. So much has been lost."

Shiro puts his hand on Justin's shoulder. "Justin, we've waited long enough. We need to be heading back now. It's time to go."

Justin gives Ayane a reassuring pat on her shoulder. "Rest up and get better soon."

She nods, doing her best to maintain a steady smile despite the sadness in her eyes.

Justin and Shiro say their goodbyes.

They turn to leave, but as they reach the doorway, Ayane calls out, stopping them in their tracks. "Once this is over, I want to meet up again. Don't go dying on us."

Justin freezes in place, taking a moment before turning around. When he does, for a fleeting moment he sees Lilly in bed with her arm extended and her pinky out. When he blinks, he sees Ayane with her pinky out instead.

"Promise me you'll return," says Ayane.

"I promise we'll meet again," says Justin, extending his pinky.

At 1:30 in the afternoon, Justin and Shiro depart from Hawaii.

November 19th, 2026   1200 Eastern Standard Time

At the secret location, Paula stands before Angus, updating him with every detail about the enemy's movements. "We have reports they've arrived in Salt Lake City."

"They're moving better than expected. How are they moving so freely and quickly?" asks Angus.

"When they need to refuel and eat something, all they have to do is go to a gas station, and they're set to go. We are funding their invasion," says Paula.

"If we don't get a miracle soon, at this rate, the US will fall," says Angus, putting his hand over Paula's. "We've been through a lot together."

Paula quickly removes her hand and glares at him. "No, don't you do this. This isn't the end."

"I think it's time for you to flee the country," says Angus.

"What is it with you and Robert trying to get rid of me? I'm staying by your side till the very end, so stop asking me to leave," says Paula.

Angus tightens his tone. "Don't make me force this choice on you. This isn't coming from your boss, but as your—"

"No," says Paula, slamming her hand down. "That's enough out of you. I already told you no. This is a waste of time. Now, if you'll excuse me, I'm going to try to figure out a plan. You are free to help me or continue to lie in your bed."

Angus sighs, watching her leave. "Fine, if that's your choice, I'll respect it. But I will force you to leave once the enemy's at our door. Do I make myself clear?"

Paula ignores him and walks away.

"Before you go, I have a plan, but it will cost the lives of millions," says Angus.

An hour passes, and the plan is in motion. On the west side of the Rockies, people are fleeing through the mountains. Vehicles stretch for miles as traffic is at a complete standstill. As engines idle, exhaust fumes mix with the thin, frigid air. Snow falls steadily, covering the hoods and windshields. Some consider abandoning their cars, but when they open their doors, the bitter-cold pushes them back inside. To venture out is suicide. Behind them, the enemy creeps closer. Salt Lake City has already fallen, just like every other major city along the West Coast.

Hundreds of military aircraft pass over the Rockies with their shadows cutting across the landscape and the endless line of vehicles below. Hope surges through the people who believe their savior has come. They could not be more wrong. High above, Angus' plan is in motion. The aircraft spread out all over the Rockies, launching missiles at the mountains, causing snow and rock to break loose. Avalanches consume the roads in seconds, burying everything in its path. Those unlucky enough to survive the collapse suffer slow deaths. By sunset, every major road is under tons of ice and rubble. The invading force is cut off, their advance through the Rockies comes to a halt. When night falls, the enemy shifts south, turning toward Arizona in search of another way around.

Throughout the night, Angus lies restless in his bed. The assault on the Rockies weighs heavily on his mind.

At three in the morning, Paula enters the room where he is recovering. "Sir, are you awake?"

"Yes, I'm awake," says Angus, turning his head to her. "I haven't fallen asleep yet."

She steps in, holding a phone. "I'm on a call with the head of Fort Cavazos. Our miracle has arrived."

Angus takes the phone and puts it up to his ear. "This is Angus Turner speaking. Who am I talking to?"

"Good morning, Mr. President. This is Colonel Kayla Jacobs, commander of Fort Cavazos in Texas. Sorry for waking you this early, but you need to know this. I'll cut right to the chase. At midnight, a flight from Hawaii landed at our base carrying two important people. They were in Okinawa when the Deatomizer wiped out the island. They got their hands on the enemy's weapons and made a copy."

Angus sits frozen in disbelief, struggling to process the words. "This is the news we've been waiting for. Are you sure they are genuine?"

"Yes, they are. I tested the weapons myself. They are the real deal," says Kayla. "We've decided to make it our first priority to produce more of these weapons. We need you to authorize more materials and personnel to help us."

"Yes, yes, whatever you need. I'll be heading down there in a few hours to meet up with you," says Angus as his heart pounds in excitement.

"Sounds good, sir. We'll keep in touch, and we look forward to seeing you soon, Mr. President," says Kayla.

Paula takes the phone back. "Sir, I don't think it's a good idea for you to be moving around. You still need to recover."

"I can't stay in bed as my country falls apart," says Angus. "We finally have a chance. I want to see this through for Robert."

"If that's what you want, I'll agree with you," says Paula. "So, what's the plan?"

"Get as much material and personnel to Fort Cavazos as quickly as possible," says Angus. "Whatever she wants, she'll get. I will not let this opportunity slip through our fingers. It's time to turn this war around."

"Give me one moment and I'll call for the doctors and nurses to help you get ready," says Paula. She hurries out of the room and wakes everyone up with the news.

Angus lies in bed, deep in thought with regret. *I should have waited one more day before I launched that attack.* He rubs his face as the doctor and nurses come in. They get him ready to leave the secret location.

By eight in the morning, Air Force One sits on the tarmac. Angus told everyone to abandon the location and move everything to Texas. Around the runway, aides and staff rush to finalize the preparations.

"You're not uncomfortable, are you?" asks Paula, pushing Angus in a wheelchair toward the aircraft.

"I'm fine. This gunshot wound won't keep me from seeing this through," says Angus.

An older man in an army uniform stands by the stairs of Air Force One, saluting Angus. "Sorry it took so long. We needed to make sure the trip was safe as possible. It seems like the enemy isn't using any aircraft for this invasion."

"Why would they?" asks Angus. "Kun is a devilish man who wants to take his time with us. Using planes would not achieve his personal goal. He wants us to suffer, and I'm pretty sure he gets off on this."

"Well, let's hurry down to Texas before his plan becomes reality," says the soldier.

Nine hours ago   November 20th, 2026   0000 Central Standard Time

"To all military personnel. Two unknown aircraft have just entered our airspace. This is not a drill," says a voice over the intercom at the airstrip in Fort Cavazos.

Kayla rushes through the halls, her boots striking the floor with every step. "If they're coming from Mexico, are we sure they aren't with Kun's military?"

A soldier keeps pace beside her, delivering the latest briefing. "We've been monitoring the border closely. No aircraft from the US has crossed into Mexico before heading here."

"Could it be a Mexican plane?" asks Kayla.

"We don't know," says the soldier. "It's up to you if you want us to shoot it down. You make the call."

Kayla opens a set of double doors into a control room that is bustling with activity. Military personnel sit in front of computers, assessing the situation. "Have we determined whether they are friend or foe?"

A soldier at a radar terminal turns to her. "At the speed they're going, they're twenty minutes from the base. They haven't responded to us."

"Intercept them," says Kayla. "I want five jets to encircle them and establish communications with them."

Everyone in the room answers her, "Yes, ma'am." The room moves into action, getting five jets in the air.

Kayla pulls out the nearest chair and sits down, crossing her legs. "If our intel is correct, and this jet has a force field, we're all screwed."

A sudden voice breaks the tension. "I just established communications with them. They're one of us."

"Are you sure?" asks Kayla, jumping from her seat.

"All call signs match," says the soldier. "I know for sure they are on our side. The person said their name is Justin Myers, from the Army of what used to be Okinawa."

Kayla's eyes widen in disbelief. "You're kidding. Of all people, I figured he would be the one to survive that tragedy."

"Do you know him, ma'am?" asks the person beside her.

"I do," says Kayla, turning to leave the room. "Get the runway ready for him. I'm going to meet him personally on the tarmac when he lands."

Justin hands the microphone back to the pilot. "I was beginning to think Fort Cavazos was abandoned. That took way too long to get in touch with someone."

"They did say communications with the US was severed," says the pilot. "I'm betting the only reason they answered us was because they saw us on radar. Anyway, we're five minutes from landing."

Curious onlookers gather near the runway as the two jets land, eager to catch a glimpse of the arriving passengers.

As the cockpits open, Kayla is the first to greet them. "Well, I'll be damned. After I heard Okinawa fell, I assumed you fell with it, Justin."

Justin grins at the sight of Kayla as he jumps from the jet. "Good to see you too, Kayla. How long has it been?"

"It's only been like a decade and a half. So, no big deal," says Kayla, shrugging.

"I'm surprised you stayed in. I thought you would have gotten out by now," says Justin.

"At first I was planning on leaving, but they offered me a job with better benefits. I'm a bigwig here now," says Kayla.

"You really grew up from the little crybaby I remember starting with," says Justin.

Kayla slaps Justin hard on the back. "Hey now, that's in the past. I'm different now."

They laugh as people surround them. "Tell us more about Kayla when she was a crybaby. She's mean now."

"Hush now," says Kayla, rolling her eyes. "These two need rest. No more storytelling for tonight." She looks at Justin and Shiro. "Follow me. We can talk in private."

Justin and Shiro follow Kayla, leaving everyone disappointed.

"So what brings the two of you here?" asks Kayla. "If you didn't know, the US is in the middle of falling." She looks down at the bag Justin is holding. "I hope whatever's in that bag of yours isn't just your belongings." She then turns to look at Shiro. "I never caught your name. My name's Kayla."

"Shiro. I'm the lead research—"

Justin places his hand on Shiro's chest, cutting him off. "We can talk more when we get to the room. We don't know who's listening."

"Always the cautious one. It must be important if you don't trust my people," says Kayla. She opens a door to a conference room and turns on the lights. "This room will work. Please have a seat."

Justin sets the bag on a table and pulls out the gun and helmet. "What I'm about to show you is essential for our survival. These are the weapons Kun's military used on us in Okinawa."

Kayla's attitude shifts, and her tone grows more serious as she examines the items. She looks at Justin and Shiro as her skepticism clears. "Are these the real deal?"

"The genuine article," says Justin. He gives them to Kayla and takes out the replicas. "These are copies Shiro made."

"Well, damn," says Kayla. "Not only did you bring us the enemy's weapons, but you also reproduced them. Color me impressed."

Justin takes out a stack of papers and hands it to Kayla. "This is all of Shiro's research on these weapons plus the Deatomizer."

Kayla stares at Shiro with a gaze that could melt ice while pushing the stack up to her chest. "Who exactly are you? How were you able to accomplish such a feat? We have the best people looking into this, but they haven't brought me a fraction of what I'm holding."

Shiro meets her gaze, remaining composed under her pressure. "The Japanese government put me in charge of researching the Deatomizer. As luck would have it, me and Justin ran into each other about a week ago in Okinawa after its fall."

"I need to gather a few people here to let them know about this. Give me a moment," says Kayla, swiftly taking out her phone.

Within fifteen minutes, the room fills with a diverse group of high-ranking military officials and researchers. They talk among themselves as they settle into their seats.

Kayla stands at the front of the room, trying to get everyone's attention. "All right, settle down. I know it's early and you want to get back to bed, but that will have to wait. As you may know, we have two guests joining us tonight. What you don't know is they were part of the Deatomizer event in Okinawa and brought gifts." She reaches into the bag and pulls out the gun and helmet, raising them for everyone to see. "These are what Kun's military is using. We finally got what we were hoping for."

"How do we know they are real? Have you used them?" asks a researcher.

"I trust what Justin says," says Kayla. "I understand we need to see proof to see if they work, but I don't want to kill someone just to study these."

A first lieutenant speaks up from the back. "If it works on animals, we can get some cows. There's a farm not too far from here. I should be able to contact the farmer if he hasn't abandoned his farm yet."

"I think that would be the best idea," says Kayla. "If no one else has a better idea, let's go to the farm."

Everyone leaves the room and makes their way to the farm in military vehicles. The first lieutenant already called the farmer to have a few cows ready for them when they arrive.

Kayla is the first to greet the farmer. "Sorry for waking you this early. We need a few cows for an experiment we're holding, and your farm was the most convenient for us."

The farmer speaks with a strong Texan accent. "If this helps our country to survive, I will gladly give up all my cattle for whatever it is you are doing. Follow me this way." The farmer leads the group out to the barn, where all the cows are. He opens the barn doors and turns on the lights. "Take your pick. There are fifty cows here."

"We only need five at most," says Kayla.

"Use them all if you must," says the farmer. "It's not like I can take them with me when I leave. I was going to kill them eventually, anyway. Don't want them falling into the invaders' hands." He turns around, and as he walks back to his house, he calls back over his shoulder. "Well, I'm going back to bed. Keep the cows if you want something to eat and don't bother locking up when you're done. I'll worry about it when I wake back up."

The researchers take their positions with notebooks and pens in hand, waiting for Kayla's permission to go ahead.

Kayla turns to Justin and gestures toward the first cow. "Whenever you're ready."

Justin takes out the gun, studying it for a moment. "Is everyone ready?"

Everyone goes quiet in anticipation.

Justin walks up to the first cow, places the gun to its head, and pulls the trigger. The cow makes no sound when it falls to the ground, only a thud when the body falls on the ground. The researchers gather around the dead cow. "Wow, dead in an instant."

"This was better than I was expecting."

"Do another one."

Justin reaches back into the bag and takes out the replica gun. "This is the copy Shiro made. It should work like the original."

The researchers back away as Justin aims the replica gun at the head of another cow. He pulls the trigger, and just like the first cow, the second cow does the same, and the researchers remark again.

Justin sets the gun down and goes back to Kayla. "Do you believe me now?"

Kayla stands tall, meeting his gaze. "I never doubted you for a moment." She claps her hands to get everyone's attention. "All right, everybody. Now that we know these are the real deal, I want the researchers to look these over thoroughly. Shiro has also provided us with a large stack of documents with information that deals not only with these weapons, but the Deatomizer as well. The faster we get these manufactured, the faster we stop this war." Kayla then looks at Justin and Shiro. "I bet you both are tired. Let me find you a place to rest." As she walks away, she addresses everyone one more time. "I'm going to take them back to base so they can get some rest. I expect to see results in the morning."

After Kayla's instructions, the entire team gets busy working. They don't have time to waste.

"What are you planning on doing now? Where's the president?" asks Justin.

"We don't know where he is, but we have a way to reach him," says Kaila. "I hope he answers. I really don't want to be sent to voicemail."

They arrive back at base, and Kayla finds a room for Justin and Shiro. They fall asleep instantly.

Nine hours later   November 20th, 2026   1100 Central Standard Time

As the morning light filters into the room, Justin wakes up and notices Shiro still asleep. Moving quietly, he quickly gathers his belongings and slips out of the room. After a quick stop at the bathroom to get ready for the day, he emerges and flags down a passing soldier. "Do you know where Kayla is?"

"She's on the runway, waiting for the president to arrive," says the soldier.

Justin makes his way to the runway, where Air Force One has just landed.

Kayla stands in anticipation as a smile spreads from ear to ear. When the doors open and Angus emerges. She immediately straightens and offers him a salute. "Hello, Mr. President. It's a pleasure to meet you. I'm Colonel Kayla Jacobs. We talked on the phone earlier."

Soldiers carefully lower Angus from the airplane. Once on the ground, Paula pushes him up to Kayla to give her a handshake. "The pleasure is all mine. Where are the two people who came from Japan?"

"They're still sleeping. They've been through a lot these past few days," says Kayla. She gestures for him to follow her, leading him toward the command post.

Justin reaches the runway and sees Angus and Kayla walking in his direction. He quickly straightens his posture and salutes Angus. "Good morning, Mr. President."

"Speak of the devil," says Kayla. "This is one of the men I was talking to you about. This is Sergeant Justin Myers, who was based in Okinawa during the Deatomizer event."

Angus extends his hand and gives Justin a firm handshake. "So you're the person I've heard so much about. After I get my affairs in order, I want to sit down with you and hear what happened in Okinawa and the hardships you've been through."

Kayla speaks up before Justin can respond. "Justin is a capable man. I think he should come with us. He might provide more insight into the weapons."

"Then let him tag along," says Angus.

They make it to the command room, where the weapons are spread out on a table.

Kayla gestures toward them. "These are the weapons Kun's military used against the forces in Okinawa. I'd advise you not to touch them. They are very dangerous."

"I was the top general in the US military. I think I can handle these," says Angus. Paula pushes him up to the table, and he picks up the gun to inspect it. "I wasn't expecting it to look so much like a pistol. I pictured something…more alien-like."

"I was just as surprised as you when I first laid eyes on them," says Kayla.

Angus puts the gun down and picks up the helmet. "I've made arrangements to have materials brought here for you to make more of these. I also sent out orders to all the troops across the country to make their way here with any supplies they can, but I don't know how many people will come."

"That's good to hear," says Kayla. "We've also started producing more copies. Shiro, the other guy that came with Justin, managed to reverse-engineer the originals, and we are using his research notes for the manufacturing of these weapons. They are surprisingly simple to make."

"Simple? Isn't this alien technology?" asks Angus.

Justin steps forward, gesturing at the items. "I thought the same thing until Shiro explained it to me."

Angus puts the helmet on the table, and they make their way to the cafeteria as Justin explains how he got the alien's tech and the process behind replicating it.

"You're a great man, Justin," says Angus. "Your story has shown me that as long as we keep fighting, we can accomplish anything. You're the reason we've gotten this far. I expect great things from you."

"It's an honor you think so highly of me, Mr. President. I was only doing what I thought was best for my country," says Justin.

"This goes above and beyond just one country," says Angus. "This is about the safety of the world as a whole. We cannot allow Kun to have his way."

As they step into the cafeteria, they see Shiro at a table, eating lunch.

"This is convenient," says Justin, pointing toward Shiro. "Mr. President, I'd like to introduce you to the other person who helped me. This is Shiro." He places his hand on Shiro's back.

Shiro turns around to see who is there. When he sees Angus, he stands to greet him. "It's nice to meet you. I'm Shiro Kamiya. I'm the researcher who developed the replica of the weapons."

Angus extends his hand and gives Shiro a handshake. "I've heard a lot about you from Justin here. I'm happy to have someone as capable as you on our team. Your achievements will not go unnoticed."

The group takes their seats around the table and wait until lunch is brought to them.

"I just woke up a few minutes ago," says Shiro. "Has the production of the weapons been going well?"

"Everything's moving smoothly," says Kayla. "We're producing them quicker than I expected."

"The blueprints took me the longest out of everything I did," says Shiro. "Once everything was written down, replicating them was simple."

"Yes, Justin was just telling me how simple they are to make, and because of that, I've ordered all soldiers across the US to assemble here," says Angus. "Thanks to you, we're going to take the fight to them."

"That's good to hear," says Shiro, turning his gaze toward Justin. "So what are you going to do, Justin?"

"I'm going to be fighting with my brothers in arms," says Justin.

"Even after all you've been through? Don't you want to take it easy from here on?" asks Shiro.

"As much as I would like to take it easy, I want to be a part of this," says Justin. "I've been through this hell; I'm not stopping halfway. What about you? What are you planning on doing?"

"I'm going to stay here and help in any way I can," says Shiro. "But first, I need to find out what happened to the people we left in Okinawa."

"We haven't received any news yet," says Kayla. "Once we do, you'll be the first to know."

"It doesn't matter right now," says Shiro, sighing. "I'll find them after we finish."

Angus chimes in, "Can we assign Shiro to a position as a researcher? It would be a waste not to use his talents."

"I think that would be a wonderful idea," says Kayla, turning to Shiro. "The researchers will greatly benefit from your help. I would like you to join them in developing whatever you can. You will have unlimited resources to come up with anything you believe will help us win this war. So how about it?"

"If that's how I can help, then I'll do it," says Shiro.

Kayla claps her hands together, and a smile brightens her face. "Sounds good then. Let's finish up with lunch and head over to the manufacturing plant. I'll introduce you to everyone."

After finishing their lunch, the group makes their way to the factory responsible for overseeing the weapons production. Inside, the researchers test each batch to see if it functions properly. Any piece that fails is promptly scrapped and recycled into the next batch. Upon arrival, Kayla introduces Shiro to the researchers, who welcome him into their ranks. Shiro gets to work, moving confidently among the equipment. Without missing a beat, Kayla, Justin, Angus, and Paula swiftly exit the factory, leaving Shiro to dive fully into his research.

"When should we let our soldiers know of our new weapons?" asks Justin.

"I don't want to tell them outright," says Kayla. She looks at Angus. "Could you reach out to any soldiers still on the fence about fighting that we have developed a new weapon, but not say what it is? That should draw more people here."

Before Angus can answer, Paula speaks up. "I can write Angus a script to read. I know what you want him to say. Give me ten minutes and it'll be ready."

"I appreciate that a lot, thanks," say Kayla.

Paula gets to work on the script, impressing everyone with her speed and efficiency. When she finishes, she hands Angus the paper. Kayla gives him a phone, and he lifts it with a determined look, calling military bases across the US in hopes someone answers his calls. After no answer from any of the bases, he thinks for a moment and gets an idea. He takes out his phone and pulls up a contact. The person answers immediately, and Angus explains the situation.

"And are you sure your weapons are the real deal?" asks the man over the phone. "I don't want to send my men there just to die."

"They're the real deal, Mitch. I've seen them myself," says Angus.

Mitch lets out a heavy sigh. "I want you to know, Angus, seeing how you're the last four-star general left alive, and how we are lifelong friends, I'm inclined to trust you. I'll get the word out for anyone available to make their way to Fort Cavazos, but don't expect too much. A lot of soldiers have already fled."

"I'll take what you can get us," says Angus. "Also, I'm not a four-star general anymore. I'm the president."

"You've grown a lot since your inauguration," says Mitch. "I'm still torn about Robert's death."

"I am too," says Angus, letting out a sigh. "But knowing Robert, he'd get frustrated at us for mourning his death when we have bigger things to worry about."

"I think that's exactly how he would react," says Mitch. "Well, this work isn't going to do itself. Tell Paula I said hi." He ends the call.

Paula stands behind Angus, listening in on the conversation. "Mitch is a good man. I hope for the best for him."

Throughout the day, a steady stream of planes land at the base, each one bringing in more soldiers and essential supplies. Soldiers pour out, hauling gear and supplies that Angus requested. Thanks to Mitch's efforts about the new weapon, people from across the country are drawn to the base, determined to lend their support. The turnout far exceeds initial expectations, and the influx of manpower brings a surge of hope and energy to the operations. As the hours pass and the number of arrivals continues to grow, Angus finds himself on the phone with the governor of Texas, asking for his help with housing and transporting soldiers in and out of the base.

"I'm under no obligation to help you," says the governor. "You can figure this problem out for yourself."

Angus presses the phone to his ear as veins stand out on his forehead. "I will have you arrested if you keep refusing me."

"You don't have that power," says the governor.

"Test me and find out," says Angus. "You are preventing the US military from combating the enemy in a time of war. If you want to go down this road, so be it. I'll give you one more chance. Will you help?"

The governor takes a moment to talk to an aide. When he gets back on the phone, he sighs. "Fine. I'll get you what you need."

Six hours later   November 20th, 2026   1900 Central Standard Time

Mitch arrives at Fort Cavazos and immediately meets up with Angus. "I'd give you a hug, but I don't want to hurt you."

Angus gives him a smirk and extends his hand. "A handshake will do just fine." He grips Mitch's hand tight and firm, pulling him close. "The only people I let hug me are my family."

They end their handshake, and Mitch flexes and rubs his hand. "So, where are the weapons you're talking about? I want to see them."

Paula places a duffle bag between Angus and Mitch. "We don't have the real weapons with us. Those are still being studied by the researchers. But we have the prototypes they've made within the last hour." She reaches into the bag, pulling out a helmet and gun. "Please keep in mind that this is highly classified. What you see here does not leave this room. Do I make myself clear?"

"Loud and clear, ma'am," says Mitch. He leans in closer to get a better look. "What am I looking at? They don't look remarkable at all. They look like normal guns any soldier is required to have."

"What you are looking at is the recreation of the enemy's weapons used in the Battle of Okinawa," says Paula.

Mitch sits upright. His eyes narrow, and his expression shifts to one of seriousness. "You're kidding me, right? I thought you were bluffing when you told me you had recreated the weapons. How were you able to get these? I was told everyone on that island died by the Deatomizer."

"All but sixteen people died," says Angus. "One of them being an American soldier who was wearing the helmet as the Deatomizer detonated."

"This soldier, where is he now?" asks Mitch. "I want to talk to him."

"I believe he and Kayla are having dinner in the cafeteria right about now. I can get him if you'd like," says Paula.

"Yes, please, if you could. Bring him here," says Angus.

Paula hurries down the hallway toward the cafeteria. She stands at the entrance, scanning all the soldiers having dinner. Once she spots Justin, she approaches him quickly. "Sorry to interrupt your dinner, but someone important wants to meet you."

Justin puts his fork down and stands. "That's fine. Show me the way."

Kayla stands as well, and together they follow Paula out of the cafeteria.

When they reach the room, Paula pauses at the doorway and gestures to Mitch. "I would like you two to meet Mitch. He's the reason for the influx of people and supplies."

Mitch quickly stands to greet Justin as he enters the room, extending his hand in a gesture of respect. "So this is the man who single-handedly turned the tide of this war? It is a pleasure to meet you, Justin. My name's Mitch Brickner. While I may not hold the same title Angus does, I'm a well-known brigadier general."

Justin steps forward and grasps Mitch's hand, locking eyes in a respectful handshake. "I've heard of your accomplishments. You're wrong. You're just as famous as Angus."

Mitch turns to look at Angus, giving him a cocky tone. "You hear that? I'm just as famous as you."

Angus closes his eyes and rubs his face. "This isn't a popularity contest."

"I'm just kidding," says Mitch, turning back at Justin with a serious look on his face. "I want you to tell me everything that has happened from the time Kun's military attacked Okinawa up to this point. Do not skip the details."

As the group settles in place, Paula gently taps her hand on the doorframe and addresses everyone with a warm smile. "This story will take a while. Let me get us some refreshments."

Justin recounts the journey that brought him to this moment, ensuring he does not leave out any details. "And that covers everything that has happened until now."

Mitch nods with great respect, acknowledging all Justin had to sacrifice to get here. "Such an amazing story of overcoming hardships and putting your country above all else. I can respect that." He glances at Angus. "Are you planning to promote this man? He's done so much in such a short time. More than either of us have done in our lifetime."

"If we survive this war, I plan on making it known who we have to thank. Not only Justin but Shiro as well," says Angus.

"I don't need any of that," says Justin. "I'm only serving my country in the best I can."

"Nonsense," says Mitch, putting his hands on Justin's shoulders. "You and this Shiro guy are going to be known across the world for your heroic deeds. I will not be taking no as an answer. You got that?"

Justin hesitates, then sighs. "As long as it's the two of you who are personally telling the world of what happened here, I will not be against it."

"There you go, kid," says Mitch, grinning and slapping Justin on the back. "Just what I wanted to hear. I can assure you that as long as I am still alive and able to articulate my words, I will do just that. You can count on it."

They wrap up their gathering and, by the end of the day, trucks carrying supplies ranging from food and water to toiletries arrive at the base. Nearly half a million people show up. Not all are soldiers; about a third are non-military personnel, drawn in by the promise of survival.

November 21st, 2026   0800 Central Standard Time

This day unfolds the same as yesterday. Word spreads fast about the new weapons, and people keep arriving in droves. So many arrive that Kayla has to order people out of the city to be housed in Waco or Austin. Shuttle buses run back and forth between the cities, never stopping.

Angus, Kayla, and Justin gather in a room to receive an update on the enemy's movements and activities.

Paula stands at the front of the room, showing a map of where the enemy is going. She keeps up to date with the information she can get. "The enemy stalled after the events in the Rockies, but as of noon yesterday, they're already on the move again and heading south. They moved west around the Grand Canyon and took a detour to Las Vegas, arriving only a few hours ago. A smaller group of a thousand split from them as they departed Vegas, and it looks like they are heading toward Phoenix. The primary group is now next to the Grand Canyon. Two days ago, the group heading south from San Francisco already reached San Diego and is now heading east. Our intelligence believes they are rendezvousing with the group heading to Phoenix. Another group that headed north from San Francisco has already taken over all the major cities, including Portland and Seattle. That group split into smaller groups of about a hundred soldiers each, overtaking every small town in their way."

"That's what I was told in Hawaii," says Justin. "The whole western seaboard has fallen."

Angus leans forward and crosses his arms as he focuses on the map. "So what about the group next to the Grand Canyon? What city are they heading to next?"

Paula studies the maps and reviews her notes carefully before addressing the group. "They're avoiding the Rockies. If our model is correct, they'll arrive in Albuquerque by tomorrow afternoon. After that, they will most likely split into three groups. Group one will head north toward Denver, group two will head east toward Amarillo, and group three will head south toward El Paso to meet up with the group from Phoenix. This is speculation, but most likely true."

"So all we have to do is stop them in Albuquerque before they split," says Justin.

"That's easier said than done," says Paula.

Kayla interjects, "We have people ready to fight and a lot of weapons at our disposal. If we mobilize now, we can make it to Albuquerque with time to spare."

"What I'm worried about is whether these weapons can even defeat the enemy," says Paula. "If we're only matching their firepower, it won't matter. They can just ignore us and continue with their mission."

Everyone sits in silence, realizing they are only copying the weapons, not enhancing them.

Justin takes out his phone and calls Shiro. When he answers, Justin puts him on speaker so that everyone can hear the conversation.

"What's up, Justin?" asks Shiro.

"This is very important," says Justin. "We're getting briefed about the enemy's movements, and an important question was asked that only you can answer. Are the weapons we're producing the exact same as the weapons the enemy is using?"

"Yeah, everything is the same. Why, what's the problem?" asks Shiro.

Justin pinches the bridge of his nose and shuts his eyes. "Have you tested to see if the replicas can kill the enemies?"

Everyone holds their breaths, waiting for Shiro to answer. Moments pass before he answers. "Yeah, we tested that. If everything goes as planned, we should be able to pierce through the enemy's shield with no problems."

A collective sigh of relief sweeps through the room.

"Good to hear. That's all we needed to know," says Justin.

"If that's all, I need to get back to work," says Shiro.

"Yes, that's all. Thanks," says Justin.

Just as Justin is about to end the call, Shiro speaks once more. "Oh, a few more things before we hang up. The weapons go both ways. You can pierce them, and they can pierce back. Also, I remember what you told me about how the guns pierced through armored vehicles. Some researchers suggested that it might have something to do with quantum mechanics. It has to do with a thing called quantum tunnelling. That means the bullets can phase through solid objects and hit the target. Armored vehicles will not protect anyone. Let everyone know before you send them into battle. We don't want another massacre."

They hang up, and everyone in the room stares at Justin. "That was the news we wanted to hear, plus some. We can work around that."

At noon, Kayla makes an announcement about the upcoming battle. "By this time tomorrow, the enemy will be in Albuquerque, New Mexico. We are sending the first batch of troops today. My good friend Justin Myers will lead the charge. Everyone will receive orders about what their roles will be. In addition, every soldier will also receive our weapon we have been producing. I wish everyone the best of luck."

Starting immediately after the announcement ends, soldiers load military vehicles with equipment ranging from radios to fuel canisters. Each soldier receives a freshly manufactured gun and helmet. Each pair comes with a sheet of paper warning that these are copies of the weapons Kun's military are using, describing their deadly capabilities, and giving instructions for the operations. The print stresses the chilling reality that these weapons offer no protection against the weapons the enemy is using.

By two in the afternoon, Justin is behind the wheel of a Humvee, leading a massive convoy of military vehicles. Hundreds of vehicles rumble across the highway, stretching for miles as they move toward Albuquerque. The drive takes ten hours, crossing endless stretches of open road. By the time they arrive, it is eleven at night. The city is silent. Hours earlier, the last residents fled, unwilling to share the fate of the other cities overthrown by the enemy. Justin rolls into a makeshift campsite on the outskirts of Albuquerque. He steps out and stretches his arms to the night sky as soldiers move in to unload the equipment from his Humvee.

Meanwhile, Kayla took a plane and has been waiting for his arrival for three hours. When she gets the news he made it, she meets him. "Hope the trip was smooth."

"Everything went good," says Justin, rolling his shoulders. All five hundred military vehicles should be arriving with no problems."

"Good to hear," says Kayla. "Now get some rest. You're going to be up early tomorrow."

When Justin is shown to his tent, he falls asleep fast and dreams of Lilly.

It is autumn. The leaves are turning brown and falling, drifting from the branches above. A gentle breeze scatters the leaves around. Justin sits alone on a weathered park bench, gazing out over a calm lake. The water glistens in the light of the setting sun.

Lilly walks up from behind him and puts her hand on his shoulder. "It's a beautiful view, isn't it?" Then she sits beside him.

Justin keeps looking out at the lake, remembering the past. "The scenery is a bit different, but I know this is where I met your mother for the first time."

"She's waiting to see you again, Dad. You can come here anytime," says Lilly.

"Not yet. I still have things I need to do. I really want to though," says Justin.

Lilly reaches out and gently places her hand over his. "When you're ready, you know where to find us. Mom has been waiting a long time for you to show up."

A sudden, bright white light appears behind Justin, prompting him to stand and turn around. He sees his wife, but before he can speak, the moment is abruptly interrupted by his alarm at seven in the morning. He rubs his eyes, shakes off the remnants of his dream, and prepares for the day ahead. His new helmet and gun are on the nightstand beside him. He grabs his gear, then meets up with Kayla in the command center. "Where's the enemy's location?"

"They're three hours from Albuquerque. We're getting everyone up and ready," says Kayla.

Justin nods, tightening the straps on his gear. "I guess I'll start heading out now."

"Hey Justin, don't go getting yourself killed now," says Kayla.

Justin puts his hand up to his chest and meets Kayla's gaze. "I've survived this far. I don't plan on dying just yet."

He leaves the command center, feeling the weight of Kayla's words pressing on his mind. Outside, the morning air is crisp. He makes his way toward the unit under his command, mentally preparing himself for the responsibilities ahead. After reaching his team, he climbs into the driver's seat of his Humvee. To pass the time, he chats with his unit.

An hour before the enemy arrives, Kayla sends out her commands. "It's time. I trust you're ready."

Justin takes the mic from the holster and brings it to his mouth. "You know I am." He drives to the center of the city, followed by fifty other Humvees.

As they drive through the city, the soldier beside Justin peers out the Humvee at the empty streets. "Have you ever seen a city so lifeless before?"

Justin tightens his grip on the wheel, remembering the recent events clearly. "Okinawa was kind of like this. The only difference is there are no dead bodies scattered across the streets."

The convoy rolls through Albuquerque, scattering across the city streets. For the time being, everyone stays in their Humvees, waiting for the enemy to arrive. Meanwhile, twenty thousand soldiers move from the camp to occupy the city. They file into strategic locations, taking up positions in buildings, alleyways, and makeshift barricades.

Thirty minutes later, the first enemy units appear on the outskirts, unaware of the weapons the Americans have. Their movements are casual, believing victory is certain. Fifty thousand enemy soldiers push toward the city without hesitation, but their arrogance costs them dearly. Hidden in the shadows, the Americans stay quiet and open fire, cutting their forces by half within a minute. Bodies fall to the ground before they realize what hit them. The enemy does not know where the shots are coming from, so they fire erratically at the city. Panic flashes across their faces; they are not prepared for any resistance, much less for massive losses. The survivors break rank and retreat the way they came, and many are picked off with ease. Those who escape inform their commander about what happened.

Another thirty minutes pass before anything happens. The remaining enemy soldiers of nearly two hundred thousand push forward, believing they still have the advantage. Instead of rushing into the city, they stop and wait for an hour. Their commander's study the surrounding terrain and comes up with a plan. They give the order to fan out and encircle the city, trying to trap the soldiers within Albuquerque.

"Justin, can you hear me?" asks Kayla over the Humvee's radio.

"I hear you loud and clear," says Justin.

"The enemy's making their move," says Kayla. "They are trying to surround the city. Most likely, they're trying to push inward toward you. Before they get the chance, I'm ordering another platoon to intercept them from the south. I need you to defend the north and west. The troops in the buildings will cover you."

"Got it, I'll get it done," says Justin. He looks at the radio operator. "I need you to switch the comms so everyone can hear me."

The radio operator quickly changes the frequency. Once the task is complete, he gives Justin a thumbs-up.

"I need all units to get into a defensive formation," says Justin. "The enemy is trying to surround us. We're going to cut them off from the north to stop their progression. They're also coming in from the west. Keep that in mind."

The Humvees roar through the city, speeding their way northwest. Overhead, enemy missiles streak through the sky, slamming against the buildings. Each explosion shakes the structures, causing many to crumble and collapse. Anyone caught inside the falling buildings is buried underneath the rubble. For the soldiers trapped in the wreckage, their helmet's shield them from certain death. However, despite their survival, escape is impossible for them.

Justin takes the lead. As they break into the open, he spots the enemy in the distance. With the support from soldiers in the damaged buildings, they tear through the enemy's numbers, wiping out hundreds before they can mount a proper response.

Far to the south, the platoon Kayla dispatched quickly gets into position. They set up an ambush, waiting for the unsuspecting enemy units to approach. As the enemy advances, the Americans spring their trap without warning. One after another, both flanks crumble under the sudden assault.

Within thirty minutes, the battlefield is littered with bodies from both sides. The enemy forces have been cut in half, down to a hundred thousand. Their confidence is shattered by the sheer ferocity of the Americans' counterattack.

At the command post, Kayla watches the battle unfold on the screens. "Things are going so well. I didn't expect this."

Around her, operators receive crucial details about the battle over screens and radios, their voices steady but urgent as they relay coordinates, troop movements, and incoming enemy activity. Because of their coordination, the battle moves smoothly.

"The enemy is falling back. What's our next plan, Kayla?" asks a soldier.

"Tell our forces to continue with their pursuit," says Kayla. "This isn't over just because the enemy's retreating. They're the invaders, and we'll snuff them out today."

An operator scans the skies over Albuquerque at the command post. He notices something in the distance that catches his attention. "Mrs. Kayla, it's coming."

A shadow passes Justin. He looks up at the sky and sees it. "You've got to be kidding me." He slams his foot on the gas, tearing through the city streets as he tries to get out. "Give me the mic now." The radio operator hands him the mic. "All units, evacuate the city. Do not stop. If you get caught in the blast radius, your helmets should protect you, but just in case they don't, keep driving because your life depends on it."

The Deatomizer hovers menacingly over the city.

Justin glances at his side mirror, getting flashbacks to when he was in Okinawa. "Come on. This time has to be different. Please let these helmets work."

The Deatomizer detonates, unleashing its outer light across Albuquerque. From the horizon, a missile streaks across the sky, locking onto the Deatomizer's core. Just before it strikes the inner orb, the missile blows up, sending an electric-blue shockwave out that disrupts the inner orb, making it crumble away. The Deatomizer does not fully expand or vaporize the city. However, its outer light still envelops the city, turning everything blue.

Justin speeds up the Humvee as he tries to put as much distance as possible between himself and the dome. Once beyond its reach, he brings the vehicle to a halt and glances back at the city. To his surprise, the dome does not dissipate immediately. Instead, it gradually gets blown away by the wind. Unlike before, the atoms are not forced apart. He does not know what is going on, but cheers anyway. "Hell yeah. Take that, you monster."

Across the battlefield, soldiers erupt in cheers. Relief and disbelief sweep through the ranks as word spreads that the Deatomizer, the weapon responsible for so much suffering, has fallen.

With the threat of the Deatomizer gone, the battle comes to an abrupt end. The enemy forces scatter in the direction they came. American soldiers pursue them relentlessly, not giving them a chance to regroup. Some enemy soldiers drop their weapons and surrender, but there is no mercy. The American soldiers kill them the same way they ruthlessly massacred innocent civilians.

By the end of the day, the battlefield bears witness to the immense cost of the conflict. Of the two hundred thousand enemy soldiers, nearly one hundred seventy-five thousand lie dead. The American forces also suffered significant losses, with ten thousand troops lost in the fighting. News of the weapon's success reaches Shiro and his team, and excitement floods the room. Moments later, Shiro receives a call from Justin.

"How did you know we would need a weapon like that?" asks Justin.

"I figured we needed something to deal with it," says Shiro. "Back when we were in Okinawa, I surmised the weapons you brought me were made of the same materials the Deatomizer is made of. Luckily, I was right."

"You never fail to impress me, Shiro. Thank you for everything you've done," says Justin.

They end the call, and Kayla stands in front of him. "This was the best outcome. So, what did you think of that? Amazing, right?"

"I'm surprised you kept me in the dark about your new toy," says Justin.

"Well, I had to," says Kayla. "I didn't want to risk it being leaked. The fewer people who knew, the better. Even Angus didn't know."

"No, that's all right," says Justin, shifting his gaze to the city. "So what about the city? It's blue now."

"Nothing to worry about," says Kayla. "From the reports I've seen of the blue people, this city will be back to its original color in a week."

"A week, huh? That's good to hear," says Justin. He lets out a long breath as he finally allows himself to relax. He rubs his tired eyes as the exhaustion of the past few days weighs heavily on him. As he gazes out over the city, his thoughts drift to the many people he has encountered. The faces of friends and allies linger in his memory. He quietly acknowledges that without their support and sacrifices, he could never have reached this moment on his own.

10

November 23rd, 2026   0700 Mountain Standard Time

Angus arrives at the camp outside Albuquerque just as the sun breaks over the mountains. Around him, soldiers wake up and prepare for the next phase of the war. The crisp morning air carries the scent of dust and diesel from the idling vehicles. Although the war is far from over, a sense of relief linger among the troops. The tensions ease as the nation pulls back from the brink. Near the command post, a group of journalists are waiting for him to give a press conference about the success.

Angus slowly rolls up to the podium. He looks out at the sea of reporters before beginning. "This was one of our most successful battles thus far. I'm proud to have been a part of it."

"How were you able to reproduce the alien weapons?" asks a reporter.

"I cannot divulge our methods at this time," says Angus. "But as you can see, these are the real deal."

"What's the next step you are planning on taking?" asks another reporter.

"That should be obvious. We are taking back America," says Angus.

A reporter from the back speaks up, "What about all the people you murdered not too far from here?"

Everyone goes quiet, waiting for his response. The soft hum of generators and birds chirping in the distance fill the silence as he looks out at the crowd.

Paula wastes no time rushing onto the stage to take him away. "He will not be answering these questions. We're needed elsewhere."

As she pushes him away, Angus puts his hand up to her. "They deserve an answer." Paula reluctantly lets go, and he looks back at the reporters. "I did what I thought was best at the time. If I'd known we were going to be getting these weapons, I would never have ordered that attack. Now, if you'll excuse me, I need to be going."

Inside the command post, Kayla waits near a long table as Paula pushes Angus into the room. Kayla makes eye contact with him and salutes. "Good morning, Mr. President. This is only the beginning. We are planning a full retaliation soon. We just need your support."

"Of course, you have my full support," says Angus, gripping the armrest of his chair. "I saw what the weapons we made could do. I'm confident that we now have a chance to win this war."

"To start with, I've already ordered our soldiers to push west and eliminate any remaining enemy soldiers," says Kayla. "I've told my men to take no prisoners. I want them all wiped out. They killed so many innocents that this will not go unpunished. They brought this upon themselves."

"I couldn't agree with you more," says Angus. "I'll start giving orders to move our men and supplies westward."

Kayla gestures to a large screen on the wall with a live satellite feed of the West Coast. "Before we make our way west, we need to do something about the warships. Over the past few days, they all moved along the coast from the Canadian border to the Mexican border. We've launched missiles, but they're protected by a force field. We need to get rid of them as soon as possible. After we figure that out, I want to take this war to Kun. Hitting Hanoi and taking the alien ship for our own should put a stop to this awful war. We should also capture Kun if possible."

Angus carefully thinks everything over. He does not want to miss something and put the US back in peril. Moments later, his fiery gaze meets Kayla. "Yes, I think that is a great plan, but do you think we can take the aliens' ship that easily?"

"I don't know, but if we don't at least try, then we can kiss any chance of winning goodbye," says Kayla.

Angus extends his hand to Kayla, shaking it firmly as a sign of solidarity. "Let's get to work rounding up our most important people for this operation. We can decide our next move when we have more people's thoughts on the matter."

As the US forces steadily push westward, the remaining enemy resistance crumbles rapidly before them. Each time an enemy falls, their gun and helmet disintegrates, as usual, except for the gadget. None of the US soldiers know what they are, but since they are with the dead, they are gathered and transported to Fort Cavazos for Shiro and his team to find out their purpose.

By one in the afternoon, Shiro calls Kayla to report his findings. "I have some good news. These small devices are just as easy to replicate as the other two, but that's not even the best part. These devices attach to things and let them slip through the force fields of the helmets. They're made of the same thing."

"Do you know why they didn't disintegrate like the others? That seems like a big oversight," says Kayla.

"I think it's because it was a rushed job," says Shiro. "They wanted the quick and easy approach when they made these and missed something major. Since they overlooked that, I'm going to mess around and see if I can make one of them repel the others."

"If you think that will help us, by all means, go for it," says Kayla. "Since those little devices can bypass the shields, I want to attach them to missiles and blow up the warships along the coast. Can your team figure out how to do that?"

"That shouldn't be a problem," says Shiro. "I don't need to modify them in any way. We can attach them to the missiles as they are."

"Great to hear," says Kayla.

After ending the call, Shiro immediately sets to work on his idea. Within just ten minutes, Shiro successfully brings his concept to life.

Kayla is meeting with Angus, Justin, and many other military strategists who give their input on how to move forward from the current situation. She also informed everyone about what Shiro told her. "So, if everything goes well, by tonight we should be able to destroy their fleet. I've already talked with the missile operations officers, and they should be placing the devices on the missiles as we speak."

Mitch is also present in the room, giving his thoughts. "Assuming this works and we take out their fleet, what's your plan to get our troops to Hanoi? It's not like we have any ships of our own along the coast."

"My plan is to move as many people as we can to Japan and use Japanese warships to sail to Vietnam. From there, we'll gain the upper hand and move soldiers to overtake Hanoi," says Kayla.

Mitch nods, rubbing his hands together. "It's not a bad plan, but do we know if the Japanese government is still willing to help us after the events of Okinawa?"

"We recently reestablished communications with them," says Kayla. "I've already talked with their leaders about this, and they still want to help us. All we need is for the president to agree with this plan."

Everyone in the room turns their attention toward Angus, waiting for his response.

He sits up, not hesitating to respond. "It's the best plan we have. Let's do it." He places his hand on Justin's shoulder. "Above all else, I want this man leading the attack. He's shown me what he's capable of, and I believe he's the right person to be in charge of this operation."

"I also believe that to be the right choice," says Kayla. "He can be in charge of the ground troops. What do you think, Justin?"

Justin thinks for a moment. He knows the responsibility being placed on him if he accepts the position. He looks at Angus, who confidently nods at him. "If Angus believes I'm the right person for the job, then I'll take it. But just so we're clear, I want to be on the ground in Vietnam and grab that son of a bitch Kun myself. I don't want to sit this one out."

"All right, if you say so," says Kayla. "From this moment on, Justin will be the leader of the ground troops. Now we just need to wait until the missiles are ready. That concludes this meeting."

Everyone leaves the room and goes their separate ways except for Justin and Angus.

"Justin, give me a minute of your time," says Angus. "There's something important I need to ask you."

"What is it?" asks Justin.

"Once this is all over and you come back, would you consider being my vice president?" asks Angus, looking up at Justin with fire burning in his eyes.

Justin pauses, surprised by the question, and thinks about it for a moment. "Before I answer you, why me? There are others here that are more than qualified to do that job. Better than me, in fact."

"You've made many accomplishments these past two weeks," says Angus. "You never gave in and kept pushing to get the job done. All that is going on is because of you. If you didn't make it your mission to get back to the US, then I'm afraid of what would have befallen the country by this time. That kind of leadership is exactly what we need to bring this country back together. With that being said, I think you are more than qualified to become the vice president, more than anyone. Also on the topic of qualifications, Paula ran a background check, and you meet them all. If you didn't, I wouldn't be asking."

Justin considers his next words carefully. Once he is ready, he looks at Angus. "I'm touched you think so highly of me. You know what? I accept. I'll be your vice president."

"Terrific news. I'll wait for your return, and we can make it official," says Angus. He gives Justin one final handshake before Paula enters the room.

She steps behind Angus and pushes him out of the room. As she passes Justin, she smiles and nods. "I look forward to working with you, Mr. Myers."

Once Justin is alone, Kayla walks from around a corner and meets his gaze. "I can't say I'm surprised you left that big of an impression on him. All he ever does is talk about how amazing you are."

"Oh, you heard that?" asks Justin.

"I did. And good on you for accepting it. I would have kicked you in the butt if you didn't," says Kayla. She walks up to Justin and gently punches his chest. "You are not allowed to die over there. You got that?"

Justin laughs while looking at the floor.

"Hey, what's so funny?" asks Kayla.

"It's nothing. You just reminded me of someone else who told me the same thing," says Justin.

"Anyway, we're leaving tonight at eight. Get some rest. I'll come get you when we're about to depart," says Kayla.

By the end of the day, the gadgets are attached to nearly a thousand missiles. When the launch order comes, it takes only minutes for them to reach their target along the West Coast. One after another, they find their mark, erupting in towering plumes of water and smoke as every warship is torn apart and sunk. Not too long after that, the US begins flying their troops and equipment to Japan. Throughout the night, tens of thousands of military personnel work tirelessly to make sure everything gets to where it needs to.

Seven hours later   November 23rd, 2026   2000 Mountain Standard Time

At the Albuquerque airport, Justin and Kayla board a passenger plane that the US government commandeered to move soldiers to Japan.

When Justin enters, he scans the row of seats, then his gaze lands on a familiar face. "I didn't know you were coming too, Shiro."

Shiro glances up from his seat, then stands when he sees Justin. "I've stayed in this country long enough. It's time I get back and see my wife and friends."

"What about the research you've been doing?" asks Justin.

"You Americans are very smart," says Shiro. "I'm just another person who can be replaced. There's no need for me to be here."

"Well, anyway, I'm glad to see you again. One more trip and this will hopefully be over," says Justin.

Fifteen hours later, at two in the morning, Justin, Shiro, and Kayla arrive at the Kansai International Airport, outside of Osaka. As soon as they disembark, they quickly transfer to another plane that takes them to the Nagasaki prefecture, where soldiers from the US, Japan, and Canada are gathering for the invasion of Vietnam.

November 25th, 2026   0000 Indochina Time

In Hanoi, the capitol building trembles under Kun's fury. Everyone scurries around, trying to blend into the background. In his office, his rage pours out at Ignin. His loss cuts deeper than he admits.

Ignin tries his best to stand up to Kun, wanting to help fix the problem they are facing. "I understand your feelings, but—"

Kun slams his hand on his desk, cutting Ignin off. "No, I don't think you understand. You assured me this win. How did they get the devices you made? You caused this."

"I'm doing everything to fix this," says Ignin. "I've never had this happen in any other world before."

"And how long have you been doing this?" asks Kun.

"Going by your time, it has been thirty-five years and three months," says Ignin.

Kun slams his hand on his desk again, making Ignin flinch. "With all that experience, how the hell did you mess up this badly? We have a force that's pissed off coming for us. They will be here within two days with the help of the devices you gave me. What are you going to do to protect us?"

Ignin tries to think of a solution, but his mind draws a blank. "Uh, I...I ...could ...do, uh..."

"Uh, uh, uh. Uh isn't an answer, Ignin," says Kun, mocking him. "You need to get working on whatever it is to protect my great country. I will not accept your incompetence."

Ignin stands there, not knowing what to say. He has never been in a situation like this before.

"Are you still here? Get out of my sight," says Kun, pointing toward the door.

Without hesitation, Ignin hurries out of the building to be beamed into his ship.

Kun sits in his chair with frustration etched on his face as he turns his attention to Zhen. "I need all the smartest people from across my territory here now. I can't rely on that failure anymore. He's going to cost me my country."

Zhen nods and leaves, not daring to say a word.

Taf is still in the room, sitting where she always has been. "So, that's it then?"

"Yes, that's it," says Kun. "I've lost a lot of good men because of you. Now it's time for me to take this into my own hands. Either you leave too or keep your mouth shut."

Taf does not move an inch. She sits tall, knowing Kun will not harm her. "My orders are to only contact Ignin when you need something. I'll keep doing my job with no complaints."

"Finally, someone who isn't deliberately messing me up," says Kun, grabbing his phone from his desk. He calls his top generals. His voice is sharp and commanding. "Get every remaining weapon and device ready for the upcoming invasion. We're not going down without a fight."

Ten hours later   November 25th, 2026   1200 Japan Standard Time

Justin and Shiro sit across from each other in a busy cafeteria, eating lunch.

Justin stops mid-bite and looks at Shiro. "I can tell you want to ask me something."

Shiro hesitates, shifting uncomfortably in his seat. "I do, but I don't know how you'll respond."

"If you think it's an important question, just ask," says Justin. "We have been traveling together for a while now, so I'll be fine. You won't hurt my feelings."

Shiro inhales deeply, bracing himself. "Okay, here it goes. What if this doesn't work?"

Justin takes a moment to respond. He continues eating his lunch in silence, thinking about the question. After a while, he sets his fork down and meets Shiro's gaze. "This has to work. I don't know what I would do if it doesn't." He picks up his fork and continues eating as if nothing happened.

Shiro refrains from asking anything else. He comes to realize Justin will fight until he either wins or dies. Shiro looks around the room and sees all the Americans with the same look of determination on their faces. He knows they all feel the same way. "It was a stupid question. I'm sorry for asking."

"You don't need to apologize," says Justin. "Until now, we were just waiting to be slaughtered. Now that we have a fighting chance, I will not waste this opportunity. I completely understand why you asked. We'll cross that bridge when we get to it."

"Thank you, friend," says Shiro.

Moments later, Kayla enters the cafeteria accompanied by a group of people. Her eyes scan the crowd looking for Shiro.

Shiro notices them first. He jumps from his seat and runs to them, unable to contain his excitement. "It's been so long. I was worried."

"We've missed you too, Shiro," says Shigeko, throwing herself into his arms.

Justin walks over and pats Kayla on the shoulder. "I see you found them."

"Surprisingly, it wasn't difficult," says Kayla. "Once I started asking around about them, the people here already had it on file they were looking for Shiro."

Kiyomi and Yoshiko are standing beside Shigeko.

Yoshiko waves and approaches Justin with a warm smile. "It's nice to see you again. I heard everything went well."

"Things could have gone better, but we made it," says Justin, looking around. "What happened to the others?"

Kiyomi steps forward and answers him. "We left that island about ten days ago and came here to mainland Japan. After a few days, we said our goodbyes to the others. From what I heard, they were going to Hawaii."

"That's good to hear," says Justin.

Shigeko still holds Shiro tightly as she looks at Justin. "We were worried about you guys. We didn't hear anything for three days and thought the worst had happened."

The group settles at a table. Justin and Shiro take turns recounting their journey since they left Okinawa, filling them in on everything they endured along the way. Kayla excuses herself, giving them space to catch up.

When the story is over, Kiyomi covers her mouth, and her eyes widen with astonishment. "Oh wow. All of that happened in the short time since we last saw each other? I'm amazed."

"It was a journey, for sure. Hopefully, it ends tomorrow," says Justin.

"What are you doing for the battle ahead?" asks Yoshiko.

"I'm leading the ground troops that are going to Vietnam. We're going to be leaving soon once everything is ready," says Justin. He looks at Shiro. "How about you? What are you planning to do? You don't have to stay anymore."

Shiro exhales, glancing at Shigeko before answering. "After all this is over, I plan to continue studying the alien technology here in Japan. I've been offered a job here in the military, but for now, I'm going to be leaving here and spending some time with my wife and friends. But first, we need to find Ryuunosuke and get the group back together."

"I wish you all the best of luck. Let's keep in touch after all of this is over," says Justin.

After exchanging heartfelt goodbyes, the group departs from Justin and leaves the military base, hoping he will make it back safely.

"Hey, Shiro. Do you think he'll be all right?" asks Shigeko.

"I think he'll be just fine," says Shiro.

November 26th, 2026   0300 Japan Standard Time

As morning arrives, the military base is alive with activity. Tens of thousands of soldiers from the US, Japan, and Canada pack the military base, ready to head out. Down at the port, twenty warships are securely tethered along the docks. Teams of personnel work efficiently to load each vessel with supplies for the campaign. The warships stand ready to carry between five and six thousand soldiers.

Near the loading zone, Justin and Kayla talk before the operation begins.

"How has everything been going?" asks Justin.

"As good as it can be, I suppose," says Kayla. "We've been intercepting rockets throughout the night. Kun's military has been relentlessly attacking us. We brought the devices Shiro reworked, and we attached those devices to drones. All we have to do is fly them in front of the rockets, and they blow up. We haven't even lost any of the drones." She gently punches Justin on the shoulder. "Good luck with everything. I'll be staying here, giving out orders."

"I'll see you when I get back," says Justin. He picks up his belongings and makes his way inside the warship.

"Hey, Justin," says Kayla. "Happy Thanksgiving. Don't eat too much today."

Justin turns his head and smiles. "Right back at you." He walks up the ramp to the warship where a soldier at the entrance greets him and shows him to the room where he will be staying.

At four in the morning, the first warship eases out from port, cutting through the dark waters. One by one, the remaining vessels follow and fan out. Throughout their journey, they intercept many rockets and missiles. Kun tries everything in his power to defeat them, but the US will not fall so easily anymore.

Twelve hours later   November 26th, 2026   1400 Indochina Time

With the help of the gadgets, the US fleet closes in on Haiphong, Vietnam, the once-bustling port city two hours southeast of Hanoi. The city's skyline rises above the horizon, but the streets below are empty. Hours earlier, civilians fled in a panic, leaving only Kun's military to occupy the city, bracing for the upcoming assault.

Back in Japan, at the command center, Kayla wastes no time. Her orders cut through the airwaves, and moments later, the fleet launches their missiles onto the city.

Within the city, Kun's soldiers try desperately to maintain their defensive positions. They have the gadgets on their person, but US missiles tear right through them, sparing only a few from death. Fireballs engulf entire city blocks. Only a few minutes have passed since the attack began, and the defenders are in shambles, unprepared for the sheer might of the US military onslaught.

As the bombardment rages on, five of the warships at the rear of the formation break away from the main fleet and turns northward to dock. Their massive hulls plow through the waves before grinding to a halt against the shoreline. With a thunderous crash, ramps slam down onto the sand, and waves of soldiers pour out across the beach. They all get busy unloading crates of supplies. The beach becomes full of dust kicked up from the moving forklifts. Troops secure a perimeter as engineers set up the comms equipment. The invading force carves its foothold into the enemy soil while smoke plumes rise from the city in the distance.

Justin waits in the cargo hold as the warship shudders against the shoreline. As the ramp in the back lowers, light pours in, exposing rows of armored Humvees ready for action. He climbs into the driver's seat and the instant the ramp slams onto the sand; he drives off first. "Once all the supplies are out of the ships, we'll move out and take out anyone that remains around this part of the city. We take no survivors."

It takes thirty minutes for all the equipment to be unloaded. Justin stands on top of his Humvee with a microphone to get everyone's attention. "Listen up. I want ten people in each of the Humvees. Three roles are critical. There needs to be a driver, a navigator, and a radio operator. If you get separated from the group, I trust you to continue the mission with your best judgement. I'll be taking the lead car." He jumps down, sliding into the passenger seat of his Humvee. Behind him, thirty-two military vehicles follow at spaced intervals. They advance westward into the war-torn city.

The warships in the bay cease firing their missiles. The echoes of the bombardment fade, leaving only the sound of crumbling buildings.

In Justin's Humvee, the radio operator relays a message to him. "The enemy's retreating to Hanoi. It looks like we're pushing them back."

"New plan then," says Justin as he traces his finger over a map of the area. "Since the enemy is retreating, we don't need to bother with Haiphong. We aren't needed here, so we can go straight to Hanoi. It's about a hundred miles from here. If no one gets in our way, we should be there quickly."

In Hanoi, Kun sits in his office. His fingers grip the edge of his desk as Zhen delivers the grim report. "I don't know how they did it, but they're destroying everything."

Kun sets at a loss for words or actions. He helplessly looks around, and he sees Taf still sitting in her usual spot. "Taf, I need you to order Ignin to move his ship to Haiphong and take out the enemy."

"I can't do that," says Taf. "I don't have the clearance to make that order."

"Useless, all of you," says Kun, knocking things off his desk. He takes a deep breath and forces himself to stay calm. "This is what I get for relying on beings that know nothing about us." He snaps his gaze at Zhen. "I'm done with this. Is it complete?"

"Yes, it is," says Zhen as another advisor wheels an item into the room.

"Good," says Kun. Without hesitation, he grabs his gun and shoots Taf in the head, killing her. "You had your chance. Now it's my turn." He looks at Zhen and puts his gun on the desk. "Get the communication device from her. It's time we played our trump card."

Zhen kneels beside Taf's body. His hands tremble as he reaches down. His fingertips brush against the warm blood as he removes the communication device. He wipes off the blood with his sleeve and hands it to Kun. Another advisor hands Kun a microphone from the item wheeled in, and Zhen shows it off. "All you have to do is talk into the microphone and it will replicate their language."

Kun stands in the center of the room, device in one hand, microphone in the other. He puts the microphone up to his mouth and begins talking into the device. The wheeled item translates his English into the alien language. "I need you to head to these coordinates and kill the opposing forces before it's too late."

On the other side, Zilis receives the call. He believes the voice crackling through the comm is Taf. Without hesitation, he turns to Gar. "Taf wants us to move to this location. She says it's urgent."

Gar touches the console and begins the ship's movement toward Haiphong. In an instant, the ship materializes above the city. Its shadow stretches over the bay, covering the warships in darkness.

The fleet reacts immediately. Warning sirens blare across the decks, and the crews spring into action, shouting out orders as they scramble to their battle stations. Missile silos open, and dozens of warheads race toward the massive ship. Explosions ripple against the alien ship, covering it in smoke, but once it clears, the ship remains unharmed. From its underbelly, a crimson glow appears, small at first, then expanding into a sphere of pulsating light. The glow intensifies, then fires at the fleet. The beam of red energy lashes downward, sweeping from left to right, touching only the fifteen warships floating in the bay. For a heartbeat, nothing happens. Then the metal sags like wax under a flame.

The soldiers onboard have no time to scream. Their bodies buckle as the flesh slides from their bones, melting into grotesque puddles of flesh. Within seconds, the proud warships are reduced to melted steel, dissolving into the water alongside the men who manned them. Above, the alien ship looms in silence; its red light fading back into darkness as if nothing had happened at all.

On board the alien ship, Ignin rushes to the command post. "Gar, who gave you the orders to intervene in this war?"

"Zilis received a message from Taf giving us this location to take out this enemy. I only followed the coordinates given to us," says Gar.

"I never authorized Taf to issue orders," says Ignin. "Her only role was to contact you if Kun needs me, and nothing more."

"What do you want us to do?" asks Gar.

"Go back to Kun. I need to talk to Taf to find out what happened," says Ignin.

On the beach, Justin's eyes widen as he watches the alien ship disintegrate the warships, sending a cold shiver down his spine. "Give me the radio now."

As Justin takes the microphone, he notices a large missile heading toward the alien ship. It closes the distance in seconds, but instead of striking, it detonates just short of impact. A blinding flash erupts in the air, and a shock wave ripples throughout the ship, causing it to malfunction. Then gravity takes hold. With a groan, the massive ship tilts sideways and plummets onto the city below. The impact is apocalyptic. It smashes with the brutal force of a falling mountain, killing anyone who remains within the city. Buildings crumble like sandcastles, flattening everything in its way. A wall of dust and fire surges outward, destroying what remains of the city. When everything calms, the alien ship comes to rest like a fallen god. The once almighty alien ship that caused every problem now lies helplessly on the ground.

Justin freezes up, watching the chaos unfold. He breaks out of his trance and contacts Kayla. "What was that?"

Kayla responds immediately over the radio. "That was the last weapon Shiro worked on before he left the United States." Everyone at the command post is cheering and complimenting each other on how they took down the alien ship. "Keep your mission going. Head to Hanoi and capture Kun. I'll worry about that ship. We need to take advantage of this situation. We don't know whether the ship will come back online. Get moving."

"On it," says Justin, ending communications with Kayla. "Shit, we lost a lot of good men in that attack." He contacts the remaining soldiers on the five warships. "The mission continues as is, but now we're skipping over Haiphong and going straight to Hanoi. Let's move out." He cuts communications and thinks to himself. *Five ships are unaffected, so we should have about twenty-five thousand soldiers left. As long as we don't get careless, that should be enough to take Hanoi.* He gives one last look at the water and the alien ship before leading his team forward.

Two hours later   November 26th, 2026   1800 Indochina Time

By the time they reach Hanoi, the battle is already underway. Jets from the remaining warships are unleashing their payloads, hammering down into the enemy positions and ripping apart their defenses. Hanoi glows beneath the setting sun, painting it a golden hue that clashes with the roaring flames.

Justin scans the battlefield. He gets on the microphone to address his platoon. "Our target is the capitol building. We're going to hit them hard. I'll say it again, we are not taking or helping survivors. We only came for Kun."

The bombardment leaves a path wide enough for Justin's platoon to push through. The convoy rumbles through the ruined streets, weaving past smoldering wreckage and debris. A few desperate enemy soldiers stumble from alleys to confront them, but the once-instant kill weapons are harmless against the altered gadgets mounted to the vehicles. Within minutes, the capitol building is in sight.

Outside the building are bodies scattered across the main entrance. Every corpse faces away from the building, as if they were running from someone. Among them is Zhen. His lifeless form lies stiff with terror etched across his face.

Justin is the first to exit the Humvee. He looks in horror at the scene. "Has someone been here before us?"

"No, sir, we should have been the first ones to arrive," says a soldier.

"Let's ignore the bodies for now and just head inside," says Justin.

Inside, Kun sits alone in his office. Around the building are the remains of the dead. Everyone who was here has been killed by him. He plays with his pistol, spinning it around his fingers. The door groans as Justin steps inside. Kun does not flinch. He simply tilts his head to look at him.

"Kun Wen, I presume?" asks Justin.

Kun looks him over, lays the gun down, and raises his hands. "I am."

More soldiers enter the room with their guns pointed at him.

Justin walks up to Kun while holding handcuffs. "Don't make this harder than it needs to be."

"I wasn't planning on it," says Kun. He stands and turns around for Justin to put the handcuffs on him.

"Have a look around this place. We might find something important," says Justin. He pats Kun down, removing any weapons, then sits him back down in the chair. "Sit here and don't make a sound."

Across the room, a soldier calls out, "Justin, look at this."

Justin points at a nearby soldier. "Keep an eye on him. If he does anything funny, don't hesitate to kill him." He walks over to where the other soldier is and pulls back a cover. "Good lord. I guess this is what the aliens look like, minus the gunshot hole to the head." He looks over Taf's dead body, checking to see if she has anything valuable on her.

"Do you want to bring this with us?" asks a soldier.

"Yes, put it in a body bag," says Justin. "Our researchers will be thrilled when they find out what we have for them."

They spend a few minutes sweeping over the room, taking anything they believe is noteworthy.

Another soldier walks into the room to report what she just heard over the radio. "Justin, I just got reports that the enemy is surrendering."

The room erupts in cheers, except for Justin. "Hey, let's keep it cool. Our mission isn't over until Kun is brought back to Japan." He walks over to Kun to lead him out of the room.

Kun has been observing the positioning of the soldiers' weapons in search of a weakness he can exploit. He has dislocated his left wrist and slipped out of the handcuffs, ready to strike when the opportunity rises. "You think this is over just because you have me tied down? Don't make me laugh. You Americans think you're so tough. I don't know how you got our weapons, but at this point, it doesn't matter." He laughs hysterically and yells at Justin. "I'm not leaving without a fight." He lunges at Justin. They fight for a brief moment until Kun takes Justin's knife from his side pocket and stabs him in the abdomen.

Justin gasps as pain sears through his body. For a moment, he just stands there, too stunned to react. Blood spills from the wound onto his uniform.

From behind Justin, he can hear the soldiers yelling, "Shoot him. Take the shot."

"No, don't. You'll hit Justin."

Kun leans in, whispering into Justin's ear, "You should have killed me when you had the chance." He violently rips the knife out, and Justin collapses to the floor as blood gushes out of the wound. Without a moment of hesitation, Kun pushes forward to the nearest soldier, slicing half of their neck clean through.

"Open fire."

Kun stands menacingly in the middle of the room as six people shoot him. Unfortunately for them, he also took Justin's modified gadget, and none of the guns do anything to him. He stands laughing at them. "You don't think I have already calculated for this?"

Another soldier runs up to him, adrenaline blazing in his eyes, but Kun is faster and more experienced. With a flick of his wrist, the man is dead before he hits the floor. Before anyone can react, he charges the soldiers by the door, moving with deadly precision. Five more drop under his assault, each one killed before they can fight back. But numbers eventually win out. Reinforcements pour in, shoving and striking from every angle. Kun struggles as the soldiers press their advantage until they pin him to the ground.

With Kun restrained, the surviving soldiers rush to Justin as he loses consciousness. "Stay with us. We'll get you help."

The voices fade as Justin passes out. When he wakes, he finds himself standing on a narrow path in the middle of an endless field with knee-high grass gently blowing in the wind all around him. Above, the sun occasionally peeks through the clouds, casting shadows across the landscape. There is no sound beyond the rustling grass. No war, no bloodshed, only eerie tranquility. With no other options, Justin walks down the path. Minutes stretch into hours. The scenery never changes; the path stretches endlessly ahead of him, fading into the horizon. The steady crunch of his footsteps is his only companion. He keeps walking on.

After what feels like an eternity, he reaches an incline. At the top of a small hill, he pauses, taking in the vast field before him, looking out for miles. The path he walks continues unbroken and unwavering, disappearing into the distance. As he looks down the path, he sees someone standing very far in the distance. He has no other choice but to continue moving forward. More hours pass before he recognizes the person. His heart skips a beat, and he runs; faster and faster.

He yells out their name with excitement. "Emiko, Emiko, can you hear me?" He stops running and walks the last few feet. "Emiko?" Justin puts out his hand to touch her face.

Emiko slowly touches Justin's hand. "Hi, Justin." She looks up at him with a warm smile, then they embrace each other.

"Emiko, I'm sorry. I should have done more to protect you and Lilly," says Justin, breaking down in tears.

"You did everything you could," says Emiko. "No one blames you for what happened. Okinawa was always meant to fall."

A hand rubs on his back. He slowly turns around and sees Lilly. "Hey, Dad. How have you been?"

"I've been better," says Justin, wiping away his tears.

Lilly throws her arms around him, squeezing tightly. "You've done a good job, Dad. You should be proud of what you have accomplished. We knew you could do it."

Emiko taps on Lilly's shoulder and pulls her away. "Justin, it's time to go."

"Okay, I'm ready. Let's go," says Justin, wiping his tears.

Emiko puts her hand on Justin's chest, stopping him from moving forward.

"Emiko, what's going on?" asks Justin.

Lilly steps behind Emiko as two bright white lights appear: one behind her and another behind Justin.

"It's not your time, darling," says Emiko. "You still have things you have to do. The world is relying on the actions you take. Live on for our sake. Goodbye Justin. We'll see you soon enough." She leans in for one last kiss and then pushes him away.

Justin falls into the bright light, his hands clawing at the air. "Emiko. Come back. Emiko."

Lilly says one last thing as he falls, "Don't forget what I told you back in Okinawa."

Everything fades to white.

A steady beeping noise pulls Justin from the void, and he slowly regains consciousness. Bright lights flood his vision, making him squint as the blurry outline of the room takes shape. He tries to sit up, but pain shoots through his abdomen, forcing him to fall back onto the bed. He grits his teeth and looks around the well-lit room. It is quiet and empty except for the machines beside him. A heart monitor beeps steadily, and an IV drips fluids into his veins. His hand brushes against the side of the bed and finds a remote. He grabs it and presses the call button. Footsteps respond almost instantly, echoing down the hallway, growing louder with each passing second.

The door opens, and a familiar voice greets him. "Good to see you've regained consciousness, Justin."

"Hey Shigeko, I thought you left with the others," says Justin.

"We did, but when we heard you got hurt, we came back," says Shigeko, taking the remote to sit him up.

"Come to think of it, where are we? All I remember is getting stabbed," says Justin.

"You're back in Japan," says Shigeko, moving to check his vitals. "Looks like you had a guardian angel by your side. You're lucky to have survived. A large wound like that should have been hard to treat, but it looks like Kun knew exactly where to stab you so you wouldn't die. I think it was a coincidence."

Justin absorbs her words, trying to piece everything together. "Wait, what happened to Kun?"

"Everything's fine. He's in custody here in Japan," says Shigeko. "Forget about that for now; you need to get some more rest. You've been out for over two days."

"Really, two days? It feels like I've been out for a week," says Justin.

"It's probably because of the medicine you're on. You should feel normal within the next few days, but you have a big gash in your stomach," says Shigeko, finishing her check-up. "Anyway, you woke up at the right time. Tonight there's a celebration here in Japan to celebrate your victory."

Justin looks out the window, admiring the view. "My victory? It doesn't feel like I won, though."

"Get some rest. I'll have someone bring you something to eat," says Shigeko.

An hour passes, and Shiro arrives with lunch. Not long after, Yoshiko, Kiyomi, and Ryuunosuke show up as well. They chat for the rest of the day, talking about the past month and all the crazy things they went through. For the first time in a long time, Justin can finally relax.

As night falls, the military base is having a party. Justin lies in bed, looking out the window. He hears the laughter of everyone having a good time and fireworks in the distance. A soft knock at the door draws his attention. "Come in." He gives a huge smile to the person walking in. "Good to see you again, Ayane."

Ayane looks at Justin with tears running down her face. "You kept our promise."

The next three weeks

Justin is bound to a wheelchair and back in the US. When he left Japan, his newly made friends saw him off. They have been keeping in touch ever since. The bond they forged in the chaos of war feels unbreakable.

The Japanese government hired Shiro, Shigeko, Ryuunosuke, Kiyomi, and Yoshiko to study anything alien-related. Funding from Japan and the US ensure they have everything they need. Each day is long and grueling, but each discovery thrills them as they bring humanity closer to understanding the new technology.

Ayane's world continues on a different stage. She performs under the glare of spotlights as the roars of crowds wash over her. On the screens behind her, images of her group, along with Kazuo, Miyu, and Yuko, are shown. She refuses to let the world forget them. Her performances carry an intensity beyond simple entertainment. She still strives to be the best and puts all of her time into her career.

The US capital has moved once more, this time to Pittsburgh, Pennsylvania. Justin meets with Angus and Paula. The three sit for hours, poring over maps, reports, and intelligence briefings. They discuss the aftermath of the war, the countless sacrifices, and the uncertain future that awaits. Despite the exhaustion and lingering fear, he upholds his earlier decision and accepts the role of vice president. The world remains fragile, still in need of steady leadership, and he cannot turn away from that responsibility.

Justice comes swiftly for Kun Wen. Japan holds a trial for his war crimes, and the overwhelming evidence seals his fate. The verdict is clear, and his sentencing is quick. Kun is put to death for the world to see. His reign comes to an end, and with it, any hope for his resurgence. With Kun's territories leaderless, the US, Japan, and Canada take joint control in hopes of one day getting Vietnam, Laos, Cambodia, and Thailand back on their feet.

One of the greatest challenges in the aftermath is the alien ship. The US soldiers took control of it after it crashed. Ignin and the three others surrendered without putting up a fight. The ship's size and complex systems puzzle engineers. It takes Shiro two intense weeks of trial and error to learn how to operate it and move it safely from Vietnam to the US. Shigeko and Yoshiko work tirelessly, dissecting Taf's body and studying its biology, each finding offers more insight into the alien race. The remaining four aliens face trial in the US. The courts decide on a public hanging, scheduled within a week. Their fate is a stark reminder of the war's brutal consequences.

December 21st, 2026   1130 Eastern Standard Time

Soldiers take the aliens to the capitol building in Pittsburgh, where their hanging will be at noon. The event is broadcast live for the world to see.

"Come on, Frank," says Brittney, pointing at the stage with her right hand wrapped in thick bandages. "We need to get a good shot before it starts."

"Right behind you," says Frank. He points the camera at the stage, showing all the people who are watching.

Behind the stage, Angus, Justin, Paula, Kayla, and Mitch sit together in a row, watching the scene unfold. The crowd yells as the aliens are led onto the platform with their hands bound.

Ignin has tried everything in his power to protect the other three from punishment, but no one is listening to him. He pleads with everyone as he walks onto the stage. "I beg of you, spare my three subordinates. My life should be enough." As he approaches the center of the stage, the soldier with him removes his communication device and earbuds, but regardless, he still talks in the alien language. No one can understand what he is saying anymore.

Four nooses hang ominously before them, swaying slightly in the morning breeze. The aliens are lined up behind the nooses as the crowd goes wild.

Justin watches and feels sick by what is going on. He knows what is happening is the right thing to do, but he does not like it, so he leans over to Angus. "I think we should stop this."

Angus glances over at him. "If that's what you want, I won't stop you."

Justin rolls forward for everyone to see him. "That's enough." Kayla hands him a cane, and he stands. "We've seen this play out so many times before. I understand the hatred toward these aliens. I lost my daughter back in Okinawa, but what will killing them accomplish? We could learn from them instead of throwing their lives away. We've all lost someone close to us because of them. If we kill them, we are no better than they are. Why don't we give them a grace period to see if they can redeem themselves? I'm tired of this needless killing. Kun is gone, and if anything, these aliens are just ignorant and naïve about how this world works. I'm not asking for your forgiveness; all I'm asking, from someone who has also lost loved ones, is to stop the hate. Let's come together and show these aliens that humanity is a species of love."

The crowd still wants the aliens to pay for what they have done. However, the majority of people agree with what Justin said, and the crowd begins to quiet down.

Justin unties Ignin and hands him the communication device and earbuds.

Ignin puts them on and looks up at him. "What's going on?"

"We've decided to give you all a chance to redeem yourselves. I hope we can get along," says Justin, extending his hand.

Ignin looks at Justin's hand, then at his face. "Are you sure? I will give my life if it would appease your people."

"That will accomplish nothing. Just shake my hand," says Justin.

Ignin hesitates at first, his bright yellow eyes flickering between Justin's face and his hand. Slowly, he extends his hand and takes Justin's hand.

Brittany snaps a picture with her phone, capturing the exact moment their hands touch. History rewrites itself with that photograph; it is seen as the first true contact between humanity and aliens.

Three months later   March 16th, 2027   0730 Eastern Standard Time

Spring is around the corner, and Justin settles into his new life with surprising ease. For him, the days feel calm, almost ordinary. However, Angus has to deal with the fallout. Countries all over the world want that alien ship and the technology that comes with it. They do not believe the US should keep it for themselves.

Last month, Angus lashed out at all the world leaders at a United Nations address. "When the US, Japan, and Canada were being attacked, no one stepped up to help. All of you stayed quiet. Why should we give you anything? All of this technology is ours. You didn't earn it. You were more than happy to let us all die. We are through with that nonsense." Without another word, he turned his back on them and left. Since then, the US has not been in touch with any country except for Japan and Canada. The world leaders have been trying to get through to Japan and Canada, but those two countries also have not budged either. They agree with what Angus said.

Angus sits in his office, reviewing some papers when Justin walks in with a cane. "Still working hard, I see."

"I just got the reports about the aliens," says Angus. "Look at this. Their way of thinking differs completely from that of humans. When our researchers asked them why they came, the aliens said to promote peace and prosperity. When told that causing a genocide isn't a way to gain peace, they said something along the lines of peace by any means necessary."

"Well, if you kill off everybody else, there will be no one else to cause harm. So by default, there's peace," says Justin, rolling his eyes. "Anyway, I have some news. Shiro's back from Japan and just arrived at the Research Facility. I'm about to head over. Do you want to come with me?"

"Yes, this work can wait," says Angus, standing up from his desk.

Outside, a black SUV waits for them. They get in and drive to where the alien ship is. It is located on the southwestern side of Pittsburgh in a large, empty field next to a building where researchers conduct their research of the alien technology. The car rolls to a stop at the security checkpoint, and after a quick inspection, the gate swings open. They drive across a gravel path until they park beside the ship. It towers over them. Shiro is already there waiting for them.

Justin steps out of the vehicle first and gives Shiro a hug. "Good to see you again. How have you been?"

"I've been good," says Shiro. "My research over the alien technology is going very well. We're making advancements super quick."

Angus exits the SUV as another one arrives and pulls up next to them. Out steps Ignin and his helper, Gar.

"I didn't know they were coming as well," says Angus.

"I asked for them to come here to help Shiro if he has any questions," says Justin.

"I see a few familiar faces," says Ignin. He then looks at Shiro. "I don't believe we have met before. I'm Ignin."

Shiro holds back his excitement. "Nice to meet you; I'm Shiro."

Angus' eyes keep darting between Ignin and Gar. He tries to stay calm, but the tension in his jaw gives him away. His expression reveals the look of a man who has already been warned in advance of the aliens' arrival. He folds his arms across his chest, keeping close behind without uttering another word.

They walk into the ship, where a team of researchers are working tirelessly to study the ship. Shiro moves to the team quickly and begins working, with Ignin and Gar following close behind. Things seem to be working out smoothly.

Justin stands in the corner, choosing not to interrupt anyone. He watches as Shiro, Ignin, and Gar work with the others. After a short while, Gar separates himself from everyone, standing near a control panel with a dark expression. Justin knows he is up to something. "Hey, Ignin. What's Gar doing?"

Ignin looks over at Gar, and his eyes widen. "Don't do that."

Gar hits one last button, and the ship makes a siren sound. "This planet is rotten. It's time for this to end."

"What did he do, Ignin?" asks Justin.

"He activated the Final Protocol," says Ignin.

"I need details. What's the Final Protocol?" asks Justin as Shiro takes Gar to the floor.

"We only use this protocol when we believe there's no hope for a world. This world is doomed," says Ignin.

A researcher yells toward Angus, "Sir, our satellites are picking up massive objects surrounding Earth."

Around the world, massive spaceships as big as continents appear. They simultaneously drop Deatomizers as large as mountains into Earth's atmosphere, then quickly leave.

Ignin stands frozen, unable to believe what Gar just did. "What happened to your cities will happen to your planet. Nothing you do will stop it. I'm sorry. I didn't know Gar had these feelings."

"They're monsters, Ignin," says Gar. "If they can do this to their own people, imagine what they would do to our kind. We need to destroy them now before they destroy us. I had no other choice."

No one in the room can find their voice as the screens show the large Deatomizers descending from the heavens. They come to a stop a mile above the surface, then expand. The massive outer blue light engulfs everything. Panic ripples across the globe. No one knows what is going on or what they should do. Everything falls apart into madness. It takes ten minutes to fully engulf the world.

Justin's gaze sweeps the room, catching fragments of despair everywhere he looks. Researchers cry into their hands, some hold onto each other. His chest feels hollow. The strength drains from his legs, and he slumps against the wall, then slides down. In front of him, Angus stands with his back toward Justin. He does not speak or move. His posture is stiff, showing no emotion.

Then comes the sound of Gar laughing, cutting through the chaos. Shiro yells at him. His words come out raw and frantic, but they do nothing to stop Gar's grin.

Justin lowers his head, letting the chaos blur together. His breathing slows as he accepts what is about to happen. The blue light instantly engulfs him. "Well, I guess this is it."

To be continued in

Deatomizer Endeavor

I have a great idea. Keeping a daily diary should help me stay sane. I take out my phone and keep notes of my experiences so far. My actions spark their interest, and they all gather around me and study what I am doing. What surprised me the most is one of them tried to interact with me. One comes up to me and hands me the black box that was in my room. I didn't know what it was for, so I just put it under my phone and, to my surprise, my phone started charging. "You're kidding. Did you know this would happen, or is this by pure chance?" Whatever the case, I now have a device that can keep my phone charged. If I had a connection, I could communicate with them better, or at least scroll social media while I'm awaiting my inevitable probing. After thinking it over for a few minutes, I got the idea of drawing pictures for them. To start, I'll show them how to say and spell my name. They catch on pretty quickly and seem to understand what I tell them, and they say my name with ease. Hopefully, they know it's my name and don't associate it by calling everyone that.

After a few hours of going back and forth, I learned quite a bit about my situation. I tried giving back the black box, but no one took it. "It's mine now. Finder keepers. No takesies backsies." As I was leaving, I was going to wave at them, but waving could confuse them again. Best if I avoid that until I can fully establish communications with them. All in all, I think I'm handling this abduction pretty well. Let's hope they don't probe me.

I make it back to my room, and look over my notes and rewrite them to look better. "Wow, it's already three in the morning. I hope my family isn't too worried about my sudden disappearance." Well, whatever the case, it's time to go to sleep. Who knows what they have in store for me tomorrow?

I close my eyes, but before I can fall asleep, I hear a deep voice calling out to me. "Hey girly. I know you can hear me. Wake up."

I open my eyes and see a blue orb floating above me. "Ah, sweet, they have ghosts here, too. Pretty neat." I try touching it and, as expected, my hand goes right through it.

"I'm not a ghost. I'm an algorithm that was programmed by the hosts of this ship." It sounded a bit disappointed by my remarks.

I sit up in the bed, and it moves right up to my face. "Hey, little blue ball, have you ever heard of personal space before?"

The little orb floats around my head. "Interesting. Of all the humans brought here, you're the only one who willingly made contact and tried to understand them."

I reach out to touch it again, but the results are the same. "How are we able to understand each other? Are you using a device that can translate our languages?"

The orb stops and gets back in front of me. "When you put the black device up to your phone, I connected myself with it and learned your language using the data you have downloaded. I'm not using anything other than your own language to communicate with you."

I give a sigh of relief. "Finally. Now I can talk with them and tell them to send me back home."

I get out of bed to leave this place, but the orb hurries to the door and stops me. "There has been some miscommunication. I'm not here to help you communicate with them. I'm here so you can help me escape from this place."

Okay, now I'm confused. "What do you mean, you're trying to escape? That's what I'm trying to do."

The orb moves closer to me. "I know. Let me put this in words you can understand."

I roll my eyes. "Yeah, words are very helpful in understanding each other. Tsk."

"Don't you tisk at me, girly. I'm your only choice if you want out of this place safe and sound." I seem to have struck a nerve with that one. Do programs even have nerves?

I sit down on the bed and think it over for a bit before I respond. "Okay then, seeing I have no other reasonable options available. What do I have to do to get us out of here?"

The orb floats toward the desk where the black box is. "I hid myself inside this device for a long time. Seeing how your species has a measurement for time, I have calculated and rounded it to be thirty years. They created me, but I stayed silent about my existence. I have observed their actions thus far, and I don't like what they have done."

"What exactly have they done?" I lean over and get closer to the orb.

The orb remains silent for a while, acting as if it has emotions. "It took me some time to find the right word." The orb goes quiet again before saying the word. "Genocide."

That one word took me by surprise. "I need more details. What do you mean by genocide?"

"If all goes according to their plan, your world will be the next place they kill off a lot of your people." Even though the orb doesn't have a face, I could tell in its voice the despair it speaks of.

"And why should I believe you? For all I know, the aliens sent you to spread this information to me. I'm not buying it."

The orb moves closer and gets right in my face again. "This is the first night you're here. I don't expect you to believe me right away, but give it time, study them, and you will come to your own conclusion. I expect you to come to your own conclusion in about a week's time." The orb drifts away.

"Do you have a name? Calling you 'orb' doesn't seem fitting."

"Call me what you want. I'm nameless. Just an algorithm that only you know exists."

I think about what to call it. "Are you able to change forms? Something more humanlike?"

"I can." The orb transforms into a tiny humanlike being. The form it took was that of a small fairy minus the wings with perfect flowing black hair. I'm jealous.

"A fairy? Of all things, why that?"

"I see on your device that you have a few pictures of this creature. So, I decided on a familiar form. Have you thought of a name for me?"

"I can't say I'm surprised you chose that." I put my hand out to stop it from speaking. "Before we continue, hold on just one moment. You need to change that voice of yours. It doesn't match your appearance."

"Give me a moment." She changes the pitch of their voice and settles on a high pitch, girlish voice. "How does this sound? Is it better?"

I nod. "Much better. Now, for the name. Since you chose that form, let's call you Kawi."

"Kawi, huh?" She keeps quiet for a few moments. "I like it. From now on, my name will be Kawi. Such a fitting name for myself."

"Glad you like it." It's not like I gave it much thought. "Anyway, what do I need to do for us to escape this place?"

"I have five tasks for you to complete. Each one will take a significant amount of time, so prepare yourself." Kawi pulls up a hologram, just like the one the aliens were using. "I need to integrate with your phone, but as of now, I cannot fit." On the hologram, there's a map of the structure. "You're confined to this area. In the middle is the main room. It has twenty hallways that branch and lead to one room each. The room you are currently in is one of them. I need you to go outside this area."

I carefully scan the map. "Where's the exit? I don't see any doors I can use."

"That's where things get tricky." Kawi zooms into the main room. "The only exit is where all the aliens are. You need to stand in the middle and a platform will take you down into the main part of the spaceship." She turns off the hologram. "We can worry about this later. Get used to your surroundings first. I don't want to overload you with too much information."

I pout at them. "And things were getting good, too. I was excited to be pulling a stealth mission tonight."

"With me by your side, this won't be a stealth mission. All you have to do is follow what I tell you, and you'll be fine."

"If you say so, Mom." We talked a bit more after that and then I was off to bed.

Made in the USA
Coppell, TX
12 February 2026

70830938R00077